GENEROUSLY DONATED
TO THE MOUNTAIN VIEW
PUBLIC LIBRARY *by Scott A.
MacDonald and Josephine T. Hucko*

In Memory of

Bob Voras

RUNNING DOGS

Recent Titles by Gwen Moffat

CUE THE BATTERED WIFE
THE LOST GIRLS
THE OUTSIDE EDGE
PIT BULL
RAGE
VERONICA'S SISTERS

A WREATH OF DEAD MOTHS *

* *available from Severn House*

RUNNING DOGS

Gwen Moffat

This first world edition published in Great Britain 1999 by
SEVERN HOUSE PUBLISHERS LTD of
9–15 High Street, Sutton, Surrey SM1 1DF.
This first world edition published in the U.S.A. 1999 by
SEVERN HOUSE PUBLISHERS INC of
595 Madison Avenue, New York, N.Y. 10022.

British Library Cataloguing in Publication Data

Moffat, Gwen
    Running dogs
    1. Detective and mystery stories
    I. Title
    823.9'14 [F]

    ISBN 0-7278-5456-9

For Janet and Malcolm McWhorter

All situations in this publication are fictitious and
any resemblance to living persons is purely coincidental.

Typeset by Palimpsest Book Production Ltd.,
Polmont, Stirlingshire, Scotland.
Printed and bound in Great Britain by
MPG Books Ltd, Bodmin, Cornwall.

One

"There's a bald eagle feeding on the point." Constance Dodge focused the telescope. "And here's a vulture! A carcass must have been washed up. Come and look."

"In a minute." Grady was agonising over the mail, making notes. "*Two* new tyres for the van? You had two punctures?"

"The spare was finished anyway."

"That van isn't cost-effective. We should sell it, and the Mercedes, buy a Volvo—"

"I've decided on a new van. I need the space if I buy furniture. And there are long party trips, like Vancouver. A car carries five at the most."

Grady gaped at his wife's back. He was furious; he'd set his heart on a new car, had even considered whether he could persuade her to buy a Jaguar. "The Merc is the oldest car in Prosper," he protested.

"No, sweetie; the oldest is Win's Rolls." The telescope swivelled.

"You're moving it!"

"There goes young Owen."

"He's not young—"

"And he's making for the Hole. He's surely not about to wade through. No, it's low tide; he's looking at the sea stars. Maybe they don't have sea stars in England."

"He comes from Wales. He was a cook."

"What does that have to do – he *is* going through. I hope Win's warned him about the tides." She shifted position, knocking a leg of the tripod.

Grady's silence was eloquent until he said, "It's two o'clock and Win is having her nap. What's the point of looking for her? You can only see a corner of her roof. She's asleep, the toy boy's off the leash and he's bored. He's exploring."

"Grady Dodge, you're impossible. Owen is Win's secretary and you know it—"

1

"He's the house boy."

"He likes to cook. That doesn't make him a servant. Win wouldn't visit with her neighbours and bring her house boy. Personally I'm delighted she's found someone to come and live in that house, and so should you be: an old woman on her own with the forest close behind. Anything could happen, could have happened."

"You had the right tense first time. A rich old woman and an illegal alien half her age—"

"He is not illegal—" Turning to confront him she caught a shadowed movement on the mezzanine. She grimaced, jerking her head at the upper floor. "I need more avocados for the party," she stated loudly. "Someone has to go to town tomorrow, and I don't have the time . . ."

Back in the master bedroom Myra Hubbell dusted the colonel's silver-backed brushes without for once coveting them, going over the conversation of which she'd heard every word. Not that it differed much from how folk talked in the forest, only in degree. Everyone had concluded from the first that Winnie Carver had taken the little Britisher for her fancy man but that was how rich people behaved: you wanted something, you paid for it; no different from Mrs Dodge and the colonel really. It was obvious who had the money here, all those expensive clothes, and the woman would never see sixty again. Why, she didn't even know what clothes she had, where they were, thought she must have lost the red sweater one time on a trip. And that bottle of scent she'd never missed. They should know what it was to have to pay for medication, consultation fees, Seth's walker, them with the insurance paying for everything. The rich had it all – although she guessed the colonel didn't have it from birth. He was mighty mean with his money – *her* money: hardly drank, begrudged them running two cars . . . He was supposed to have worked in the Pentagon. Myra doubted that; you'd have to be clever to work for the Government, which Grady Dodge was not. It could be that he hadn't been a colonel, they'd have guards at the Pentagon, maybe he was a captain in charge of the guards. Myra sniffed; there was none so savage about status, and mean with cash, as those who'd clawed their way to the top. She should know, she'd worked in most of the houses in Prosper, knew the difference between old money and new.

Flicking her duster over the glass baubles on a window sill she saw air showing through rusted holes in the wheel arch of her car.

So Winnie Carver's swanky Rolls was the oldest vehicle around? Her own Subaru could give it a year or two but who ever considered the maid's car? Come to that, who considered the maid, except to keep an eagle eye on the levels in the bottles of Scotch? Prosper. There was a laugh. The settlement had been founded by Win's grandfather when logging was a major industry hereabouts, and now look at it: a handful of rich retirees, and a few women and kids and one sick old logger in the forest living on welfare and their wits and struggling.

Owen Hughes sat on a log and looked back at the passage through South Point that they called the Hole in the Wall. The water had been no more than ankle-deep but then low tide wasn't till three o'clock so it would be ages before the Hole was impassable. Win had been adamant, warning him never to go through the Hole, that he'd be cut off by the tide. She had this tendency to smother him, watched him constantly, although at the start it had been understandable. When he arrived here he'd seen this great expanse of ocean: in morning light, in the sunset, under the moon, and he'd thought of swimming until his strength gave out, of floating and going to sleep. The water would wake him as he sank and it took four minutes to drown but that would be a penance. Jessie had taken longer to die after the car hit her, and perhaps she cried for him until he came home and found her on the doorstep. "It's only a cat," they'd said – all except Win, touring Wales, staying at the hotel. Dear Win, to whom cats were people too, who had understood and told him firmly that he was coming back with her for a holiday on the coast of Washington. And when they'd arrived she had seen him looking at the ocean and she'd *known*. But that was then, and the new world had conspired, if not to enchant him, at least to distract. And there was the other side to the experience. It was not a holiday but then he wouldn't have known what to do with a holiday.

Win had her moments of perceptiveness, had seen how she could benefit both him and herself. He didn't begrudge the opportunism, he admired her for it, and the job was amusing. Realising his potential, she said; he'd been wasted at the hotel. She was right of course, but he still missed his lovely Jessie.

He stood up, a small neat man with the sharp features of an alert weasel, forty-two years old, bereft but starting over in a different world. He'd been much impressed with the old frame house with its marvellous kitchen, with the books, his own bathroom, the Rolls. And there was always the ocean and the acres of golden poppies and of course the cats. He disliked the forest, it sent a frisson through his dark Welsh soul, but the rocks and the little sedums reminded him of home although it was odd to hear quail calling and to see a whale go cruising by.

The neighbours treated him with courtesy; they would speculate on his role in Win's house but were far too polite to approach the subject. Constance Dodge was having a party tomorrow which should be fun. It was a long time since he'd thought of anything being fun, something to look forward to. He realised that this afternoon he was almost at peace with himself, walking the empty beach of this wild cove where the sea stacks stood proud above water so quiet that there was scarcely a tatter of foam about their feet.

Southward the grey sand stretched for a mile to another rocky headland and all along the back of the strand, behind the jumbled bulwark of bleached logs, the forest crowded like a tropical jungle, but this was temperate rain forest and the trees were conifers, not palms. They clothed the slopes above the crumbling cliffs, some leaning, many fallen, and when he looked more closely he saw that what he had taken for shrubs were alders which were growing like weeds. In one place the cliff had collapsed, a bare brown scar marking where the land had slipped. There was movement at the foot of the slope.

Eagles rose at his approach: four of them, rising heavily to perch in the branches of a dead tree. The fifth bird left it to the last minute before it flapped away to a stack with a crown of firs. He stared after it: a naked red head, could it be a vulture? He was more intrigued by that than by the eagles which he saw every day, scavenging along the shore for seal carcasses.

And this was a seal pup, he saw, the skin rolled back neatly to expose the rib cage – wait, this was no seal, there was a leg pecked clean and certainly no flipper . . . There was a paw, a pad, pads rather. It was a dog.

Momentarily horrified he remembered that in America there were coyotes. He hadn't seen one yet, hadn't known there were any in the vicinity, although Win said there were cougars, the American lion. That he had to see: a big cat. He looked from the paw to the landslip, surprised that a wild animal should have been caught in it. Now he saw that there were pieces of wood protruding from the surface but, starting to climb, he gave up after a couple of steps. The slide was waterlogged and he sank to his ankles in glutinous mud.

The wood had been worked, it wasn't branches; there was even part of a door. He could see a hinge. His eye travelled up the slope; there must have been a building on the edge of the forest. Could it have been occupied? Was this carcass a dog after all? There was a skull, the bones picked and ragged; eagles had powerful beaks. He reckoned the animal had been about the size of a large collie.

He was thoughtful as he returned to the Hole in the Wall, vaguely aware that he'd been in the cove quite a while for the tide had turned and the breeze had got up. The waves were choppy and his chinos were soaked, wading through the tunnel.

As he came up through the poppies to the house he saw Win leaning on the deck-rail, tension in every line. He sighed. She was going to scold. He mounted the steps and her eyes were on his wet trousers. He got his word in first.

"Who lived in the cabin in Stack Cove?"

The brown cheeks sagged and the faded eyes were suddenly wild. He was dumbfounded, he hadn't expected her to take it so much to heart. "For Heaven's sake!" he protested, "I watched the tide; it's only knee-deep inside the Hole even now."

She was breathing deeply and he was concerned. "I'm sorry but truly, if you know the time of low water there's no danger. At least, I didn't think so – and here I am!" He spread his hands, laying on the charm, begging forgiveness.

"With an onshore wind you could have been cut off." It emerged raggedly then, with apparent carelessness, "What was that about a cabin?"

"There's been a landslide and it looks as if a cabin was carried away. There's a door showing in the mud."

"Is that so." She made to turn away.

"Was it inhabited?"

"Of course not. It's inaccessible. It's probably that old hunting cabin. The woods are full of deer. Why do you ask?"

"There are coyotes too. There's the body of one at the foot of the slide."

She turned back. "A body?"

"Carcass, I mean. Like a dog, but it could be a coyote."

She stared fixedly. "Couldn't you tell?"

"Not really. The eagles and – a vulture – with a red head?" She nodded, her eyes boring into his. "They'd picked it clean – virtually. The only way I could tell it was canine was the paw. Just one left. There was part of the skull, shattered."

She looked tired, he thought, but then people in their seventies

. . . maybe she hadn't slept this afternoon, or was still worrying over his being cut off by the tide. Daft really, there were heaps of places where the cliffs were no more than banks; he could have taken to the forest.

"You need a drink," she said shortly.

It was a bit early, but she was the boss. Obediently he followed her indoors. "Go and change," she ordered, "and then I have something to say to you."

Now what? She was going to send him packing for visiting that bloody bay? But she had the intuition of an animal, sometimes. "No," she said, as he made for his room. "Nothing to do with you. I have to explain why I didn't want you to explore in that direction. Incidentally, why did you?"

"Why, I saw that someone – must have been Virginia – had gone through with Henry, so I just followed her tracks. If they could, I didn't see how it could be dangerous."

"Virginia went through the Hole? No. She always turns back at that point. We all do. You're saying her tracks were on the other side of the Hole?"

"There were tracks – at least, the dog's tracks – at some point in the bay, which was why I associated the carcass with dogs. But you could be right; I don't remember seeing human footprints in the cove, just a dog's. Coyote's, I mean."

"We don't have coyotes here."

"Oh. So you're saying that the carcass is a dog?"

"Go and change, Owen." She transferred her attention to the Burmese cat stalking by *en route* for his empty food bowl. "And no way are you eating now, so don't push it."

He caught the edge in her voice, turned and followed Owen; if he couldn't wheedle food out of her, he'd settle for soft words from the other one.

Paul Manton winced as claws scrabbled on wooden planks. He lowered the National Geographic and waited, knowing exactly what was about to happen.

The big poodle hurled himself against the screen, announcing his arrival noisily. There was a bellow from Virginia: "Cut it out!" Feet pounding up the steps. "Back off, you bastard, one of these days you'll go right through—" The screen door crashed open, the dog plunged past her, stopped on the Turkey rug and shook himself luxuriously, ear fringes flapping, water showering.

6

"Gin! Can't you leave him outside? Look! All over the rug—"

"Hubbell's hounds are loose again. Here, on our own beach! I saw the tracks. Win's boyfriend went through the Hole, following them."

Paul was wiping water from his magazine with a handkerchief. Henry lapped noisily from his bowl by the fridge in the huge open-plan room. Virginia, who had her priorities straight, swooped on the bowl, rinsed and re-filled it, scarlet nails and rings flashing in the sunlight. She turned back. "Those hounds are lethal; they could attack a man. Owen's a townie: he walks through the Hole – no regard for the tide – and loose dogs in the forest—"

"He's not a townie; he was raised in the Welsh mountains some place. Of course that doesn't have to mean he knows about tides. Did he come back?"

She was running her hands through her hair. The question checked her: arms raised, sweat and sand patches on her shirt, Levis she'd outgrown revealing too many bulges and thighs like tree trunks. He regarded her fondly. Virginia Manton had the reputation of a termagant but not among her intimates, least of all to her husband, who might knuckle under to her ostensibly while going his own way on the quiet. "Well," he prompted, "did you see Owen come back?"

She sat down. "I didn't see him going, only coming back just now," she smiled slyly "tippy-toe through the poppies, soaked to the crotch, and Win waiting on the deck, breathing fire. He must have escaped while she was asleep."

"What's the fuss? If he came back he didn't meet any killer dogs."

"What worries me is low life letting their savage brutes run over our land. You figure Henry could cope with those hounds? Let alone Win's beloved cats – none of 'em would stand a chance. You know something? I'm going to start carrying the Colt."

"You'd never dare."

"Just watch me."

"Oh yes, shoot the dogs, but how are you going to deal with Kent Hubbell when he comes here looking for the shooter? He's served time for wounding, remember; it was only good luck that guy survived. If he'd died Hubbell'd be a murderer."

"For all we know he is; he just hasn't been caught yet. A man who beats his wife's capable of anything, not that she doesn't ask for it: Stagg Harbor's hooker, and not averse to crapping on her own doorstep in—"

"Now look, we've had enough—"

"OK, OK. All I know is I have to find a maid and no way am I going to employ her mother-in-law. This place can look like a dump, I'll clean it myself before I let Myra Hubbell inside it again. Not that there's all that much wrong with Myra – apart from her partiality for single malts – but she's the thin end of the wedge. Misty's the thick end – very thick. What a family! Kent, old man Hubbell—"

"You can't blame the old man for being sick."

"Myra blames you for not helping—"

"Jesus, you were a nurse, Gin; how can a surgeon, retired at that, help an old guy with multiple sclerosis?"

"It's how Myra thinks, a mind-set. All doctors are the same to them: magicians. Her husband's got MS, you're a doctor, even retired you've got contacts; you should know who can cure him. You *spurned* her." Virginia paused for effect. "And her daughter-in-law," she added, getting up to go to the kitchen.

"Good job I did," came his voice, thinking, as he returned to his magazine, "or there'd have been murder in Prosper." He relished the image of his formidable wife advancing on Misty Hubbell: a cheap scrubber certainly but possessing something . . . allure? His guts contracted.

"Peaty or pure?" Virginia asked.

"What's that?"

"You were miles away." She smiled knowingly. This woman knew his thought processes. "Tomatin or The Macallan?" she prompted.

"I think I'll have a beer. It's warm weather."

Misty Hubbell dabbed Connie Dodge's Chanel between her breasts and stoppered the bottle carefully. There was no hurry. The pickup wouldn't start and she had to wait for Myra to come home when she could borrow the Subaru. Her attention was caught by her reflection in the mirror. Maybe she should tint her hair, although that pale shade looked bleached anyway, 'ash' they called it at the salon. It would look better with a tan, but her pale skin went red in the sun, never tan. The blue of her eyes passed muster – some guys asked if she was wearing coloured contacts – and with shadow and eyeliner they looked huge. She thought her lips were too full so she reddened them only slightly, with Damask Rose. On the whole she was looking good, not that it mattered; it wasn't the face or the big boobs or the long legs that men went for, it was the rest.

Misty wasn't high on IQ. She wasn't a proper hooker because she didn't trade, although she accepted money when it was offered. She did love to screw, and her reputation went before her. If men could have her for nothing, they did. She was the macho man's dream.

Myra, drinking her first cup of coffee after her return from the Dodges' place, sighed as her daughter-in-law came to the door in her scarlet stilettoes and the black frock with white polka dots, the long V plunging between her breasts. "Now what d'you want?" she asked.

Misty was twenty-four but she could pass for much younger. Today she looked like a teenager in her big sister's clothes. "The pickup's broke," she said. "I'm out of cigarettes. Can I take the Subaru?"

Myra's eyes lingered on the new gilt purse. "The keys are in it," she said gruffly. "At least you don't get drunk." Misty didn't rise to that. "I have to be at work at ten," Myra said meaningly, both knowing that Misty wouldn't be back till the small hours. She added, as if it were an after-thought, "When's Kent home again?"

"God knows."

The screen door slammed. Myra frowned. She didn't dislike the girl, she'd have made a good wife except for this wild streak. Maybe she'd grow out of it. And Kent put up with it; wasn't as if Misty deceived him, couldn't, could she, Stagg Harbor being so close? They both of them knew where they were coming from, her with her nights on the town, him coming home at long intervals, hearing new gossip in the bars, taking his belt to her. They stayed together for all that. Eventually there had to be kids (Myra's thinking faltered as to their parentage); Misty would settle once there was a family.

"You there?"

She started, blinked and stood up. She drained the last of her coffee and made for the bedroom. "I'm here. You want something?"

Two

The small town of Stagg Harbor was six miles from Prosper but only as the eagle flew. Impassable headlands barred access by way of the coast even for an adventurous hiker, while inland was the impenetrable forest, probably more inaccessible now than before the old growth was logged a century ago. It wasn't so much the new growth of hemlock and cedar, spruce and red alder that kept hikers and hunters at bay, but the sappy green understorey, not to speak of the ground that was nowhere level, pitted with holes and seamed by water-courses, all of it masked by rotting fallen trunks and the ubiquitous greenery.

Stagg lay south of Prosper but in order to circumvent this huge block of forest, initially the road from the settlement ran east, parallel with the Blacktail River but so deep in the timber that the water was invisible except near the start where the road crossed to the north bank. Upstream of the bridge there was a stretch of white water and a gorge where fine rock scenery was inaccessible to anyone other than a kayaker. Even when a landslide tore through the forest in the forties, taking the road and a swathe of timber with it, the water was still way out of sight below. The bare slope was convex, steepening above the gorge.

Six miles east of the coast the Prosper road met the highway and one turned southwest for Stagg Harbor. At the junction was Angel's Camp: a gas station, a crude bar and a cluster of tacky cabins patronised by fishermen in the season but ignored by the wealthier inhabitants of Prosper. If any locals went there they were the people who lived in the forest.

Another group of ramshackle cabins stood in the trees upstream of the bridge, surrounded by the remains of rusting vehicles. If the gentry could ignore Angel's Camp, the existence of this rural slum so close to home angered and embarrassed them. They salved their consciences, to some extent, by employing Myra Hubbell, at least until recently in the case of Virginia Manton.

10

Driving to Stagg the morning after she'd realised that Hubbell's hounds were loose again, Virginia saw Myra approaching the road from her cabin. They exchanged stiff nods.

Beside Virginia in the car, Amy Nelson waved brightly. "Car broken down?" she wondered. "Who's she with today? She comes to us tomorrow so it has to be Bill Selhorst today. Or is it you, Ginny?"

"I wouldn't have her in the house," Virginia said tightly, swerving to avoid a leggy rooster. "She's Misty's mother-in-law."

Amy flushed. "Misty's not to blame," she said stoutly. "It's a condition. She needs help."

"You can say that again." They rattled across a plank bridge with a wrecked pickup in the creek below. "Look at the oil in that water!" Virginia was vicious. "Corruption set in here when Win's granddaddy upped sticks a hundred years ago."

"No one's to *blame*," Amy insisted. "It wasn't economical to go on logging when there were more accessible forests elsewhere. I'm sure old man Carver meant well."

"Your mission: defending the underdog." Virginia glanced sideways. The girl had new glasses: large with red frames, too big for such a small face; David should have chosen something more suitable for her, but then David wasn't concerned with appearances. Neither of them was.

Amy had married young. Plain, determined and passionate, she shared his interests with her older husband. David Nelson was a naturalist, currently employed in trying to ascertain the number of cougars in the forest in relation to the deer. The introduction of wolves had been suggested and most people thought there weren't enough prey animals to go round. Prosper wasn't bothered; they didn't want wolves and were pretty sure David's research would decide against them. In any event the job meant a harmless man was employed and it was healthy to have new people in the community; there was someone fresh to talk to other than spouses, and neighbours they'd known for decades.

A vehicle appeared ahead and Virginia lifted her foot. It was a two-lane road on this section but automatically one slowed down to have a good look at the other driver.

"It's Myra's Subaru," Amy said. "So that's why she's walking to Prosper." They were inclined to refer to the houses on the coast as Prosper, ignoring the cabins in the forest.

Virginia's face was set; she knew it had to be Misty in the Subaru.

The car approached at a moderate speed. Virginia's lips stretched, her eyes fierce. Misty grinned cheekily as she passed.

"That frock!" Amy exclaimed, twisting to stare. "How low did it go, for God's sake?"

"Probably to the navel. I didn't peer."

"You think she's been out all night?"

"Amy, you are *too* naive!"

"But – what about her husband? Kent?"

Virginia didn't answer. Amy leaned back on the expensive leather and shivered.

They went their separate ways when they reached town, Virginia dropping Amy at the health food store before finding a place to park close to the supermarket. Land was at a premium on this rugged coast and although Stagg had a fine harbour, snug inside a twisting estuary, only the boats had plenty of space; cars had to squeeze in where they could. Besides, it was Friday, tourists and yachtsmen were starting the long weekend and Stagg was humming.

Virginia and Amy met again at Brewster's restaurant: a white wooden building overhanging the water, a place famed for its seafood. Over their drinks they speculated on the party Constance was throwing that evening and for which Virginia had been asked to find ripe avocados. They agreed on a fancy luncheon since the party was just drinks, and they ordered extravagantly, Virginia's treat. They both had crab gumbo; Amy, stern environmentalist, rationalising that the oysters, at least, were farmed. Afterwards she sat back, sighed sensually, caught Virginia's ironical eye and looked away guiltily.

The tables on the outside deck were filling up with boat people. They were identified by their creased but expensive casual clothes and sneakers, not to speak of the means to lunch at Brewster's where even the coffee cost a bomb. Virginia's gaze passed over the men and the slender girls in designer shirts to linger on the older women. Her eyes widened.

"There's a Fassett sweater just like Connie's," she declared. "Bat-wings and all. Funny, I had the idea his stuff was custom-made."

Amy stared at the woman wearing a sweater in rich reds and shades of blue. "They sell kits," she said, "but Connie bought hers in New York. Maybe that lady made hers."

Virginia snorted. "Not wearing that rock," she said, stooping to vulgarity – a tendency of hers after the second drink. The diamond on the woman's ring finger was indeed ostentatious for casual wear. New money, she had it so she flaunted it.

Virginia wore her rings for safety's sake, distrusting home safes. "I don't think that lady knits," she said. "I guess she bought it in Seattle. There has to be an outlet."

"I'd love one." Amy was wistful. "I wonder, could I convince David to give me one for Christmas. Shall I ask her where she bought it?"

Virginia shrugged. "Wait for an opportunity."

It came when the woman went to the powder room. They rose and trooped after her, and while Virginia entered a cubicle Amy fussed with her hair.

A lavatory flushed and the stranger emerged, smiled pleasantly at Amy and stepped up to wash her hands. Amy stared into the mirror like a small child. "I've been admiring your sweater," she gushed. "I'd die for one like it. Did you buy it in Seattle – or San Francisco?"

Virginia appeared, alert as a pointer. The woman included her in the conversation: "Actually I found it here, in Stagg Harbor. Isn't that odd?"

"Where?" Amy was incredulous.

The woman focused on this ingenuous girl so she missed the dawning suspicion in Virginia's eyes. "It was a – private transaction," she admitted, seeming a trifle embarrassed. "You know Clarissa, the receptionist at the hotel next door? She sold it to me—" She was about to add more, possibly to elaborate, but she checked. She took out a comb and concentrated on her hair.

Amy broke the silence. "I wonder where she could have bought it," she mused. "The boutiques in Stagg aren't exactly upmarket. But if there is an outlet I mean to find it."

"We both do." Virginia seemed intent on her reflection, applying lipstick.

The stranger observed the large capable hands and assessed the value of the rings. The diamond was smaller than her own but the ruby and the emerald were respectable pieces. "I have to come clean," she said. "Clarissa told me she bought it at a garage sale. Gave twenty dollars for it. She had no idea of its worth of course. I gave her thirty. There!" Her face was a travesty of contrition.

"Well, you've gotten yourself a bargain," Virginia barked. "Congratulations."

"My husband says I'm a better horse-trader than him." The woman

13

was obviously relieved at the reaction of this formidable matron. She nodded to them. "It's been nice talking to you, ladies." She returned to the restaurant with just the slightest roll of firm buttocks.

Virginia paid the bill and made for the hotel next door, Amy trailing behind. The hotel was a white clapboard building with cupolas and a wraparound veranda, a tourist trap for well-heeled tourists with its brass bedsteads and gardens modelled on those of some great English estate: lush masses of colour this June day. Virginia ignored the flowers.

Their pace slowed at the porch. Inside the open front door Amy sidled into the shadows of the dark lobby leaving Virginia to approach the desk. Clarissa (her name on a label on her breast) showed no interest in the pair initially; they carried no luggage and they were women. Clarissa's interest was reserved for men.

"We have a query," Virginia said loudly. "We've been talking to a lady to whom you sold a sweater: red with batwing sleeves? I want one like it. Where did you buy it?"

Clarissa gaped, then shut her mouth with a snap. Her eyes signalled indignation and, aware of it, aware of her position and, belatedly, of this woman's potential influence, she swallowed. If those rings were real stones . . . "I bought it in a garage sale. The folks are gone now," she added wildly. "They left town."

"You're sure of that?"

The girl wavered. "I've done nothing wrong" – even Amy caught the uncertainty in the tone – "I go to a lot of garage sales and – and thrift stores." An obvious lie; like most girls of her age she wouldn't be seen dead in a thrift store. Virginia surveyed her carelessly, pricing her outfit. "I don't remember," Clarissa faltered. "What was it like again?"

"Shades of red and blue, and black. Batwing sleeves, heavy roll collar. The lady gave you thirty dollars for it."

"Oh, I remember that!" The shrewd little face cleared. "I bought it from a girl."

"For twenty dollars."

"I guess." Further enlightenment. "And it was *her* bought it in a garage sale! That's why I was confused. I buy a lot of stuff—" She checked, aware of the repetition.

"What else did she sell you?"

"Nothing." It was bitten off. Clarissa was scared.

"Misty Hubbell?" Virginia asked, eyebrows raised.

"I don't know her last name. It could be Misty. Drives an old pickup. She told me she bought it in a garage sale: the sweater."

"It was Myra, wasn't it?" Amy said as they walked to the car. "Myra gave it to Misty. What are we going to do?"

"Difficult," Virginia admitted. "We have to tell Connie, but there's the wretched party. Myra's helping, probably there right now, after she finished at Bill's place. Damn! Maybe I'll leave it till tomorrow, get the party out of the way. There's no knowing what Myra would do: she's unpredictable and, after this, worse than I'd thought. That family is the pits."

Three

B ill Selhorst was greasing his mountain boots, taking a sensuous pleasure in working the dubbin into the old scuffed leather, thinking of it as an animal's cracked hide. His daughter sat cross-legged on the deck and watched him indulgently. Their kinship was obvious in the small faces: broad brows and wide grey eyes, thin mouths and pointed chins; but where Bill, in his seventies, resembled a leprechaun, Robin, in her thirties, was stunning. This evening, in deference to the occasion, she had piled her hair up with Spanish combs, allowing tendrils to escape and cling to her neck. The sun, heading westward now, touched the hair and her skin with gold. She was Titania in palazzo pants and a top in ivory silk.

"We were asked for six," she said meaningly.

"You go and change. I can be ready in five minutes."

"*Dad!*"

He looked up. "You *are* changed." He studied her gravely. "You're very smart. Is someone else invited?" He meant someone he didn't know about.

"This is casual wear in Tucson, Daddy. I don't dress for men. Where are the men in Prosper anyway – apart from yourself?"

He set the boot beside its fellow and stood up easily: a spry little man, still loose-limbed even if the eyes were faded below brows bristling like a schnauzer's. He was brown rather than tanned, having lived all his life in the open, and for much of the time had lived hard. It showed in the seamed face. It was said that on one of his expeditions he'd been so short of food he'd been forced to eat his own leather boot laces. He'd been known as Hurricane Bill in his prime, the result of sitting out a prolonged blizzard in an ice cave on Hurricane Ridge. Now he considered her question. "There's the Welshman," he pointed out. "He's amusing, near your age-group too."

She would never convince him that she didn't find her visits to Prosper boring. She divided her time between her parents, who had divorced amicably when she graduated from university. She had no career; since majoring in English she had bummed around, in her own words, dabbling in arts and crafts, making jewellery, restoring furniture, silk screen printing. If driven to it she might agree that wealthy parents were a disadvantage but she was happy to play the field, occupation-wise. She was currently helping her mother in her Tucson gallery, but a recent affair with an ecologist had left her with an enhanced awareness of the environment. She was considering applying for a job with the Sierra Club or some organisation to save whales, or cougars, or something.

Bill's money came from family land in Texas which had been found to be sitting on a lake of oil. He was tolerant of his daughter's lifestyle; he could hardly be otherwise when he had found his own niche at fifteen, exploring his daddy's open range on a pony with a rifle in its scabbard and a bed-roll behind the saddle. He'd been exploring ever since. To hell with work; what he did – in the Pamirs and the Atlas, China or Chile – was harder grind than that of any labourer in the oil fields. His days of hard climbing were over but he still favoured the steep side of any mountain in preference to the tourist route.

Robin didn't climb and maintained that he was reckless but she had forced a compromise from him. At seventy he had agreed that in future he would not climb alone. From that time any visitor to Prosper was liable to be pressed into service as his companion.

"I've got my eye on young Owen," he said, emerging from his room and joining Robin where she waited on the deck. "He's from the Welsh mountains. I'll try him out on Sentinel Ridge."

"Is it steep?"

"It's horizontal." He smirked as he preceded her down the steps. No need to tell her that it was a knife-edge. He'd better smuggle a rope into his pack in case Owen turned out to have no head for heights.

It was no more than a few hundred yards to the Dodges' house but a quarter-mile by tracks through meadows of wildflowers now at their best, with drifts of orange poppies, a host of yellow composites and a scattering of the blue-eyed grass that is no grass at all but a tiny iris.

"The otters are back," he told her.

"I didn't know they'd left."

"Hubbell's hound was loose for a time in the spring. It went in the

17

water after them. Never caught 'em of course but they disappeared for a while."

"Is that the dog that killed one of Win's cats?"

"The same. The trouble is that with Hubbell working in the Cascades, Misty's in charge, and she's not bothered if a dog slips its collar."

"She still sleeping around?"

"Am I the person to ask?"

"So who is?"

"I would think any of the bartenders in Stagg."

"She'll get AIDS."

Bill shook his head dolefully. "I don't think the possibility would ever occur to her. Did you know that Myra had to walk here today? She lent Misty her car last night and she hadn't come back this morning."

"I hadn't realised. Myra's stupid. She's a slave to her family, and that includes her daughter-in-law. How's Seth these days?"

"He's hardly mobile, even with a walker."

"That'll put a curb on his activities. No more peeping into bedrooms."

Bill halted and stared at her in amazement. "How did you learn that?"

She laughed. "Everyone knew Seth Hubbell was the local voyeur, a flasher too on occasions. Actually I didn't know until one July Fourth after a party at the Dodges', and Nat Dodge and some of us were skinny-dipping. It was a full moon and Nat caught old Seth – not so old then – hiding behind a rock, down there below Win's place. We thought it was funny but Grady told Nat that Seth had been caught more than once looking into cabin bedrooms at night. He wouldn't do it down here of course."

"Well, it's history now, poor old fellow."

"Dad! You'd forgive murder if it suited you."

Constance Dodge saw them approaching and went to switch on the gas to broil the clam puffs.

"I thought you were planning on having Myra to help out this evening," Virginia said, following her.

"Listen." Connie drew close. "She had to walk to Bill's because she'd let Misty take her Subaru last night, and the girl hadn't returned this morning. Then she came over from Bill's to give me a hand here and by five she was panicking in case Misty still wasn't home, and

Seth had been alone all day. So Grady gave Myra a ride home and I told her not to come back till tomorrow. I don't like her handing round stuff anyway. It's not like a formal party."

"If it was, Myra Hubbell's the last person I'd hire for it, considering—" Virginia bit it off but the venom was unmistakable.

"Myra's not to blame for Misty's lifestyle," Constance pointed out. "Anyway, Misty had come back," she added absently, peering at the clam puffs. "Grady said she was sitting with Seth on the porch."

"That fits. No one could imagine Misty without a man." Virginia drifted away. This wasn't the time to tell Constance that her maid had stolen her sweater. It could wait till morning. Her attention focused on the Selhorsts, grudgingly approving Robin's outfit – with the mental qualification that only a woman who was anorexic could wear it.

"I find this place unbelievable," a voice said.

She turned to find Owen Hughes at her elbow. Her eyes went to his glass: no ice, if there was water it didn't show. And evidently not his first whisky. "Meaning?" she asked.

He looked through the glass wall to the sparkling ocean. "The juxtaposition," he breathed. Virginia blinked. "The wild coast," he elaborated, the mobile face relaxed and dreamy, "this room, the rugs and the parquet, the Edward Hopper, Wagner – the Wagner's wrong: savage, nasty, but there's that book on Delacroix . . . of course he can be savage too, but even Wagner and Delacroix have their own kind of sophistication."

"You've been drinking."

"Who hasn't? I write best after a couple of whiskies –" he paused, took a gulp of his drink and went on "– meaning that I can deal with Win's writing. With a few drinks under my belt I'm quite a competent copy editor."

"What do you find unbelievable?" Virginia asked, seeing that she was stuck with him for a while and after all, he was different, given that she could understand what he was talking about. "What was that about juxtaposition? A good word." It was a jibe but it went unnoticed.

He looked up at her. She was wearing low heels but he was no more than five foot seven. "You're living on a volcano," he told her. "Prosper's a tiny enclave surrounded by hostile elements: the ocean in front with submarine earthquakes and tsunamis, the forest behind, and God knows what that contains." He stopped and stared at her.

19

"Go on."

"Well, that's it," he said lamely, and looked away. He took another gulp of his whisky.

"You were in Stack Cove yesterday," she said. "What did you find there?"

"What would you expect me to find?"

"Something sinister? Otherwise why go over the top about the dangers surrounding us, the volcano that we're living on?"

"It's the ambiance. I'm a Celt. We believe in magic."

"What do volcanoes have to do with magic?"

"It was symbolic. I'm drunk. You must excuse me." He moved away: normally a neat little guy but at this moment giving the impression of clumsiness.

Constance intercepted him. "Owen, try these clam puffs, and there's guacamole on the side. You won't be eating properly till you arrive home, you know." Grady hardly drank himself but he was lavish with alcohol for his guests and the Welshman had been drinking steadily. "What were you so intense about with Virginia?"

"My dark soul talking," he confessed. "I find this place intimidating. Don't get me wrong, I love living here, it's just – the wildness, you know?"

"But you're not a townie."

"Far from it. North Wales is all mountains, but they're bare, bleak places; you can see where you are. The forest here troubles me. It could be a tropical jungle. Thank God there are no snakes."

"And then there are the tides. I saw you go through the Hole yesterday."

He was still, his eyes narrowed. "I followed tracks," he said carefully. "A dog's tracks."

"What did Win have to say about that?"

"That people in the forest let their dogs run loose, or they don't care if they slip their chains."

"Did she tell you that a hound killed one of her cats back in the spring?"

"Yes." He appeared quite sober now. "Yes, she told me that."

"So we don't talk about loose dogs," Constance said calmly, although she had initiated the subject. Her tone lightened. "I envy novelists this – catharsis? The ability to write out negative emotions: anger, resentment, all that, to exorcise them."

He smiled with singular charm. "How do you exorcise violence?"

20

"I play Wagner very loudly, my dear, one of the advantages of having no close neighbours. You've finished your drink so now you're free to sample the guacamole." She relieved him of his glass and he moved obediently to the sideboard with its canapés and dips. Owen had been properly brought up and usually did as he was told by autocratic women. He looked for Win and saw her on a sofa flanked by the Nelsons, neither of whom would think to mingle at a party, and who were now talking across the old lady. Win summoned him with her eyes. He picked up a plate of canapés and crossed to the sofa. The Nelsons stopped chatting and accepted food distractedly.

"What was Constance saying about tracks?" Win asked, as if making conversation.

"A dog's tracks in Stack Cove." Owen was dismissive. He smiled at Amy. "A grand place for dogs to run," he enthused, "seeing that there's nowhere you can take them inland: no paths."

Amy glanced at her husband. David Nelson was twenty years her senior but he still had a young man's body and, to Owen, the eyes of a Welsh preacher, a fanatic's eyes. "We were just talking about trails in the forest," Amy said.

"I didn't know there were any."

"There aren't now," David put in. "They're all overgrown. There's one goes up to the reservoir that supplies our water, and there was another from the bridge, used to go all the way to the cove, an old hunting trail. The loggers did a deal of hunting."

"Not now." Win was grim. "Not on my land." She owned three thousand acres of timber and there were No Hunting signs all along the road to Angel's Camp.

"We have to do something about those dogs," David said, evidently knowing what was in her mind. "They kill for amusement, not food, and they go for the fawns first. They have to be shot."

Owen and Win exchanged glances but it was Amy who said, "There's a leash law, for heavens' sake! Can't the sheriff order Hubbell to keep his brutes chained? Although that's cruel," she added, "keeping a dog tied up – unless it's hunting. But if hunting's illegal –" she turned wide eyes on David "– why keep hounds at all?"

"They can hunt elsewhere." He gave a mirthless smile. "And there's always poaching."

Amy glared. "I don't know why those people stay there in the forest. There's nothing for them, they're all on welfare—"

21

"Not true. Myra works. Kent's still got a job."

"And Misty? You call what she does work?"

"I have to speak to Robin." Win stood up, Owen extending his hand to her. "Sitting too long," she murmured. "I must circulate. Good boy." She patted his arm. "Come and talk to the others."

Paul Manton was flirting outrageously with Robin, watched bemusedly by their host. "I have to break up that corner," Constance remarked, pausing by Bill, glancing at his drink. "Robin must give everyone the benefit of her charm. Paul and Grady are monopolising her."

"Paul is. I don't know about Grady. He looks puzzled. Doesn't Nat bring girls home?"

"Not girls with Robin's looks." Constance sighed. There was a time when she'd hoped that her son and Robin were serious but it had come to nothing. She assumed that Robin was too insecure, too impulsive to be tied to an ambitious young lawyer. The girl – woman now – had the looks and the poise to make a brilliant hostess but she lacked dedication. Constance knew all about dedication to family. Aware of her eyes on him Grady looked startled, then guilty, recalled to his duties as host.

It was nine o'clock when Win made the first move to leave, to loud protests from Grady. "We have to go." Win registered polite surprise. "Owen and I usually put in an hour or so before bedtime."

"Before – What the – What do you *do*?"

Someone giggled in the stunned silence. Owen broke it. "Madame is now into bodice-ripping," he explained, deadpan. "I'm the collaborator."

"Collator," Win corrected, "meaning secretary. Actually I prefer to call it historical drama. A new departure."

The front door closed behind them but they were silent as they crunched across the gravel. The moon was in its second quarter and, once clear of the house, Owen slowed at sight of its bright track on the water.

"That was a mistake," Win murmured. "Collaborator!"

"It was a joke."

"I know, but if they'd been dogs their ears would have pricked. You're my secretary; it's for your own good too, you know."

It was two o'clock in the morning when Misty came home, tired, dishevelled and frightened. She parked the Subaru outside Myra's cabin and clipped up the porch steps, heedless of waking her father-in-law. She knew Myra hadn't gone to bed, a blue light flickered in the living room.

"Turn this thing off." But she did so herself, kicking off her shoes and dropping into a chair beside the set.

Myra had known something was wrong when the girl came to the door instead of going straight to her own place. She sensed disaster. Misty was ugly with fatigue, her lipstick smudged, her eyes desperate. "That red sweater," she burst out, dropping her voice at an anguished signal from Myra, throwing a glance at the closed door of the bedroom. "Did she never guess?"

Myra shook her head weakly, speechless.

"Clarissa says they were asking today, knew everything: how much she gave for it, hell, they knew about me! The stupid cow, she told 'em!"

"Mrs Dodge? She was where? Who's Clarissa?"

"You know. Clarissa at the Schooner in Stagg. Not Mrs Dodge: Virginia. Had to be her, covered with rings, Clarissa says. And another with her, musta been the Nelson woman. They wanted to know where it come from: the sweater."

"She was wearing it? You said – I told you to sell it to a tourist, one who wouldn't be coming back."

"I did. She did." Misty paused, and lied. "I gave it to Clarissa, told her not to flash it about, sell it to some woman off of the boats. But whoever bought it musta come back and it was just our luck Virginia recognised it. She'll have told Connie Dodge."

Myra stood up and went to a battered cupboard. Reaching in past a clutter of clothing and picnic plates she retrieved a bottle. She found a mug and poured a measure of bourbon. She drank half of it, leaning against the sink for support. Misty glowered at her, waiting.

Myra returned to her chair and said carefully, "Virginia Manton came in while we was baking. She didn't say nothing and Mrs Dodge were never out of my sight nor hearing. There was phone calls but if any was from Virginia Mrs Dodge kept quiet and her manner never changed towards me. Told me to come back tomorrow morning – this morning now." She stared at the blank television screen.

"So why's Virginia keeping quiet? You figure she'll tell the doctor first, ask him what to do?"

Myra thought about it. "She'd never ask him. He might be clever with his hands, had to be, what he did, but his brain's between his legs." She regarded her daughter-in-law fixedly. Misty looked defiant, awaiting an accusation, but Myra was on a different track.

"I wonder how we can get out of it," she mused. "The colonel couldn't take his eyes off of your legs when he brought me back yesterday afternoon."

Misty ignored that. "Anyone could have took it," she pointed out, panic keeping her blinkered. "It were in a box in the garage, you said. No one ever locks their garage; if the big doors are closed, they leave the side door open."

"You're not thinking straight. This Clarissa said you had it. That means I give it you. I'm going to lose my job – with all of 'em, not just Connie Dodge. Oh, my God, if they call the police –" Myra stared at the bedroom door "– who'll look after Seth?"

"I can—"

"Don't be stupid, girl; you're in it too. Let me think. Go home now, get some sleep, you look half-dead. We'll talk in the morning."

Four

G rady Dodge jerked upright and swung the telescope to the left as the front door opened. Myra wiped her feet on the mat and said good morning, noting that the 'scope would have been aimed at the Selhorst woman down on the shore.

"Mrs Dodge had to go to Stagg," he told her. "She said you'd know what to do."

Myra nodded. "Was it a good party?"

"Oh yes. Fine. The hors d'oeuvres were fine." He was always nervous in her company, whereas Myra was always distant, stressing that she knew her place, and so further embarrassing the old fool who she was certain had never known what it was to have a servant in the house until he married money. However, gestures were immaterial today; what mattered was that, assuming Constance had gone to Stagg Harbor to find the woman in the batwing sweater, she hadn't breathed a word of the affair to the colonel. Had she done so he'd have been putting on some show of indignation.

She started to clear the debris of the party. Constance hadn't even troubled to load the dishwasher. That was a signal: contemptuous, knowledgeable. Constance knew — and she'd gone to Stagg to find the proof.

Myra didn't hurry over her chores. She behaved as she would at any other time: cleaning, polishing, vacuuming where the guests had been, running the machine through the master bedroom — which was in better shape than the living room. Constance had been raised to put her things away tidily, and the colonel would have died before he allowed any woman other than his wife to touch his clothes. So shy indeed that he'd disappeared into his workshop after she'd arrived. Now Myra switched off the vacuum and bustled back to the kitchen. No sign of him but a sound of hammering from the shop. She could use the telephone. Afterwards she returned to the bedroom, opened a drawer and took out a small, sealed box.

In the shop Grady was uncomfortable. He knew that someone

should always be on hand when Myra was in the house but he'd thought that was because of her liking for whisky, and he'd devised a clever trap of pencil marks on the labels. So he'd retreated to his workshop but was uneasy in case Constance should come home and catch him there. When he heard the front door slam and an engine start he sighed with relief and laid down his tools.

It was two o'clock when Constance returned. Her van was gone, both garage doors were raised, exposing the interior with all the valuable equipment – mower, irrigation pipes – and the stacks of boxes containing winter clothes, from one of which the sweater had been removed. She was furious.

She went to the garage and reached inside to retrieve the house key from its concealed hook. She wondered if, in the past, someone other than Myra could have come across these open doors: some itinerant gardener, a salesman or a religious nut, who had seized his chance . . . Lost in the scenario she mounted the steps and inserted the key in the lock. It wouldn't turn. Now what? She was tired, hot and exasperated before she reached home. Disorientated, she tried to force the key before stepping to one side and peering through a window.

The big open-plan space was neat, in perfect order. Myra had cleaned up as if nothing had happened. And the woman had to know. The girl Clarissa would have told Misty that Virginia had questioned her, surely. And where was Grady? She giggled hysterically. Gone off with Myra – in his wife's van? Then she remembered that he'd given the woman a ride home yesterday. Maybe she'd had to walk to work today as well. With a derisive snort at the untidy structure of such lives, she twisted the door knob. It turned and the door opened. He'd left the place unlocked. So what was missing now?

Old Hubbell was in front of the television set when Constance arrived. Kent's dog had alerted Myra before the grey Merc came sliding through the trees. Which was how she thought of the car, and its driver: slippy like a rattler. "You stay here," she told Seth. "I got business with Miz Dodge." Talking as if he were mobile but she liked to humour him.

He showed a spark of interest but only because it was a variation of routine. They had a visitor. Some days he would have been out of his chair and working his way to the window behind his walker, see what was happening. Today wasn't one of those; good days were getting fewer. TV wasn't really holding his attention, he just sat there and stared. He couldn't see much through the cataracts but the images moved, and they were coloured; put him in front of it like a baby and it would keep him occupied. If the cataracts were cut out he could take an interest in things again, enjoy life. As Myra came down from the porch, a look of mild enquiry on her face, she was wondering exactly how much it would cost for the operation.

"You got a problem?" she asked as her employer stepped out of the car.

Constance had been home for an hour. Grady hadn't returned, for which she felt a certain relief. She didn't need distraction at this moment, she needed a clear head. She had showered, drunk a small whisky, considered calling Virginia, rejected it, and driven to the senior Hubbells' cabin. The whisky was for support, not in a confrontation with Myra, but to help block out the thought of Seth Hubbell who, despite his having been the kind of dirty old man children were warned against, was now a sinking wreck. For all that, Myra's question caught her off balance.

"You could say that." She clamped down on anger. "How come a woman in Stagg is wearing my sweater?"

Myra raised thin eyebrows. "How would I know?" It was years since maids called their employers 'ma'am'.

"She bought it from a girl at the Schooner Hotel, and she had it from your daughter-in-law. How did *she* acquire it?"

"Someone's not telling the truth," Myra said calmly. "What girl at the Schooner?"

Doubt niggled at Constance's mind but she wouldn't show it. "I've spoken to her. She's willing to testify."

"I don't understand." Myra showed no sign of being flummoxed; she understood well enough.

Constance said coldly, "It's criminal. There'll be a charge of theft; Misty received stolen goods, and sold them on. There was more than just the sweater." It was a statement, not a question. "And that alone was worth hundreds. What else is missing?" Her voice rose with her anger. The dog started to bark.

"Keep your voice down," Myra ordered. "Hubbell's having a bad day."

"You don't have to come back," Constance said tightly. "Whether you have the face to show yourself at my friends' houses is your problem. I wouldn't advise it." She threw a glance at the cabin. How dare she mention Hubbell! "You should have thought of his welfare before you started appropriating my property." Clever, that;

27

'welfare' would have suggested to her that she could stand to lose benefit.

"I've taken nothing of yours," Myra said with dignity. "Nor has Misty. I won't be coming back, you may depend on that, and I have to find out where I stand with you calling us thieves. And maybe saying so to your friends. Isn't that slander?"

"Try it," Constance grated, moving to her car. She stopped and turned. "You won't," she said quietly, "you're not that stupid."

Myra smiled faintly.

Constance drove home. She was puzzled, wondering how the woman could appear to be so confident. There had been no sign of fear, and she needed the money. And even a short term of imprisonment would mean old Hubbell having to go into a home. Her attitude was more than puzzling, it was disturbing.

She needed to talk to someone. If she couldn't prevail on the sheriff to search Myra's cabin ("There has to be more than one red sweater in town, Miz Dodge . . .") at least she could make sure than no one in Prosper would employ the woman again. No doubt she had ways of entering the houses, would have scouted them in advance. Would she have dared to have keys cut, borrowed them and had copies made? Should they change the locks?

It was Saturday afternoon. Most people would be home, Virginia and Win certainly, but what was needed here was someone with knowledge of the law. Nat, of course, although he was into torts and civil action, not criminal stuff, but Nat sailed his boat at weekends, would be out of touch. Bill Selhorst would have no idea what to do, Paul Manton was interested only in good living, David Nelson was the most undomesticated . . . Grady was a broken reed . . . And where had he been? He must be there by the time she reached home.

Grady was deep in the relative merits of a '94 Jaguar XJ6 at twenty thousand, and a '95 Volvo at sixteen. He knew which he'd choose, and knew without doubt that Constance would go for the Volvo. She said Jaguars were vulgar.

"Difficult," agreed Norm Riessen, squeezing more oranges while Grady stared moodily at his empty glass. "Both done 34,000, but one reliable, the other – well . . ." He spread his hands, looked wistful. "The Volvo's a lady's car, take her friends to town and stuff. The Jag's more what you'd call a masculine beast, know what I mean?"

"But pricey," Grady pointed out.

"Ladies like its lines." Norm contradicted himself smoothly. He was drawing a picture, allowing Grady to place himself in the frame, at the wheel of a man's car. "What d'you think, Misty?" Norm asked.

"I'd adore a Jag," Misty said.

The three of them were the only occupants of the bar at Angel's Camp. There had been other customers, tourists passing through; they'd gone, leaving the dark room quiet, somnolent, even friendly. Grady had stopped here for gas a few times in the past and chatted to Norm but he'd never been in the bar before. He wasn't drinking now of course, only orange juice; he might have a Scotch before he went home, just one, it looked effete otherwise, drinking juice, particularly in front of a woman.

Norm Riessen had called to say he'd heard Grady was thinking of selling the Mercedes and he might have a buyer, a friend who would consider an exchange. This guy, a dealer in Tacoma, had acquired a Jaguar and was on the lookout for a buyer. He had plenty of other makes, which was how the Volvo came to be mentioned.

Grady, who knew that Constance wouldn't consider buying a used car, least of all a Jag, had nevertheless welcomed the excuse for a jaunt, had felt quite boyish as he drove through the forest, amused to find himself pushing the van as fast as it would go in order to try to avoid his wife as she returned from Stagg. At Angel's Camp he parked deliberately behind the bar where the van wouldn't be seen by her as she passed.

The tourists had been in the bar when he entered so he'd ordered an orange juice and waited until Norm was free. He was surprised to find Misty there, seated on a high stool, a red skirt revealing smooth thighs. Her skin glowed in the dim light and he wondered if she oiled it with something. She told him that Norm had brought her pickup in with his recovery truck so that he could fix it. Riessen was an able mechanic. "Hubbell could fix it," she assured him. "But he's out east in the Cascades."

"Yes, I know." Grady reddened. He smoothed his moustache. "You'll have a drink?"

Misty bloomed with pleasure at the attention. Rather pathetic, he thought; they weren't used to men with manners. Norm served her with what Grady registered as some kind of cocktail but his thoughts had reverted to cars. He was wondering if he might persuade Constance of the advantages of buying a used motor; one

29

owner, low mileage, she'd save thousands. And then he might win her over to the idea of the Jag.

Norm returned his change. "Have one yourself," Grady told him. In this kind of place you didn't tip the bartender. But of course, Norm wasn't a barman, he was the owner. Grady blinked, recalled to the present, noting that the man chose a beer, nothing expensive. He wondered if Misty and Norm were an item, as they termed it nowadays; Norm was a good-looking specimen, well built and fit: an open face, pale hair – plenty of it and cut short, although not aping the military. All the same he held himself well, like an old soldier. German extraction, with that name, but fully Americanised, probably third or fourth generation. Well-disciplined, Germans; he'd served beside a few of them during the war.

They continued to talk cars, man-talk. Misty sipped her drink and listened. Norm knew every car in the area. He saw Constance's grey Mercedes go by but his eyes didn't flicker. Misty finished her drink and Grady bought her another, as a gesture to make up for leaving her out of the conversation.

"What *is* that?" he asked, relaxed and curious. "Some kind of cocktail?"

"It's a Screwdriver." She laughed engagingly. "Cool and smooth: just the thing in hot weather." She glanced at her glass but didn't suggest he taste it. Too familiar. She smiled again.

"Here," Norm said pleasantly, and passed a second drink across the bar. "On the house. Try it."

"It's delightful," Grady said, tasting it. "But it isn't gin."

"Vodka," Norm told him, mixing one for himself. "Some folks don't care for the taste of gin."

"Quite. I'm a whisky man myself," Grady said, contributing his share to the topic although, to be truthful, he wasn't into any kind of alcohol. He'd seen what it could do to a man, knew that long before a fellow was incapable, even near the commencement of his drinking, there was a loss of control. "I don't drink much," he confided.

Norm nodded. "I like that. Liquor separates the men from the kids. We had a bunch of problems like that in 'Nam and it was the senior ranks that held us together: older guys, experienced, knew drink and action don't mix. *They* didn't fall apart under fire."

"A pity there aren't more like that around now," Grady said. "There'd be far less violence without drink and drugs – and bad manners." He glowered, recalling slights that had escalated to insolence. "There's no discipline! In the schools, in the family;

d'you wonder there's so much crime?" As always when incensed, his thoughts were leapfrogging. "More than half the thefts are to finance a habit."

"Well, at least Prosper's crime-free." Misty giggled, put down her glass and slid off the stool.

Grady watched her make her way to a door marked 'Does'. The men's was marked 'Bucks'. He turned guiltily but Norm had his back to the bar, re-filling her glass. He placed it on the counter and deftly filled two more.

"I haven't—" Grady began, indicating his unfinished drink.

"Need plenty of liquid this weather," Norm said comfortably. "There's only enough spirit in that to give it a sting in the tail."

"That's good. You should call it a Scorpion." Grady stroked his chin and eyed the door marked 'Does'. "You and her – known her a while, have you?"

"Just good friends." Norm knew exactly what the other had in mind even if he didn't know it himself. "She gets lonely, does Misty; likes company."

Grady turned and looked out of the window at the empty highway. "Got quite a reputation," he murmured.

"She's a good girl. Clean-living."

"My, it's warm!" Grady gulped down his drink. Misty returned, her eyes passing lazily over Grady, over Norm, fastening on her Screwdriver.

"Hot day," she said.

"A shame there's nowhere to swim," Norm mused, as their eyes made momentary contact. "All that ocean and no proper beach—"

"—lying in the sun," she murmured.

"The kids used to go in off the rocks below my place," Grady said. "But you're right, we don't have a riviera."

"What's a riviera?" Misty asked.

He reminded himself that country schools wouldn't teach these people much, if anything, about Europe, and he was right. She knew nothing of any country outside the States; Canada and Mexico to some extent, but although she knew Spanish was spoken in Mexico she didn't know that Spain was part of Europe. She was familiar with a version of England from television but the reality was a closed book to her. He found it amusing to instruct her, to tell her about Switzerland: St Moritz and Klosters where the British royal family went to ski, Venice and the palaces on the canals, Rome,

31

Paris, Athens . . . some of these known to him from his military service, others recalled from hearsay.

Misty appeared entranced. Norm put in a comment here and there, and kept the drinks coming. Grady grew warmer as he talked and, sweating, told Norm to stop squeezing oranges and give him sparkling juice from a bottle. It annoyed him to have to wait while the fellow fiddled with fresh fruit, and it was quite unnecessary. Norm complied readily. The fizzy stuff disguised the vodka better although he doubted it needed disguise any longer. Grady literally didn't know what he was drinking.

"Athens!" Grady proclaimed. "There's a frieze—"

"A freezer?" came her clear voice.

"Frieze! Frieze, like—" He swung round to find one here, flourishing an arm towards the ceiling. There was a crack, a confusion of movement and an impact.

"Oh, my God!" Her voice again. "Not his head! Quick, what do we do?"

He opened his eyes, surprised that they'd been shut. He saw legs, glossy and rising for ever; other legs in shabby denim. Hands cradled his head, he smelled scent. He sat up. "What happened?" He was totally at a loss.

"You moved too quickly and the stool slipped," Norm lied. "You cracked your head on the floor."

"Musta thought I was on a horse." Grady giggled. "A horse would have moved with me, a good horse, that is. You ride?"

Norm didn't answer. They got him on his feet but his legs seemed to be made of rubber.

"Funny thing," he said, "I'm finding it difficult to stand, but there's nothing wrong."

"Have a drink," Norm said. "You've been out in the sun too long."

"You figure?" Grady stared at him. "Whatsa temperature?"

"It's just right," Misty assured him. For some reason she was kneeling, rubbing his legs. Her blouse had come unbuttoned and he could see her breasts. He tried to remember when he had last seen firm breasts.

She looked up. "I'm restoring the circulation. Is that any better?"

"Dreamy," he said. He could hardly keep his eyes open. The prospect of being able to lie down was utter bliss.

"You'll feel better in the air," Norm said. "Come on, let's take you outside."

With Misty on the other side, Norm managed to work him out of the bar, legs dragging, but when the air hit him, warm and cloying, he begged them to let him lie down. "I can't make it," he gasped, not sure what he meant, but knowing home was somewhere else, knowing he couldn't reach it.

"Not here," Norm urged. "There are people about." Grady was too far gone to put the lie to that. "It's just a few more steps, then you can lie down. Open the door, girl!"

Misty ran ahead and opened the door of the nearest cabin. Taking all Grady's weight, Norm shouldered him inside and pushed him on the bed. Grady opened his mouth to say something, grunted, and his eyes closed.

"All yours," Norm told her. "For what it's worth."

Five

At six o'clock Virginia knocked at the Dodges' door and walked in. "Hi, Connie! Paul says you have something to show me. Why, you're doing kebabs! After all that cooking yesterday!"

Constance turned from the kitchen counter. "It's something to do while I wait. I'm going crazy, Gin. Sit down, fix yourself a drink. I'll join you soon as I throw these in the fridge."

Virginia stared, and then she caught on. "You fired Myra! You went to Stagg and you found that woman – don't tell me you bought the sweater back from her!"

"At four hundred dollars? You have to be joking." Constance came and sat down heavily. "You didn't get a drink." She sounded exhausted.

"In a moment. Tell me what's happened. You look ghastly."

Constance glanced towards the front windows. "You wouldn't have seen Grady I suppose?"

"No. I've been out for hours. I took Henry inland for a change, let him run on Spruce Peak."

"Yes; Paul said. I told him I had something to show you because I needed you to come here; I needed to talk."

"You did confront Myra?"

"No. Yes. She's part of it, but really, there's another – well, not a problem exactly, it may not be anything, but I'd rather Paul didn't know, not yet anyway, in case . . ."

Virginia pursed her lips. "It's not often *you* don't make sense, Con. Is this about Myra or not?"

Constance was embarrassed. She inhaled sharply and let the breath go in a long sigh. Virginia went to the kitchen, dropped ice in glasses, poured two good measures of whisky and returned. Constance had regained control. "I've fired Myra," she said flatly, "and we'll have to let Bill and Amy know. That woman was defiant and – sinister. Far too confident."

"So?"

34

"I wonder whether we should have our locks changed, all of us."

"Or buy Rottweilers." But Virginia wasn't taking this part seriously. There had to be more to it than the help turning out to be a petty thief. She waited, sipping her drink.

"You didn't see Grady leave?" Constance's voice was too high.

Virginia's jaw dropped. "What in hell does Grady have to do with Myra Hubbell?"

"Nothing! It's just that because of her, her stealing that sweater, and God knows what besides . . . I came home to find the house unlocked: every door, would you believe, the garage wide open, my van gone. No note, no indication as to where he'd gone, and that was three hours ago!"

"Would Myra know? Did she come this morning?"

"She came. But you think I'm going to ask her if she knows where my husband went? I was at her cabin, fired her on the spot, no argument, told her I'd seen the sheriff, and Clarissa had agreed to testify."

"She did?"

"Actually no, she wasn't at all keen. And the sheriff says I have no proof the sweater belonged to me. I couldn't find the woman who you saw wearing it; I guess they left." She smiled wryly. "Small wonder if she knows the value of a Fassett sweater."

"Then you don't have a case against them – because they're both in it: Myra *and* Misty."

"If I could convince the sheriff to have their cabins searched – but the police aren't interested; they think I'm exaggerating the value. What's one old sweater, and worn at that, is how men would think. There'll be more stuff missing, you may be sure of that, but I haven't the energy to start looking at the moment."

"You're worried about Grady."

"It's so unlike him, Gin. Did Paul ever go off like that, with no note or anything?"

"Never." Virginia smiled tightly. "Always a note, telephone calls, flowers or chocolates when he came back."

"Ah yes, but you mean when he—"

"Was with girls? Oh no, dear, he was always at conferences, conventions, whatever; surgeons spend a deal of time attending functions. I always knew exactly where my old man was and who he was with. In the daytime, that is. I didn't phone him at night. He could have his playtime so long as he was careful about the playmates he chose. That's how Henry arrived: a standard poodle puppy with a pedigree as long as your arm; had to be a far more expensive present than any of his ladies received."

"Gin! You never told me that."

"You knew the substance. There was no need to elaborate until now."

It took a moment for that to sink in, then Constance shook her head. "No, not Grady. You don't know him."

"I wouldn't think it of him either, but if it isn't a woman, then what?"

They were at a loss. Grady had no absorbing interests; he enjoyed small projects: a greenhouse for Constance's succulents, shelves, cupboards, fencing, nothing ambitious.

"It could be he needed something essential from Stagg," Virginia ventured. "To complete some job. And met someone – and stayed in town. Did you look in the shop, see if he left a note there?"

"I'd have passed him on the road." But they went to the shop. There was no note. There was a shelf on the work bench, a bracket partially screwed to its underside, the screwdriver beside it.

"Nothing here," Virginia said.

"He always replaces his tools; he's obsessive about that."

"So he was interrupted. By Myra?"

"By the phone?"

"Who called?" Virginia was struck by a thought. "Could it have had to do with your sweater – like, trying to recover it?"

"He didn't know. I hadn't told him. Just reminded him to watch Myra. I always did. Never did trust her. No, nothing and no one was so important that Grady would down tools and leave the house – unlocked – without writing a note. Or calling to say what's happened." Constance looked at her watch. "It's nearly four hours now." Her voice was not quite level.

The phone rang in the Nelsons' house as Amy was peeling eggs for a kedgeree. "See to that, David," she called. "I'm busy. Don't take long. Supper's up."

He was reading a paper on the distribution and spacing of bald eagles' nest-sites. He moved to the telephone, his eyes still on the page. "Yes?" he asked absently, lifting the receiver. He listened for a moment. "She's busy," he said, and continued to read. After a while he said, "I don't employ her . . . well, I guess . . ."

36

"What is it?" Amy asked, bringing the kedgeree to the table. "Employ who?"

David shrugged. "Myra Hubbell."

"Oh, it's Myra! What does she want? Let me speak to her."

She snatched the phone from him. "Yes, Myra, what – Oh, I'm sorry, Constance, he didn't say—" She listened, interjecting occasionally: "You *did*? . . . Why, of course, you had to . . . I see that . . . Er, yes, I – I'll have to speak to David . . . yes, of course, no question . . ." Then, desperately, "What does Bill say?"

She came to the table slowly. David had helped himself and was already eating. He looked up from his reading. "Problems?"

"I didn't tell you, but Myra stole a sweater out of the Dodges" garage. Con's fired her. She told me not to have Myra here again. She's going to call Bill, with orders. She's treating us like kids!"

"We don't have anything worth stealing."

"David! The stereo, the computer, your cameras?"

"They go for clothes. You just said."

"They! You mean that class, don't you?" She was suddenly furious.

"Don't get upset. Fire her."

"I never fired anyone in my life. And she's got a husband who'll probably be dead by this time next year; she's got a daughter-in-law who's a nymphomaniac; she's so poor she can't afford decent clothes, and she'll never have tasted proper food in her life. They'll exist on junk food. They live worse than native Americans; they don't even have the kind of welfare Indians have." She banged the table with her fist. "And don't read when I'm talking! It's rude."

He sighed. "I'm sorry, but what can I do?"

"Listen to me, for one thing. They're disadvantaged, these people you call 'they'. You don't steal unless you're poor – and hungry – and you can't afford for your husband to have a cataract operation, let alone all the drugs he should be having for his MS. If it was you going blind I'd steal to raise the cash."

"We're insured. No –" as she drew in her breath to blast him, "– I mean, we're prepared for emergencies; we do without luxuries so we can keep up the premiums. We were brought up that way, Amy."

"And whose fault is it they can't afford insurance? Blame the logging industry, not the Hubbells. It's like the Indians, whose fault is it – don't put on that long-suffering look with me, David Nelson—"

"It's always someone else's fault. That's their alibi, don't fall for it. You're an intelligent woman."

"Oh, you're impossible!"

For a time they ate in silence. David refrained from glancing at the paper beside his plate. After a while she said sulkily, "So what do I do? Give her a month's money and tell her not to come back?"

"How much do you pay her?"

"Five dollars an hour, four hours a week. That would be eighty. Should I make it up to a hundred?" David's eyes strayed. "But the sweater was worth four hundred," Amy mused, doing sums in her head. "And they sold it for – what was it – twenty, thirty? What about that?"

"Give her what you think fit." He wasn't listening.

Robin put down the phone and went out to the deck. Bill was watching a quail calling excitedly from a rock. "Fox about," he told her. "I can smell it."

"Guess what." She ruffled his hair. "Constance got mad at Myra and fired her."

"Why would she do that?"

"I told you, Dad: the sweater Myra stole. You think it's funny?"

"You're laughing."

"Well, that's me. I'm surprised at you, you should be setting me a good example. And Constance says you have to get rid of Myra."

He sighed. "They'd run my life for me if I let them."

Robin bit her lip. She wished he would let them; she worried about him when she wasn't there. The environment here wasn't what you'd call friendly to old bones: the forest, the beach, the tides . . . "I guess Myra's a minor problem," she said. "All the same, you have some valuable stuff lying around."

"You figure she's going to steal my sweaters?" Hardly: he wore them until she threw them out, and then they were too ragged for the thrift store.

"I was thinking of binoculars, your camera, even some of your curios, if she knew the value of them. That ivory chess set: it's irreplaceable."

"And illegal, no doubt. No way could he sell it."

"She wouldn't know that. She'll have to go, Dad. Do you want me to speak to her?"

"Not yet." He lifted the binoculars. "There goes the fox. A bit near the nest for comfort. It's a vixen. Want to look?" He held out the binoculars.

"I can see without them. Shall I scare her off? She'll get the eggs."

"Nestlings now. Leave her alone. Her cubs have to eat too. Don't interfere."

She glared at him. The cock quail launched himself from the rock, lurched in the air and plummeted into a patch of brambles where it fluttered helplessly.

"What happened?" Robin cried.

"Watch."

The vixen had been searching methodically for the quails' nest, now she was wired: dodging round the brambles, rearing up on her hind legs, looking for a way in, her coat red in the late sunshine.

The bird found a way out, ran silently and fast for some distance, then splayed a wing and started to flutter and call in great distress, but it kept running. The vixen raced round the bramble patch in hot pursuit. The quail started to lift off the ground in long flying hops, drawing the fox away until they disappeared behind a straggle of trees.

"The fox will come back," Robin said.

"No. That ploy is nearly always successful: the broken wing trick. Now if you'd scared her away, she would have come back. No emotion involved then, d'you see, just instinct: to wait till you've gone. But thinking she was about to catch an injured juicy adult bird that was crying out in panic, that *engaged* her. You saw her, she was consumed by greed. No, not greed; the need was the cubs' need, not hers. Now what have I said?"

She was staring at him. "You even think like an animal."

"I am an animal. So are you."

"You know what I mean." She leant on the rail, looking from the Dodges' house to the forest beyond the river's mouth. "I need exercise," she said. "D'you mind?"

"You want company?"

"I thought I might drag Owen out. It can't be much fun working indoors all day."

He watched her go benignly. It couldn't be much fun tied to an old man all day either. He picked up the binoculars and looked to see what else was happening this pleasant evening.

Robin found Win's house deserted. Inside the living room the cats were excited by her arrival, mewing soundlessly and pawing at the windows. Robin liked cats and, going to the door to call them out, found the cat-flap immovable, bolted.

It made sense. Both cars were in the garage so Win and Owen were walking but, driving or walking, they'd bolt the cat-flap for safety when they left the house. In this part of the world small animals stood little chance if their home was beyond reach of a fast sprint. Bald eagles took fawns, and cats weighed less than fawns.

There was only one place to walk if you didn't go to the shore. She went round the side of the house and climbed the bank at the back by way of rough steps cut in the brick-hard soil. The forest started at the top of the bank which was overhung by eaves of juniper, but where the steps ended there was a hidden break. Robin pushed aside the feathery branches to reveal a path that was little better than a raccoon's run.

Now the forest closed in, all in shades of green with only the occasional pale flower, and even the tree trunks deeply verdant in the faint light. The sun was invisible. Here and there, very high, a patch of bark showed bark-coloured, but mostly the pillars of spruce and cedar were covered with lichen and from their branches long drapes of moss hung like abandoned bees' nests.

No birds called and no insects sang but, listening for it, Robin heard the water, and the ghost of a path dipped to a gully so choked by ferns that the creek was invisible.

Stones rocked under her feet, then she was wading, pushing the great sword ferns aside so that she could see where to step. Ahead the path climbed. She wondered where Win and Owen could be. Could they have gone all the way to the cove and were now disporting themselves in some tide pool? She giggled. Maybe Owen was, after all, more than a secretary. And good for Win, she thought stoutly, he's a sweet guy. But suppose they wanted to be private, like – skinny-dipping? She paused, thinking about that. This was Win's property, she could be invading the old lady's space, an embarrassing thought. She stood and pondered, and through the silence she heard someone approaching – something, she corrected in her mind, people didn't move fast in the forest.

Whatever it was wasn't on this path. There must be another, parallel; the sounds were coming from above. Something was up there, and approaching fast. She shrank back against a big spruce, touching it, rigid, trying to pinpoint the sounds: so loud, why couldn't she see the source?

There! A tawny flash, a deer: leaping, anguished, black eyes starting, muzzle dripping – it dashed by without seeing her. But the noises continued: more of them and, running silently, intent and terrifying, came a large dog.

Robin filled her lungs to shout, then clapped her hand to her mouth. Following the dog – which delayed reaction told her was a hound – came something like a wolf – a German Shepherd, of course – and then, plunging heavily, but no less ominous, even more so, two Rottweilers. None of them saw her as they passed.

For a few moments she stayed immobile, holding her breath, clutching her mouth. Then she looked round wildly for a weapon. There was nothing, only rotten branches. One loose dog you might cope with, but a *pack*? Fortunately they'd been running south, away from Prosper. But Win and Owen, where were they? She was torn between the need to alert them and the craving for the sanctuary of four walls and a locked door. And a rifle.

She started back reluctantly, seething with rage. She'd gone only a few hundred yards when, distantly and behind her, she heard gunfire. Then there was silence again. She broke into a dash for home.

Win and Owen came round the side of the house to find Bill Selhorst in occupation of the deck, a rifle across his knees, Robin sitting beside him, a Colt .45 within reach on the little iron table.

Bill stood up. Win climbed the steps and placed her own rifle on the table. Behind her Owen leaned a very solid stick against the rail.

"How did you know?" Win asked.

"Dad said it had to be you firing," Robin said. "I came looking for you. The dogs passed me, chasing a deer. I came home and told Dad. He said if you had a rifle there was no need to come and rescue you."

"But we came over to wait for you," Bill put in. "And find out what's going on. We've called everyone else, told 'em to be careful, told Virginia to keep the poodle inside."

"You called the sheriff?"

"Yes. Did you get any of 'em?"

She shook her head. "I couldn't get a clear shot for the understorey, but I scared them off the deer. She got away."

"Until the next time." Bill was grim. "Damn Hubbell! His hounds will pick up any other dogs running loose and form a pack."

"It's Misty that's the problem," Robin said. "She's in charge of the hounds when Hubbell's away."

"What does she have to say?" Win asked.

41

"She's not home," Robin told her. "I went up there and Myra said she doesn't know where she's gone. Out for the evening, I guess. Myra said the dog will come back when it's hungry. The other one didn't though, did it?"

Win stared at the ocean. Owen had gone indoors. Now he emerged with a tray of tall drinks. They relaxed a little; loose dogs, even packs of them, were not a unique feature of this coast. You went armed when a pack collected, and you shot to kill, and devil take the owners of the dead dogs.

"I was looking for you," Robin repeated, savouring her Tom Collins, addressing Win. "Constance fired Myra because the woman's been stealing. She called us to warn Bill not to have her in the house again. I told her not to come back when I went there to tell her the hound was loose."

Win sipped her drink. "Bad blood," she said. "The whole family. Always were a problem."

Bill's eyebrows twitched but he said nothing. Robin broke the silence. "What were you doing in the forest anyway, Win? And armed. If you knew the dogs were in there why didn't you call the sheriff, get the brutes hunted down professionally?"

Owen licked his lips and stared fixedly at his drink. Win said coldly, "My granddaddy would have gone out himself and shot loose dogs running his deer. I shut the cats in the house and we went walking, Owen and me. Oh yes, we knew there were dogs about, there are tracks along the shore. So I took my rifle – for defence. I didn't think there'd be so many of them though." She looked at the cats around her feet and her face softened. "My hostages to fortune," she murmured.

Six

It was the cold that woke Grady. For a moment he was stricken by panic, not daring to move. The only thing he could connect with was the dawn, but even that seemed alien. He was accustomed to a hint of brilliance this time of year even before sunrise, and an expanse of ocean when he turned his head. Here there was a sombre greyness, a feeling of enclosure – and a window hung with tacky net.

The room was tiny, the bed – he realised he was in a bed – was uncomfortable. A blanket scratched his chin and, as full consciousness returned, he felt queasy. He sat up carefully and got out of bed, grabbing at the mattress for support.

He was naked. He had scarcely time to find that an inner door opened on a bathroom before he reached it and threw up in the basin. He stayed there a while, retching, cleaning up, but not using the shower. A shower seemed too intimate, too time-consuming when there were important things to get straight. It was an insanitary hole anyway, with cracked tiling, a soiled plastic curtain and an unpleasant smell.

He returned to the room. His shirt and chinos were folded on the back of the only chair, his shoes neatly placed side by side. A used condom lay on the stained carpet. He stared at it as if it were a rattlesnake. He would have preferred it to be a rattlesnake.

He remembered everything then, up to a point; he could feel their arms round him as they dragged him across the yard, he saw Misty holding open the door of the cabin, this cabin. He gave a dry sob, scrubbing at his face, longing to be home, safe with his big, strong, reliable wife.

There was no sound, no birdsong. Peering past the net curtain he could see the back of the building that housed the bar and, bliss! Something familiar: his van – Constance's van, rather. Set back in the trees was a mobile home, which would be Riessen's place. There was no sign of people, not even a dog. Angel's Camp slept.

He was still wearing his watch. It said five-thirty. Seized by a suspicion he turned to his chinos, but his keys and wallet were there, and twenty dollars. He thought he'd had more originally, not much more. Possibly ten dollars were gone but drinks could have accounted for that. She hadn't taken anything, not even what she would consider her entitlement.

He dressed clumsily, flushed the condom down the lavatory, looked round carefully to make sure he'd left no possessions behind, and crept out to the van.

As he drove down the Prosper road his eagerness to be home faded as he imagined walking in at six o'clock: Constance up already, unable to sleep, turning from the stove: *'Where have you been?'* His guts gave a lurch.

He lifted his foot from the accelerator. The van came to a halt and he stared at the road that ran inexorably towards further humiliation and God knew what dire consequences. There had to be a way out of this, but for the life of him he couldn't think. He knew only that he could not go home without a story, an alibi, false but – did it have to be false? His eyes sharpened: he was a military man, a strategist. He started to turn the van.

At seven o'clock Virginia was walking Henry towards the Dodges' house when the front door opened. Virginia raised her eyebrows in query but Constance shook her head. She looked drained. "Come in for a coffee," she said. "Bring Henry."

"Hubbell's damn dogs!" Virginia tried to divert her friend's attention from the missing husband. She was carrying a pistol in a holster on a gunbelt. "It's preposterous that we should have to go armed on our own properties. I know Bill's reported it but Paul's going to put a bomb behind the sheriff. Sunday morning though and we have to wait till the law sees fit to drag itself out of bed. Like at noon."

"There's someone on duty," Constance said wearily. "I called them about Grady. To ask about accidents. I called the hospital last night as well. No one had anything to report."

"Is there something I can do?"

"Short of driving up and down the roads . . ." Constance shrugged. "And the Highway Patrol have been alerted, but they won't be covering the trails."

"Why on earth would he be on a trail? Oh, you mean if he left the van. But Grady's no hiker – and he couldn't take the van on trails. It's not four-wheel drive."

"Thank God he took it, otherwise we'd be searching along the shore, looking in Stack Cove, thinking tides, even those dogs."

Virginia bit her finger, trying to think of some explanation that they hadn't considered already. She wondered whether to mention that Paul was adamant that it couldn't be a woman. She was forestalled.

"I almost wish it were a woman," Constance said. "At least I'd know he was safe. And we could have the mother of all fights when he came home, and he'd buy me a puppy and we'd be back to normal." She tried to smile, rubbing Henry's woolly head.

"Maybe it is a woman." Virginia clutched at a straw.

"Fat chance."

They pondered miserably, going round in circles until Henry became restive and Virginia left. At eight-thirty the telephone rang. Thinking of the police, the hospital, Constance picked it up with a sensation of cold despair.

"My *dear!*" came Grady's breathless voice, "I'm so *sorry!* You must have been crazy with worry!" She was speechless. "Are you there, Constance? You're all right? You haven't—" He sounded beside himself with concern.

She took a grip on herself. "I'm here. Where are *you?*"

"In Stagg. I broke down. I couldn't call you. I've only just this minute been able to reach a phone."

"For heavens' sakes, Grady! What happened?"

"All I did was go for a drive: up to Lily Lake – well, Spruce Peak actually – but I got mired at the lake. Had to spend the night there. I walked out this morning, hitched a ride to Stagg, and we're going up to recover the van now."

"I'll come and fetch you."

"No need. Once this guy's pulled the van out he'll follow me down to the highway and I'll come straight home. I don't think the van's damaged, it's just deep in the mud. The ground looked firm enough and I was no more than a foot or so off the trail. I never expected—"

"Grady, be quiet for a moment. The Highway Patrol is looking for you. You'll need to inform the sheriff and tell him to call off the search."

"Oh. You reported me – missing." His voice was faint.

"Naturally." Constance waxed firm as he weakened. "You left no note, left the house unlocked, you didn't phone." She paused. "For all we knew you could have been the victim of foul play." She gave a snort of angry laughter. "I'll leave you to settle things. Do you have your Mastercard?"

"Mired the van!" Virginia shouted down the phone. "At Lily Lake? I didn't see him. Henry and I were up on Spruce, remember? What can I say? However, it's a relief for you. Do I come and hold the towel for when he arrives and the fight starts?"

"Don't be silly, Gin." Constance was returning to normal. "All's well that ends well. My, I'm full of clichés this morning."

"You didn't get any sleep. Go back to bed for an hour."

"Maybe I'll do that." But she wouldn't; she was going to play *Tannhauser* while she waited, and then roast him alive.

Dale Sumner was a sheriff's deputy and a distant cousin of Kent Hubbell so he was an appropriate choice to pay a more or less social call on Misty, ostensibly to warn her to keep her dogs secure but actually to keep his ears and eyes open and to ask pertinent questions. Grady Dodge's disappearance had turned out to be a false alarm so that was history; on the other hand the sheriff's wife had told him that if the red sweater had been a designer item, it could well have been worth four hundred dollars. In which case Miz Dodge would be on his back again this coming week, and those folk at Prosper had influence, financially and politically. Dale Sumner was to look for proof of theft.

A hound announced his arrival. He came in his own car, unmarked, himself in civilian pants and shirt. Misty observed his approach with approval: a heavy guy with a beer-belly and a meaty face full of good humour. She'd been expecting him, one of them anyway. She felt fine, she'd had a good sleep and she'd dressed in the short red skirt and draped top that emphasised her breasts. She opened the screen door and posed provocatively. Both of them knew exactly what she was about.

Sumner beamed his appreciation, his eyes shadowed. He was bald under the cap but Misty had nothing against bald men. "You gotta problem," he told her, shouldering past the screen and dropping on a shabby sofa that sagged under his weight.

She ignored that and brought him a beer without being asked. She hoisted a buttock on a corner of the table and swung one leg like a child. Her pump dropped on the floor. "Tell me about it," she said.

"Where's the other hound?"

"There's only one. What's the problem?"

"Kent has only one dog? I thought he had more."

"The other disappeared."

"What you're saying is it run off and never come back. When was this?"

"Weeks since. Kent don't know yet. He's going to kill me when he comes home." She didn't seem disturbed.

"You got more than that to answer for," he said meaningly.

"So? This'n were loose yesterday but it come back. It's chained now. The collar were loose and it pulled its head through."

"Tighten the collar, girl."

"I did. What happened? Did it kill someone's chickens?"

"It was loose with a bunch of others. The Selhorst woman saw them. She was lucky they was running a deer or they coulda turned on her: a Shepherd and two Rottweilers and your hound."

"They didn't touch her?" He shook his head. She shrugged. "Well then, how did she know it was Kent's hound?"

"It was loose. You said so yourself."

"OK, but it's done no harm—"

"It were on Miss Carver's land. You got her to reckon with."

"Kent's not feared of an old woman."

"Now, Misty, that's no way to talk. Those folk are millionaires and they stick together. These cabins are on Carver land, and Myra works for them."

"Not no more, she don't." Misty glared at him. "She left Win Carver when the old cow took up with that fella, young enough to be her grandson, and Connie Dodge fired her yesterday, said she stole some old rags from the garage, put out for the thrift store, shouldn't wonder. And Connie'll have spread it about: yak-yak-yak to all her friends. And Myra with a sick husband, what's she gonna do now for work?"

"How is Seth?" Sumner asked. "Still chasing little girls, dropping his pants?"

"That Opal Crane! She's a worse gossip than Connie Dodge; she's an animal, breeds every year, like a 'coon. And every one of those kids has a different daddy, you know that?" Misty grinned. "Why, one of them littluns got a look about him just like you, Dale Sumner."

He didn't turn a hair. "Any of 'em look like Seth?"

"You know as well as I do old Seth never done no harm, he never touched no one, least of all a grown woman—"

47

"He touched all right—"

"Only littluns—" She broke off, then went on, collecting herself. "Seth's finished, burned out. Even with all them littluns over the road he's helpless, can't move without a walker. He's near dead, Dale, leave him be."

He shook his head. "You got some queer morals out here in the forest," he said sadly, and stood up.

"Where you going?"

He looked surprised and she relaxed, the bathroom was through the bedroom. She went to the fridge for more beer.

Sumner flushed the lavatory and glanced over the rough shelves that had been nailed to the log wall. He could see nothing that seemed out of place in a logger's home, such as a big bottle of French perfume. But women's stuff had such fancy names he doubted that he'd be able to identify anything filched from a posh house anyway.

He sauntered through the bedroom – bed not made, invitingly open, sheets rumpled. His eyes raked the dresser, the top of a chest. All kinds of make-up here: lipsticks, eye-stuff, curlers, combs – and there *was* a bottle of scent: Chanel, it meant nothing to him. All of it much used except for a little green box still in its sealed wrapping.

"You get a kick out of a girl's make-up?" Misty asked from the doorway.

He picked up the green box. There was a tiny gilt polo player on it. He looked at Misty. "Present for Kent," she told him and turned away. "I'll give it him before I tell him one of his hounds is missing."

"Maybe we should go outside," he said. "Myra will have seen me arrive."

"So what?" But she followed him out to the porch, carrying fresh cans of beer. They sat on plastic chairs and Sumner considered the path to the senior Hubbells' cabin.

"She wouldn't be bothered about you being here anyways," Misty said, following his gaze. "She's got enough on her mind with the Dodges slandering her."

"Slander, is it? Who you been talking to? Myra could never make it stick."

"Listen up, Dale Sumner: Kent's momma never stole nothing in her life; you figure she'd drive into town, sell a sweater to a lady off a yacht? You have to be joking."

"How did you know she'd sold it to someone on a yacht?"

"She – that Connie Dodge, she told Myra when she fired her."

"But you were the go-between. 'Least, that's how the story goes."

"And you listen to stories. I know how that one started. Clarissa at the Schooner: she had it in for me ever since—" She stopped and eyed him, defiance fading. She grinned broadly.

"Stole her fella, did you?"

"Maybe I looked at him in a bar. Some women are just possessive, but that Clarissa, she's neurotic. Like others I could name, not a million miles from here neither."

He pricked up his ears. "Tell me about it."

"And be arrested for slander?"

"No witnesses, and I'm not carrying a wire." His eyes were warm, inviting gossip.

She looked coy. "There are" – she counted on her fingers, long and fine and tipped with scarlet varnish – "five men down there" – she gestured towards the coast – "and two of 'em with great big buffaloes of wives. But possessive! You wouldn't believe!"

"You're talking about the colonel."

She gaped, then snorted with laughter. She sobered and thought about it. "Maybe – but not in the way you mean. He's Connie's lap-dog certainly but he'd never dare look at another woman; why, I don't think he knows what they're *for*." She giggled. "No, it was the doctor I had in mind. And what d'you expect? Ginny Manton would keep that man in a cage, but he's a sly bugger . . ." Her eyes glazed. "Generous though."

This was deep water: fascinating but nothing to do with thefts from Miz Dodge. "The colonel went missing," he told her.

"Grady Dodge? He's missing?"

"No, he's been found. He'd gone for a drive, a hike, whatever, mired his van, had to spend the night in the forest. Miz Dodge called us this morning but he walked in soon after."

She was playing with her hair. "Have another beer? Then I gotta be moving."

He declined, saying he'd promised to take his boys fishing, he'd called only to make sure the hound had come home and was securely chained. There was the other hound, but that wasn't his problem, fortunately. As he drove away he wondered where she was going: Stagg, Angel's Camp, or somewhere further afield. She hadn't put that red skirt on for the neighbours. He was worried about Kent's reaction when he came home, worried not because Misty slept around (the guy knew what she was when he married her) but because of the missing hound. Kent would never forgive Misty for losing it.

He didn't go far. He needed to look in on Opal Crane, make sure she kept her eyes skinned for those dogs. All her littluns running loose, and Opal herself not strong on intelligence, no man there to protect the family. Who'd stay anyways when all the other kids except his own came from someone else?

However, Opal did have a dog. As he approached the big old cabin in its clutter of rusting cars a chained animal, part-Doberman, gave tongue between strangled coughs, trying to choke itself in its efforts to reach him. He wondered how Opal trained the babies not to go near it. A bunch of them, the oldest a girl who looked no more than six years old, were grouped at a distance. "Hi, guys," he called, trying to sound avuncular over the baying of the hound. They said nothing and their expressions didn't change; even the toddlers were stone-faced. If he took one step towards them they'd turn tail and run.

He climbed wooden steps, careful to avoid a splintered gash, knocked on the frame of the screen and announced himself. Now, from somewhere inside, he could hear the frenetic yapping of yet more dogs.

An inner door must have been opened. A pack of small terriers dashed through the house and hurled themselves at the screen which, opening outwards, gave way before them. Sumner bellowed curses, and there was a sudden silence. The hound was still, the terriers backed off in a snarling circle. He growled commands and they retreated further, glancing uncertainly from him to Opal Crane, now standing in the doorway with a baby on her hip.

She was obese, and the baby, like her, looked unhealthy: too pale, with fat cheeks like pig-lard. Opal's hair was lank and her stained T-shirt so voluminous it was impossible to tell whether it was just fat down there or she was pregnant again.

As Sumner started to speak the terriers erupted, followed by the hound, but for all the notice Opal took of the din she could have been deaf. She waited, not asking him to step inside. He wouldn't have done so but it would have been polite to suggest it. Perhaps even Opal appreciated that her cabin wasn't the place for a deputy, and wearing clean clothes.

He had to shout. "You know about the dogs running loose in the forest?"

She nodded. He caught the word 'telephone' and the glance

towards Prosper. Someone down there would have had the sense to
call her. He gestured to the children. "Keep the kids close to home,"
he ordered.

She indicated the hound and in a momentary lull said, "Them
dogs won't come here. They'd be scared."

"You watch it, Opal." He was grim. "Your brute's chained. Them
others is loose and there's four of them." Three if Hubbell's hound
didn't slip its collar again but hell, what was the difference between
four killers and three? You needed only one to savage these babies
like they was rats.

Opal was grinning. "You know somep'n, Dale Sumner? That dog
o' mine, he'd break the chain if them others as much as showed a
whisker."

Yes, to join the pack. He shivered and turned away. A grubby little
Jack Russell made a dart at his leg and he kicked it off the porch. He
wasn't a brutal man but he had quick reactions and anyway he was
wearing trainers.

The screen door slammed, whether in anger or dismissal he didn't
care. Keeping his eye on the small dogs he returned to his car,
the six-year-old girl skipping behind him, the first sign of natural
behaviour anyone, or anything, had shown. He turned round. "There
are bad dogs in the forest," he told her. "You keep the others close
to home, you hear me?"

She didn't even blink but eyed him as if he were an alien. Her
siblings waited and watched; they weren't like kids at all, more like
little cubs. But not quite. This one had extended an arm. "What's
that for?" he asked suspiciously.

She cupped her hand and rubbed thumb and finger together. There
was a strange look in her eyes.

"No!" He wrenched open the driver's door and flung himself into
the seat. He glared at her, torn between anger and concern. He looked
at the cabin, considering whether to go back and confront the mother,
or return to Stagg and report . . . Report what?

She hadn't moved except to lower her arm. She was frowning
now, annoyed. "Who gives you money?" he asked.

She turned and walked back to the others. He thought, rationalising,
OK, so guys give her money: to stay out of the cabin, keep the
others out of the way? Opal might have a certain delicacy where her
couplings and the kids were concerned. There needn't be anything
bad going on. He'd seen too much abuse in this job, that was the
trouble, you came to see it everywhere.

Seven

"He refused to do it unless I agreed to pay cash," Grady said. "But three hundred dollars? That's one hundred fifty an hour!" Constance was furious.

"Sunday morning," Grady countered. "And there was his gas, and having to winch the Plymouth out of the bog. Someone had to recover it, Con."

"Why are we members of Triple A? We're insured, Grady!"

"Not for off-road breakdowns. Insurance wouldn't pay for a recovery truck to go up to Lily Lake." The tone was patronising but he was unaware of it. However, she was too tired to argue further. She went to the bedroom where the safe was, and returned with the cash.

"I'll take the Merc," he told her. "Don't touch the van, I'll wash it when I come back."

He drove to Angel's Camp. There was one car outside the bar, and inside Norm Riessen was talking to the fellow who must be the driver. In the gloom the shape of him looked familiar. As Grady hesitated at the door Riessen said pleasantly, "Morning, sir. You want gas?"

Grady exhaled with relief at the nonchalant tone, but relief was followed by suspicion. He went back to the Merc. Riessen emerged and came over to activate the pump.

"It'll only take a few gallons," Grady said, looking past the other to the windows of the bar. "Listen, er – Norm, don't mention that I was here yesterday. I don't want Mrs Dodge to know that I'm interested in a Jaguar. If I'm to persuade her at all I have to be diplomatic." He tried to smile but it was more like a grimace.

"Shan't breathe a word," Riessen said absently, his eyes on the pump's dial.

"I spent the night at Lily Lake," Grady told him. "I mired my van there."

"Is that so?" Riessen replaced the nozzle. "Suppose someone

remembered seeing you here?" Grady gulped, staring. "We had a number of customers around noon," Riessen pointed out.

"But no one knew me. I was just another motorist, not even a local so far as they knew."

"You talked to Misty."

"Anyone would." It was a strangled whisper. This was going wrong. The fellow was hostile, and showing it with some deliberation. Grady fought for control.

"And you were drinking orange juice," Riessen went on, "which is unreasonable in a guy of your appearance. You look a red-blooded man to me." The insolence!

"What was in it?"

Riessen opened his eyes wide. "Vodka. You were drinking vodka Screwdrivers."

"*And?*"

"And I'm waiting to be paid for the gas. And the police are watching you." Grady's jaw dropped. "Joke," Riessen said carelessly. "That's Dale Sumner inside – you didn't recognise him without his clothes, huh? Without his uniform, I mean. That'll be – call it ten bucks; she didn't take much."

Grady mouthed at him soundlessly. "The Merc," Riessen said, impatient now. "She took eight gallons."

Grady took a ten-dollar bill from his wallet. "What was in the drink?" he asked tightly, his eyes on the bar.

Riessen regarded him with contempt. "I didn't spike it. You're a guy can't hold his liquor, and that's it. If we hadn't put you to bed in the cabin when you fell off of the stool, you'd have woken up on the bar floor this morning."

"You tricked me!" Grady was livid.

"There's the deputy." Riessen gestured. "What's the charge? You didn't pay for the cabin neither."

Grady went back to his wallet and proffered another ten-dollar bill. "That's all I have," he hissed.

"You got more than that." Riessen had seen the hundred-dollar bills.

"This is for the guy who winched the Plymouth out of the mire."

Riessen took the ten, laughing. "You actually went up there and mired yourself! And now you're paying for it. I guess I'll let you off – this time." He walked away, chuckling.

Grady wanted to follow and beat him to a pulp, but there was nothing he could do, he was hamstrung. He imagined Riessen telling the deputy what was so amusing, relating the whole sordid episode.

He drove away carefully, plotting what he might do, what he could say if they spread the story. Deny it, of course . . . or would it be better to ignore it? Prosper was far enough removed from Angel's Camp to dismiss it as the kind of gossip poor white trash were prone to: an occupational hazard of the upper classes, attracting scandal. And would Riessen want such a story spread around? He drove slowly, reason asserting itself. If it did get about, even if it reached Constance that he'd been dead-drunk, he could counter that by suggesting if the juice hadn't actually been spiked, that it was Riessen who had introduced the vodka. Triple measures? Everyone knew that Grady didn't drink; one whisky of an evening was his limit. To be swilling vodka in a sleazy bar was quite out of character; it had to be spiked, his friends would say.

As for the horror that was played out in that ghastly cabin – his mind shrank from even considering a disclaimer. And then it occurred to him that no way would Riessen publicise *that*, least of all tell the police. Anyone, in fact. Because Colonel Dodge had influence, and he'd see to it that the fellow was run out of the county for keeping a brothel.

"What's Virginia picked up?" Owen stopped slicing bread and stared through the kitchen window. "It's a bird. Oh no! It's – it's—" Wiping his hands on his striped apron he opened the screen, his eyes fixed on the kitten cupped in Virginia's hands. "Jessie," he breathed, and his eyes filled with tears.

"Jessie?" Bewildered, Virginia relinquished the black and white scrap.

Win appeared, accompanied by the tortoiseshell queen. "Why, this is surely too young to be weaned." She stroked the tiny head with a finger.

"She's the image of Jessie when she was a kitten", Owen told her.

"Not quite, dear." She had taken the mite from him and inspected it. "This is a tom."

Owen reclaimed it. "You have a dirty face," he crooned, "like a draggled pansy."

"You can spare the compassion." Virginia was grim. "I was drying him off and Henry came over, only interested, you know, just for a sniff. He's a very gentle dog. And this beast struck out – he's got claws like grapnels. Henry's still staunching the blood."

"Like baby crocodiles." Owen was all admiration. "Fighting fit as soon as they emerge from the egg. Besides, he won't have seen a standard poodle before."

"Where did you find him?" Win asked.

The Mantons had been driving home after brunch in Stagg Harbor and they'd seen the kitten on top of a picnic table in the rest area south of Angel's Camp. They thought someone must have dumped it from a car. "Wicked," Owen hissed. "They should be shot."

Virginia said there was no way the Mantons could keep him; Henry was still skulking under her bed when she left. So, she said, pleading gruffly, Win would take him, wouldn't she?

"No question," Owen murmured without a glance at Win. She started to suggest a little minced chicken when, prefaced by a loud click, Owen's voice, curiously formal, issued from the stereo.

"By its light she saw a slender form suspended from a beam, part-butchered. Snow crunched outside the—"

Win had crossed to the stereo without haste and thrown a switch. Owen blinked at her, seemingly unable to tear his attention from the kitten who was trying to burrow inside his shirt.

"This is your bodice-ripper?" Virginia was amazed. "Sounds more like a horror story to me. You're a dark horse, Win."

Win looked uncomfortable. "Owen was just reading a section to see how it sounds. Very effective – I think – but then he has an excellent reading voice." She glanced around as if there was something she should be doing. "It's historical actually," she said wildly, "not horror. But there were terrible atrocities before the land was settled."

"But that's a *human* body hanging from the beam!"

"She never talks about work in progress," Owen said quickly, and then, "Chicken! The only cooked meat we have is this spicy stuff I was making sandwiches with."

"That will do." Win poked at the chicken breasts on the counter. "Scrape the sauce off and mince a tiny portion. I'll warm some gravy."

Virginia shook her head in amazement as they applied themselves to the kitten's meal. The animal could have been a visiting senator. "Aren't you going to introduce him to the cats, see how they get on?"

"They won't," Win said. He's too young to know about pecking orders and he'll get slapped down for trying to make the running."

"They'll grow to tolerate him," Owen said comfortably, "or else." He grinned cheekily as Win stared at him. He was excited and happy.

"Grady came back," Virginia said absently, dipping a finger in the discarded sauce.

"Was he away, dear?" Win spooned jellied gravy into a pan.

"He mired the Plymouth at Lily Lake and had to spend the night up there."

"Constance will have been worried."

"Angry is more like it. However, he's still in one piece. He's out in the Mercedes; we passed him on our way home from Stagg. Making his peace with the police no doubt. The sheriff had alerted the Highway Patrol to be on the lookout for him. Oh yes, and Paul reported those loose dogs." She clapped a hand to her hip. "There, I forgot the pistol! However, there was more than one hound baying when we passed the old cabins so I guess Hubbell's brute came back. Be thankful for small mercies: at least Opal Crane's Doberman has never slipped its collar."

"Not to our knowledge." Win was harsh. "I'd hate to think what would happen with all those small children running around if it did." But she was looking at the cats and, glancing at Owen, Virginia was startled to see his face convulsed with – was it anguish or hatred, or both?

"The costs could be phenomenal," Grady said.

Constance regarded him shrewdly. "You're inconsistent; a few days ago you were talking in terms of a new car, now you're bothered about costs in a criminal action? I merely bring the charge, Grady; the State brings the prosecution."

"I was thinking more in terms of the Hubbells bringing a counter suit: for slander. No –" he held up a hand as she went to interrupt, "– you have no proof, Con. The girl at the hotel – Clarissa – refuses to testify; and why do you think the woman from the yacht faded out of the picture? She doesn't want to be involved either, that's why."

"Who've you been talking to? Did you see the sheriff in town?"

"You told me yourself."

"I didn't know! This is news to me; I mean, the receptionist definitely refusing to testify."

"Ah." He thought about it. "I had coffee in town. That's it: town gossip. The girl's scared of a court case so she says Misty's a

56

liar, and she – Clarissa – knows nothing about any sweater. If the yachtswoman won't come forward there's no one to say it passed through Clarissa's hands. They say Misty's got it in for her, something to do with boyfriends. Best thing to do is drop the charge, write it off to experience."

Constance picked faded flowerets from a vase of delphiniums, then aligned magazines on top of a chest. Watching her uneasily, Grady said, "And there's Myra; you don't want a case of unlawful dismissal on your hands."

"I don't believe this! You're taking their side."

"Just being realistic. They're poison. Steer well clear of them."

"I'll call Nat, see what he has to say."

"He's sailing today. For my money he'll tell you to forget about it, and he'll send you a new sweater."

"That's not the point. And you're not giving me any support over this."

"I surely am. I promise you I'm trying to spare you the expense and humiliation of tangling with that type. They're all right as servants, if they know their place, but when they turn on you, they can be venomous. Leave well alone."

The first phone call came when they were spending a conventional Sunday afternoon on the deck with the newspapers. Constance had gone indoors for a pitcher of lemonade when the phone rang.

"I have to go to town tomorrow," she said, returning. "We're out of lemons and I need a few other things."

"Who was that?"

"What? Oh, the phone. No one."

He glanced up at her as she filled his glass. She thought he looked unwell, probably the result of last night; it would have been cold at Lily Lake and there was only an old car blanket in the van. "Would you like me to make you a toddy?" she asked.

"Why?" He was astonished, even angry: a curious reaction to a question about a drink.

"You don't look too good. Maybe you caught a chill last night." Her voice rose uncertainly as she peered at him.

"I think we're at cross-purposes," he said stiffly. "All I asked was who telephoned, and you said no one, which is a palpable lie—" He stopped, gaped and gave a wild laugh. He shook his head. "I do feel just a little fragile. You're suggesting I'm coming down with something, is that it? Maybe I will have a toddy, yes. My throat is sore. Just a minute –" as she turned back to the room "– someone had to phone, honey, or are you saying that the bell rang on its own, like a wire shorting?"

"There was no one on the line. I lifted the receiver, announced myself twice, and the line went dead. Of course there was someone at the other end: had the wrong number obviously, and not enough manners to apologise. Typical."

The second call came at five o'clock. Constance was watering her fuchsias at the front of the house. She heard the phone and through the windows saw Grady enter the room from the deck and cross to the instrument. Her attention returned to the hanging baskets. They made a glorious show along the façade of the house, dripping masses of bloom in shades of purple and crimson, and a colour that was not quite white, more like the palest shadowed silk. She surveyed them fondly; they and the plants in the greenhouse were all one could grow in this country where deer ate everything within their reach. She put down her watering can and went to gloat over the succulents and her few small cacti.

"The *echeveria* is blooming," she told Grady as she served supper.

"Splendid!" It was over-hearty. "*Echeveria*, that's neat!" His eyes were popping at her, his forehead shone with sweat and she caught a strange odour. She stopped dividing the stuffed squash.

"Grady, do you feel all right?"

"Of course I'm all right!" Overdoing the amazement.

"How's your throat?"

"My *throat*?"

"Your throat was sore. Has the toddy eased it?"

"Of course." He didn't relax, rather he sagged like a collapsing balloon. "You worry too much. I'm fine. Fine."

She had identified the smell; it was familiar, she just hadn't connected it with him, not here and now. It was whisky, but no glass was visible. She passed his plate in silence, and watched as he served himself with vegetables. She had been married to him for forty years and she knew the signs, knew before but blocked them out. He was hiding something. He'd tell her eventually. She didn't think it was drink, as in alcoholism; certainly he'd been at the whisky tonight and was hiding that from her, but a sudden craving for a stiff drink, as she knew herself, was more likely to be a symptom than the problem.

"Who phoned?" She asked, helping herself to broccoli, not looking at him.

"Wrong number."

"Again? Did he apologise this time?"

There was a pause. It stretched. "Did he say anything intelligible?" she asked.

He jerked to attention. "Not really. He mumbled something and rang off. Drunk probably. We must have a number similar to someone else's."

"That has to be it," she said comfortably, thanking God that one of them possessed some sense, hoping that whatever scrape he'd got himself into, it wouldn't escalate too far before he caved in and asked her to pull him out of it.

Eight

The police rang Paul Manton late that Sunday evening with the information that the two Rottweilers had returned to their owner. They were guard dogs from a builder's yard outside Stagg Harbor and they'd escaped when burglars cut a hole in the chain link fence and got away with power tools valued at several thousand dollars. The dogs had been knocked out with tranquilliser darts. Apparently the German Shepherd was still at large and since no one had reported it missing the assumption was that it had been abandoned. It was also assumed – or rather hoped – that with Hubbell's hound now secured, the Shepherd would be no problem. Solitary loose dogs usually kept clear of people; it was when they formed a pack that they were dangerous.

"It may keep clear of people," Virginia said darkly, "but there are pets, and I shall carry a pistol until the brute is captured or dead." And they set about phoning everyone else, starting with Win, so vulnerable with all her cats.

On Monday morning Grady elected to go to town with Constance. He needed screws, he said, and what did she think of buying a mobile phone? "A good idea," she agreed. "You go to Radio Shack while I go to the market."

"I'll be some time. I have to make a trip to the hardware place. I'll meet you at Brewster's around noon."

She dropped him at Radio Shack and continued to the supermarket. Grady strode into the store, stopped short and marched out again. He went to the bank and withdrew five hundred dollars. He returned to Radio Shack, asked for the most reliable cellular phone, used his credit card for the purchase, and made a casual exit through the rear door of the building.

A pickup was parked in the service lane, Misty Hubbell at the wheel. "You're late," she said as he came to her window. "Get in." Jerking her head towards the passenger side.

"I can't. My wife is here. Stop phoning my house. She wants to know what's going on."

"So use the mobile." Her eyes were on the box he was carrying.

"I only just bought it. Give me your number." There was a phone beside her on the seat. She gave him the number and he noted it on Radio Shack's receipt.

"You brought the money," she said.

He gave her the bills from the bank. "There's only five here." She fanned them carelessly and slipped them in her purse. "I need ten."

"You said five hundred!"

"The price went up. It's for Seth's operation."

"I don't give a shit what it's for. How can I get a thousand dollars without explaining to my wife?"

"You shoulda thought of that before you took me in the cabin."

"*I* took *you*!"

"Keep your voice down."

"Are you saying I took the initiative?" he hissed. "For Christ's sake, I was incapable. You're a whore!"

"There was a witness." Her eyes danced. She'd taken care with her make-up and to a passer-by she would have looked young and sweet, flirting with a man more than twice her age. To Grady she was obscene.

Her face sharpened as he studied her. "The other five," she said, and it was a threat.

He inhaled deeply. "No."

Her purse was on her far side. She must have guessed what was in his mind because she pushed it along the seat, out of his reach. "So where is Mrs Dodge?" she asked, glancing towards the rear of Radio Shack. "Are we waiting for her?"

Grady said coldly, savouring his Pyrrhic victory, "You can do what you like. I'm about to tell her the whole story. You spiked my drink. Riessen was in it with you." His voice rose again as a possibility dawned on him. "Of course! The fellow's your pimp. What miserable lives you people lead."

"You don't know the half of it," she said dolefully. "I'm HIV positive. I'll wait here while you go to the bank for the other five hundred."

When Constance entered Brewster's restaurant she was directed to the dim corner where her husband sat facing the entrance, a drink and a box containing a mobile phone on the table in front of him. He stood up at her approach and drained his glass.

"Let's eat on the deck," she said, controlling her face. She was sure the drink had been whisky.

He sidled out from the table and took her arm. "We're going home," he told her, the tension in his voice obvious.

She allowed him to usher her through the restaurant but once outside she turned on him. "I want to eat—"

"Where's the car?" No explanation, no bluster; he gave the impression of being hard and decisive and because he was neither of these, she was mystified.

They walked to the Mercedes in silence. "You drive," he said.

She drove out of town. "I was looking forward to my lunch," she told him. "Do I have to wait for an explanation until we reach home?"

"Yes." After a pause he added sadly, "I'm afraid so."

This was a different Grady. He was involving her too soon. As they passed Angel's Camp she heard him sigh; it occurred to her that what she had taken for decisiveness could well be despair.

Prosper looked like a sanctuary as she turned into their drive, the settlement bright and shining in the noonday sunshine, Virginia coming up from the shore, Henry bounding after her. She waved and Constance waved back.

To Grady, Prosper was like a dream, one he had had but had lost. He had woken to reality and to nightmare. He saw Virginia and her bouncy dog, glimpsed the other houses: every one of them occupied by happy, healthy people without a care in the world; and he was about to die, horribly. A sob escaped him. Constance swallowed, appalled, but she parked carefully, watched to make sure he could walk straight, picked up the groceries, trying to establish some vestige of normality by handing him a full sack.

"Sit down," she ordered once they were indoors. She left the shopping on the counter, poured two large whiskies and came to sit opposite him. Her mind was on cancer, but she would surely have known if he'd seen his doctor, so she wondered if he had discovered some abnormality, like a swelling, and jumped to conclusions. "So what's the problem?" she asked. "Let's see if we can work it out."

His face was empty of expression. He could be considering how to tell her but he showed no sign of having heard the question. She tried again. "Is it some – condition that's worrying you? It's probably curable."

"Not this one," he said dully.

She moved without haste, settling beside him. He started to turn, she put her arms round him and he collapsed, breaking down like a child.

When he recovered he told her about the episode at Angel's Camp, finding it less shaming in the telling than he'd anticipated although he left out the condom, which was too revolting. Other points he forgot or thought were unimportant, but he wasn't thinking coherently. It was Constance who elicited the fact that the whole sordid incident had started with Riessen's telephone call about a Jaguar that was for sale, and that this call had come after Myra had finished her cleaning and left the house.

"So she could have phoned the bar and told him you were alone," she said, and smiled wryly. "I wasn't here to prevent you leaving."

"Myra's not on the phone," he reminded her.

"So she phoned from here. Would you have known?"

"I was in the shop."

This wasn't the moment to point out that if he'd been keeping an eye on the woman as he'd been told to do she couldn't have used the phone. "And then again," she mused, following her train of thought, "Myra and Misty could have concocted a plan beforehand, so she must have phoned Misty too, but *she's* not on the phone—"

"She's got a mobile."

"This is diabolical! They're all in it; you were set up for blackmail, to stop me bringing a charge of theft against those women! And it worked!" She was incredulous. "You convinced me yesterday that I hadn't a case. You idiot!" She checked and continued gently. "That second phone call, when I was watering the plants: you told her I wasn't going to bring charges."

He nodded miserably. He was at her mercy. "It was incidental: the thin end of the wedge. Always the same with blackmailers, isn't it? Once you pay, or meet their demands, whatever it is they want from you, then they up the ante. On the phone it was: meet her in Stagg and bring five hundred dollars. This morning it had gone up to a thousand."

She was frowning. "Grady, how do you know you had intercourse with her if you were so drunk?"

He screwed his eyes shut. "I know."

Her thoughts were chaotic. Her hands went to her mouth and her eyes were huge. She smoothed out her expression and took his hand in both of hers. "It's too soon," she insisted. "There can't be any signs yet."

"She told me she was HIV. Just now, in Stagg, outside the back of Radio Shack. What a place to pass sentence of death on a man!"

"No!" I'll kill her, she thought, I'll cut her in little pieces, I'll—

"You can't do anything," he said.

"Paul!"

"What? What about him?"

"Go to Paul. A test. Have a test."

"He's a surgeon, honey."

"He'll know people. We can get it done quickly: same day. You can buy anything if you pay enough: jump the queue, find a private laboratory. Tell Paul to come over now. No, I will."

He was there within minutes, flushed from the heat and the urgency conveyed by Virginia who had answered the phone. Grady came to the door and took him into the main room. Through the windows Constance could be seen on the seaward slope, poking at a crevice in the rock, planting something, out of earshot but within call if needed.

Grady didn't sit down so Paul remained standing. They regarded the ocean. "I want a test for HIV," Grady said tensely. "How do I arrange it?"

Paul wondered whether he should ask Constance to come and interpret.

"Yes, she knows." Grady had guessed the thought correctly. "It was she who suggested you might be able to help." He added lugubriously, "I don't think it'll do any good: the test. I mean, if you contract it, you've had it, right? No such thing as catching it early, checking the rot."

"When did this—" Paul coughed and started again. "When do you think you might have contracted it?"

"Saturday night."

Paul was flabbergasted. The night he'd gone missing . . . The old devil was with a *hooker*? "In Stagg?" he blurted.

"I'm asking about the test, man!" Grady was poised on a knife-edge.

Paul pulled himself together. "I can tell you where and how to make an appointment. In Seattle, of course, and discreetly; I promise you it will be totally confidential, you'd be surprised how many—"

"To hell with all that. How soon shall I know the result?" Grady gestured wildly. "It's knocked her backwards."

"It'll take around fourteen days."

"*What?* I can't wait that long. Listen: we'll pay whatever it takes: private lab. test, drag someone out of retirement; Con says—"

"It's not a question of money, Grady; it's the length of time it takes for the virus to enter the system. If you were tested right now the result would be negative. In fourteen days – that is, if you were infected – the virus would show. But then, if the result is negative, you're in the clear. We'll make an appointment for tomorrow but there's nothing we can do to cut out the waiting period afterwards. I'm sorry."

"I'll go and tell her."

Paul didn't try to stop him. She had a right to know, she could be at risk too. He watched Grady scratch at the screen like a blind animal before he found the handle to pull it aside. His shoulder hit the jamb as he went out and he held the guard rail as he negotiated the steps. Constance saw him coming – she would have been keeping an eye on the house. She dropped her trowel and stood up. He approached her raggedly, like a man in the first stages of the disease, a very old man.

They came up the steps together, not touching, Constance so collected that she looked brittle. "There's nothing can be done to speed up the result?" she asked, but it was a ritual question, not a plea. He shook his head, as concerned for her as for Grady. "No amount of cash would help?" She was expressionless but the hopelessness was there in her voice.

"I wish it could, Connie."

Her chin rose. "Then may we ask you for names and telephone numbers?"

"I'll arrange that side of things." Paul looked at Grady. "Walk up the drive with me. You could do with a breath of air."

Grady gave him a ghastly smile. "I've got what I wanted from you. I can't take questions. You don't need to know."

The guy was in shock. Paul nodded, making every allowance for the rudeness, and then Constance was at his elbow, pushing him to the door but emerging with him, starting to stroll up the drive. "It was Misty Hubbell," she said.

He stopped and gave a fierce snort. "*Misty?*" His eyes glazed.

"He stopped for a drink at Angel's Camp and they slipped vodka in it."

"What makes him think she's HIV?"

"She told him so." Words started to pour out of Constance. "She was blackmailing him, first to get him to persuade me to drop charges of theft because Myra stole my sweater, and today: it was cash today. Five hundred, and then another five hundred. He knew she was about to bleed him dry so he said he'd tell me. That was when she told him she was HIV; she thought he'd never dare tell me *that*." She sniffed. "She's a poor judge of character. What it did was send him over the edge." There was a pause. "And me," she added.

"My dear!" He took her hand, full of concern. She blinked at him, bewildered. "Hang in there," he urged. "Don't let go."

"Oh, I'm with you. I didn't mean her bombshell devastated me, quite the reverse. If she was just an ordinary blackmailer I'd have been content to see her run out of the county. But she isn't an ordinary blackmailer – and I'm going to destroy her."

"I know how you feel, but the priority now is to arrange that appointment in Seattle. Let's concentrate on that, shall we?"

Patronising bugger, she thought, turning back to her own house, all men were the same. She longed to talk to Virginia but the immediate task was to find some way of reassuring Grady, and how did you do that without raising false hopes? And she had to consider what to do about Misty.

Six miles to the east a yellow Corvette Stingray turned off the highway, passing the bar at a moment when there were no customers and Norm Riessen had seized the chance to bring in a fresh stock of Cola from the back. Kent Hubbell seldom passed a bar on his home patch but he didn't have much time for Norm Riessen, too smooth for his liking. Besides, he had a skinful already, was drinking as he drove, in a hurry to reach home. He had the rest of the day nicely planned. He would check the hounds, clean his gun – no, sleep first, sleep off the beer, but Misty before that. He grinned, finished the beer, crushed the can and tossed it out of the car. She'd be home, she'd *better* be home. Then sleep, and in the evening they'd be out, him and the hounds, find him a tender little doe . . . liver and bourbon at midnight, hang the carcass ready to take back and party with the guys, and the maids from the motel . . . there was a little Philippino – shit!

He braked, his eyes starting from his head. A big buck had leapt straight off the bank and across the road. He could hear it crashing down the slope; if he'd had his rifle he'd have shot it, not to eat but because it nearly had him off the road. He drove on, seething.

The hound started to bay as soon as he turned on his track. The anger faded and his eyes shone. He was a striking fellow; six foot and broad in the shoulders, he had the broad nose and full lips that hinted at African blood way back, although no one had ever dared put it into words. The yellow Stingray suited him with its aggressive lines and long snout. His accessories had to fit: his car, his clothes, his dogs, even – he glanced at the cabin as the screen door opened – even his wife: in a shiny red skirt up to her crotch.

Only one dog was giving tongue. He stopped the car, got out, staring, and walked towards it, seeing now the other stake, the loose chain on the ground. This hound was trying to reach him, choking itself in a frenzy of welcome. Hubbell turned and looked at his wife.

"It freed itself somehow," she said. "It never come back."

"When?"

She licked her lips. "Not long since. I didn't call you because I thought it'd come home."

He moved towards her. She started to run but she knew she didn't stand a chance.

Nine

S eth Hubbell's eyes flickered as a shape passed the window. He called for Myra but she was outside, chopping sticks for the cook-stove. Kent came in, glanced round and went to stand between his father and the television set.

"Where's Ma?"

"Out back." Seth was intelligible, it was one of his good days. He was resentful too. There was no present for him after his son's absence for weeks, months, no notice taken except to ask where his mother was. He frowned, his ravaged face looking more than ever as if it was composed of blobs of putty.

The screen door banged and Myra straightened from the chopping block, one hand dangling the axe, the other rubbing her back. "What you been doing to yourself?" she asked. The Hubbells weren't strong on greetings. There were long scratches down Kent's cheek, oozing blood.

"I was home."

"Why'd she have to do that?" She came closer, peering. "What you done to her?"

"What's she done with my hound is more like it."

"Nothing. It slipped its collar and took off. It come back."

"It did? She said it didn't."

"That one did." She gestured to his cabin where the hound was whining. "It was the other one that didn't. They was both loose at different times. This one here were running with a pack of 'em: Rottweilers, a Shepherd. Folks in Prosper is all carrying guns. And Dale Sumner were here."

"About the dogs or the sweater?"

"Huh! She told you about that, did she? I dunno; Misty talked to him, and he were across to Opal Crane. Misty told you about – the rest of it?" Myra looked shifty; how much had the girl told him?

"She's told me everything – except Dale Sumner were over there."

68

He frowned, forgetting the hounds for the moment, then he grinned nastily. "I know what she done to Dodge."

"It were my idea; the Dodges would have had the law on us for that sweater, son. We had to stop them some way from bringing a charge."

"I guess you done that, but what's with the three hundred? You coulda gotten three thousand for the asking. Them folks is millionaires, Ma; you shoulda known how much to ask, you work there, you seen the insides of their homes. Now what?"

She was gaping at him. "You're out of your mind. Three thousand? You don't know nothing about them, you gotta start low and build up slowly." The cunning little bitch, she was thinking; he'd got the truth out of her and probably taken the cash but she'd kept back two hundred. "That money's for your dad's operation, have the cataracts cut out so's he can see properly again."

"Three hundred's going to go a long way towards that. I'll visit with Dodge, see if we can't come to a better arrangement."

"Wait a minute –" he could spoil everything "– maybe you should leave it until—"

"This is man-to-man stuff, Ma. *Colonel* Dodge has took advantage of my little girl – his maid's daughter, no less—"

"Daughter-in-law—"

"He's given her presents. Why" – a thought struck him – "he could have give her that sweater! Now why didn't you think of that?"

"What presents—" she began, but he was gone, swaggering off to his own place. After a moment she heard an engine snarl and saw the bright flash of his car slip through the trees. She went across to see what kind of shape Misty was in.

Constance was running out of steam but she managed to keep going. She had borne up before Grady's continued expressions of guilt, had heard as much as she could take about Misty, but when he started to become repetitive she'd brought him a watered whisky and escaped to the kitchen. The need to raise his voice destroyed the intimacy of the confessional. He slouched on the sofa and started to sulk. She put *Rigoletto* on the stereo. His eyes lit up. He loved Verdi.

She dredged the snapper with flour, thinking that he was easy to distract – too easy. She couldn't rid her mind of the pictures he'd drawn: the dim warm bar, the drink, the whore's skirt. She picked up the chopping knife and played with the fantasy of chopping Misty. The lust and violence of grand opera blended with the mood. She poured herself a brandy and sipped it, staring at the ocean and relishing the fire in her veins. She was consumed by hatred. She picked up a red pepper, admired its glowing skin and sliced it in half.

"Who's this?" came Grady's voice from the sofa.

She was alert immediately, turning from the counter, knife in hand. Grady was staring through the window beside the front door, looking befuddled. His glass was empty. A yellow car was standing on the gravel and Kent Hubbell was approaching the house.

"Stay there," she ordered. "I'll deal with this."

She put down the knife and switched off the stereo. Grady's revolver was still on the cherry-wood table beside the door: their precaution against the loose dogs. She glanced at it in passing, wondered if it were loaded, and opened the door.

Hubbell tried to see past her. "Yes?" she asked frostily.

He smiled but his eyes were insolent. "You see my hound?"

"It's Hubbell, isn't it?" She stared pointedly at the scratches on his cheek. "Your mother isn't here."

"It's your man I come to see." He took a step forward, she reached behind the door, but her movement left him space to push inside. She drew back, the revolver trained on him. He hadn't seen it yet, he was advancing on Grady who was on his feet.

"Stop right there!" Constance said in a high voice. "You turn round and leave this house immediately."

"You're in deep shit, old man," Hubbell told Grady, who was flushed and speechless from anger. He spluttered and found his voice.

"You have the gall—"

"Turn around, Hubbell," Constance repeated. "This gun is loaded."

He looked at her then. He shrugged. "How're you going to explain my body to the police?" He sat down opposite the sofa. "We have to talk, you and me," he told Grady. "Send the old woman out."

"Call the police," Grady barked, in his commanding officer's voice.

Constance thought quickly. Her husband's indiscretions were known to several people now, and he'd done nothing unlawful. On the other hand here they were being threatened in their own home.

"The charge is rape," Hubbell said, watching her. "He raped my wife. There are witnesses."

"Try again." Constance felt that she had the upper hand even if the revolver wasn't loaded.

"Harrassment before that." Hubbell was undeterred. And there's all the presents he give her—"

"Stolen by your mother, and passed to your wife to sell."

"And now you're giving her money." Hubbell shook his head in reproof at Grady. "Three hundred dollars to keep her mouth shut. That weren't right. My wife's worth more'n that."

Constance laughed and glanced at Grady who was beside himself with rage. He said, "I gave her five hundred, and she demanded five more. You're married to a hooker, man!"

"He knows," Constance said. "What he didn't know was that she conned him over the payment. It was five hundred, Hubbell, not three, and you've arrived too late on the scene. You've taken over the job of blackmailer but you're pre-empted. I already know what happened, and blackmail can't work. So there's the door." She gestured with the revolver.

"You don't get it." Hubbell was beginning to look tired. "Misty will go to court and say he raped her. She wouldn't have nothing to do with him 'spite of all the presents. She's married to me . . ." He broke off. He'd lost the thread.

Constance, watching like a hawk, knew he'd been drinking and that the last of the energy was slipping away.

"She told you all this?"

"That, and more. She give me chapter and verse, how he—"

"What you have to do now," she said loudly, overriding him, "is get her treated for HIV." He looked blank. "That's the virus that leads to AIDS," she told him. He shook his head, trying to follow. "There's a clinic in Stagg," she went on kindly. "She should go to your doctor and he'll make an appointment for her. You, too, of course."

His mouth was slack. He looked from one to the other, then back to Grady. "She – she . . ." He couldn't finish. He stood up and blundered to the door, disregarding the gun, Constance, and the vase of delphiniums which he knocked to the floor. The vase smashed; water and multi-coloured blooms were strewn across the parquet.

The door stood open as he'd left it. He virtually fell into the Stingray. Gravel flew from the spinning tyres as he roared away.

"He'll kill her," Grady said.

"If he hasn't done so already. Those scratches on his face are fresh, and they weren't put there by his mother. You didn't give her presents of course. I guess it's time I took an inventory, find out what else has been stolen."

"He mentioned witnesses. It can't be possible—"

71

"He was bluffing. There was no rape, honey; you were dead drunk." Only, if *he* wasn't lying . . . She shied away from the thought. She was still at the open door, looking up the drive. "He's done time for wounding," she murmured.

It was curious that she could view the prospect of beating Misty herself with such vicious enjoyment, but the thought of Hubbell doing it was – disturbing.

Amy and David Nelson, driving home after the fortnightly trip to the solid-waste disposal site, saw a vehicle ahead with no room to pass. David, who was driving, was unperturbed, slowing down, then easing forward because the other vehicle had stopped.

"It's Misty," Amy said. "Why doesn't she shift? Don't just sit there, woman," she muttered. "Reverse. Hell, Dave, she's expecting you to go back and there's space behind her—"

"See her back, honey." David had a poor opinion of women drivers.

"She can drive well enough – oh, all right." Grumbling, she got out and went to the driver's side of the pickup. David saw her recoil, her hands raised in a gesture of – horror? Denial? He hesitated, his hand on the door, but Amy was listening intently, absorbed. He waited. After a minute there was movement in the other cab and Amy was climbing inside, behind the wheel. She reversed to the grassy verge. He advanced, braking as he drew level but Amy was shouting at him: "Go on! Go on! Block the road!"

"Block – whatever for?"

She started to scream at him. She was frantic. He moved forward and stopped. She came running. "Don't move," she cried, scrambling in. "Wait!"

He was used to her outbursts. Like her he turned his head and saw the pickup pulling away fast.

"Oh, my God!" She collapsed in the seat. "You saw her face?"

"I didn't see anything, not with you screaming—"

"Hubbell beat her, Dave! That beast – she's all swollen up, and cut—" she touched her lips "—and her poor eyes – she'll be black with bruises tomorrow. Dave, he beat her head on the floor!"

"Is he coming after her?"

"That's why we're blocking the road. It's to give her a chance to get away. Once she reaches the highway he won't know which way she's gone. She said to wait here ten minutes."

He gasped at that. "She did – she told you to wait here—"

"Asked – *pleaded* – she's desperate – why, she's in such a state she couldn't even reverse the truck! You didn't see her."

"All right, but I'm not going to be a sitting duck for Kent Hubbell tearing up this road in a rage. I'd better make it look as if we've broken down." He released the hood catch and got out to remove a spark plug.

Amy spent the waiting time pacing the road and railing against wife-batterers while her husband listened for the sound of an approaching engine, not without qualms. When the ten minutes were up he replaced the plug and they continued, but they saw nothing of Hubbell on the road.

"Perhaps he isn't going after her," he said as they passed the track to the Hubbells' place.

Amy snorted. "He won't be there at the cabin. She let the hound loose."

"What!" He was appalled. "Jesus, Amy, why didn't you say? It'll meet up with that Shepherd, like as not."

"It wasn't important. She released it to hold Hubbell back, she figured he'd go look for that first before he came after her."

He didn't curse, he wasn't a cursing man, but he was coldly angry. "Now I have to go out and—" He stopped.

"And what?"

"I was going to say, and track that hound, but then that would mean shooting it, and there's Kent Hubbell out in the forest – armed? – and him looking for the same hound."

"You stay home." She was firm. "You call the sheriff. About the dog, that is; I doubt he'll be bothered about what happened to Misty."

They came to the start of their track and looked down at the Dodges' house as someone emerged and walked unsteadily to a yellow car.

"It's him!" Amy gasped. What's he doing *there*?"

David said nothing. The Stingray came bouncing over the potholes to tilt at the turn as a rear wheel mounted bedrock. The car roared down to the river, turned right and disappeared in the trees. "There's Connie at her door," Amy said. "So at least we know he hasn't murdered *them*. I'm glad you blocked the road. Not that it did any good but it was a nice gesture on your part. Misty may be a hooker but that's no excuse for what that swine did to her."

Dale Sumner was in the office when David called the police. The call was handed to the deputy because he was the man who knew the area, had even been following up the loose dog angle yesterday morning. He asked David if he was sure that the animal had escaped. Maybe Misty had taken it along as company on a trip, or loaned it to one of Kent's friends. Which could mean poaching, it being closed season, but neither Sumner nor David referred to that possibility.

"I don't know." David was testy, realising that Misty could have been spinning stories. "It wasn't with her in the pickup when we met her on the road. She said she'd freed it deliberately."

There was a pause. "Now why would she do that?" came Sumner's voice, intrigued.

"Look –" Amy was glowering at him "– it was my wife she talked to. Ask her." He relinquished the phone with relief, but that was short-lived; now there was this problem of the dog amongst the deer. He listened absently as Amy poured out the story: the savage beating Misty had received, her flight in the pickup – loosing the hound first in the desperate hope that Hubbell would go hunting that instead of herself. "It's Misty you should be concerned with," she insisted, "not some loose dog."

"I guess you're right there," Sumner said, speaking out of turn. "I don't give much for her chances when he finds out she set it free on purpose. Hounds is valuable animals—"

She inhaled sharply but David shook his head at her in warning. "He's got his priorities wrong," Sumner said, interpreting the pause correctly, "However, if she's gone to a friend, relative, whatever, he'll be back at work by the time she comes home. Things will have calmed down. The dog's what matters as of this moment but no way can we search for it in the forest; even Hubbell can't, but he'll be trying. He stands the best chance of finding his own brute."

Hubbell was looking, not methodically but in a fog of rage. He had left the Dodges with no specific idea of how he would deal with his wife, only a compulsion to hit, break, destroy. And when he careered into his yard and skidded to a stop, there was no pickup, and no barking. There was no dog. The chain was loose, clipped to the collar, and the collar was unbuckled.

He went to the cabin for his rifle. That was gone too. Because she was a woman and the only time he'd seen her violent was when she raked his cheek this afternoon, his first thought was that she'd taken the rifle to kill herself. He didn't like that. He wanted to pull the trigger. He wasn't unarmed. His magnum was in the trunk of the Stingray.

He went to his mother. He said nothing about Misty, nor did she. His mood terrified her. It was best to let the hound distract him, maybe he'd forget Misty after a while. He'd gone too far this time; the girl looked such a fright she'd never be able to show herself in public till the bruises faded. It wasn't what he'd done that bothered Myra so much as what he might do to Misty. So she focused on the problem of the lost hound and told him that the animals usually went to the shore, most likely going through the Hole to the cove. She'd seen Win Carver's fellow down there last week when she was cleaning at the Dodges' place. It looked like he was following tracks, and he went through the Hole.

He frowned. "Which one was that?"

"His name's Owen. He's foreign. They say he's her toy boy."

"I mean the dog. Was that the first one as went missing, the one that didn't come back?"

"No, that went months back. It's this hound that's been marauding lately. Killed Win Carver's cat – no, that were the other one when it got loose in the spring."

"One of my hounds killed Carver's cat?"

"So I heard."

He went to the Carver place. There was no sign of life at the house and the Rolls that she drove was gone, leaving only a little Volks in the double garage. He tensed as shadows moved at a window but it was only cats.

Taking the magnum he went down to the shore. It was low tide and there were only a few inches of water in the Hole. There were the tracks of raccoons but none made by a hound. He walked through the tunnel and came out in the cove. It was evening now and the water like pressed silk, the offshore stacks gold in the late sunshine. Birds were feeding quietly on the exposed weed and the only sound was the whisper of water off South Point.

He walked along the wet sand, staring at the great logs above the tide-line, at the wall of jungle behind and above, at a fresh mudslide with spars protruding. The old hunting cabin must have been carried away. The mud was still water-logged and he searched along its base for prints with no success. And then he saw the bone.

A thin stream trickled from the base of the slide and there, lying in the water, was a rib. He picked it up; it was too small for a lion or deer, too large for a raccoon. It could have come from a coyote but equally it could be from a hound. The skull would tell, but he searched and found nothing else, not even another rib.

He put the bone in his pocket and then, needing to damage something, anything, he fired at the gulls. He brought one down, grinned as he visualised the folk at Prosper, startled and intimidated by the gunfire, and then he wondered if the noise might attract the hound. Unlikely; had it been his rifle the animal might associate the sound with him, but he didn't have his rifle, *she* had it. He started back.

The tide had turned and he had to wade through the Hole. He climbed to the Carver place in the gathering dark, the afterglow reflected luridly in the windows. The door to the deck was locked, even the cat-flap secured. He drew back and kicked it open. There was a small clatter as a metal fitting fell on the floor. He threw the rib bone through the gashed opening and drove away.

Win and Owen were coming back from a lecture on the pioneer trails at Stagg's Little Theater and a late supper at the Brewster. Owen was driving staidly – Win didn't like speed – enjoying as always the experience of being in charge of this beautiful piece of machinery. There was a long straight before Angel's Camp and the turn to Prosper. He glanced in his mirror, saw an empty road behind him and was about to signal when a vehicle emerged from the side road without stopping and turned towards them, headlights blazing. Owen dipped his own lights but the other driver didn't. He came on fast.

"That will be someone who's drunk too much in the bar," Win said tightly. "Probably no manners when he's sober either."

The car passed, dazzling them. There was something about the faintly glimpsed shape of it that made Owen glance in the mirror. He saw it slow down, swivelling in a skid, saw lights wheel across the trees and then they were in the mirror – and suddenly dipped. "Turned the wrong way," he muttered. "I do that in a strange place: stop for a meal, come out, and go south instead of north." He turned the Rolls smoothly and started down the road to Prosper. The vehicle with the dipped headlights swept round the corner and crept up on them.

"*Diawl!*" Owen was incredulous. "Is this a hold-up?"

Win had twisted in her seat. "Keep in the middle of the road. Don't let him get in front." At this point there was room for another car to pass.

"Damn! We've passed the bar. If only . . ." His voice died. The other car was directly behind them. Headlights flared and a moment later there was a report. Something like a stone hit the back of the Rolls.

"He's firing!" Owen shrieked.

"Keep driving," came Win's voice, loud and steady. "I've got him covered."

He'd forgotten the rifle. She'd brought it this evening, saying, with the Shepherd still loose, she didn't like being on the roads in the dark without a weapon. Now she was kneeling on the seat, sighting through the rear window.

"I don't think the glass will break," he said, in a voice like a small boy's.

There was another report but no metallic clang. "Pull over," she said, "but gently. Let him pass."

"But if he gets in front—"

"Put your window down."

"*Win!* He'll fire—"

"*Do it, boy!*"

The window came down and cool air entered as the Rolls edged to the right. The following car then came up on the left.

"Lean back!" Win shouted and he glimpsed the rifle barrel by his right ear. Flinching away from it he risked a glance leftwards, saw pale metal, a dark figure behind the wheel, even a glow from the instrument panel before there was a shattering discharge beside him, a flash, an echoing flash – and the steering wheel was turning in his hands. "Push him over!" Win shouted.

A Rolls runs almost silently. In the crazy moment when he remembered that the only sound you should hear was the ticking of the clock, he heard the smash. Disorientated, he prepared for the pain – but there was the road in the headlights, the Rolls was moving and Win was saying with deep satisfaction, "Good for you, dear."

He slowed down. "No!" she cried. "Keep going. He may have survived."

"I can't drive. I'm shaking."

"You can so. We can't stop and change places. Take deep breaths. It's a straight road, no traffic – now. You can drop your speed a little."

"Who was it?" he whispered.

"It was a yellow Stingray. Kent Hubbell drives one."

"The guy whose hound—"

"The same. Are you feeling any better?"

He was, surprisingly. "What are we going to do?"

"Report it when we reach home."

"But – you fired." There was silence. "Did you hit him?" He was diffident.

"I hope so. I saw him jerk as I fired. But he fired too. I assume I hit him. Anyway I pushed him off the road, made him crash."

"I did that. I was driving."

"I had my hands on the wheel. You want to take all the credit?" She was amused.

"I share the responsibility. Whether he died from a bullet or the crash we killed him together."

"So? It's manslaughter."

"He may not be dead. We should go back, Win. You've got the rifle, there's nothing to be afraid of. He could be terribly injured."

"So was my cat. Keep driving."

It had been a quiet night in the bar. Norm Riessen had cleared up and was about to lock the door when, coming from Prosper, the Stingray sped past, clear as day in the security light on the forecourt. He watched it swing round the turn with no more hesitation at the stop sign than it took to change gears. As it roared down the highway he saw a car approaching from the south and wondered if Hubbell was on his correct side. There'd be the mother of a crash if he wasn't.

The other vehicle came on smoothly, signalling a left turn: someone from Prosper who'd been out for the evening. Behind it the Stingray had swung round and was coming back. Riessen switched off the bar lights and withdrew into the shadows.

Win Carver's big Rolls passed and a moment later the Stingray came creeping after it, like a predator closing on its prey. Engine noise receded, not quickly because the Rolls would be holding back the other, although it was easy to pass for some distance, but then in the dark – there was a shot.

Riessen opened the bar door. He could still hear an engine, and within half a minute there was another report – surely a magnum. A little longer interval this time: then two reports so close together he wasn't sure that it wasn't one and an echo, although this time the sound was different from the other two times. Then there was a crash, about which there could be no mistake, and silence.

Ten

The Selhorsts, father and daughter, came up from the shore and approached Win's house. They could see people in the kitchen but it was Owen who came to the door as they climbed the steps. Bill was staring at the place where the cat-flap should be, now with a rough plank nailed across the opening.

"Mussels!" Robin said, lifting her bucket. "Bring a bowl, Owen. You can have *moules marinières* tonight. We've more than enough for ourselves."

"What a kind thought." Owen turned and collided with Win. They recoiled with profuse apologies. Robin thought they both looked drawn. "You're working too hard," she told them.

Win licked her lips and glanced at Bill. "Why have you nailed up the cat-flap?" he asked and, looking at the inside of the door, "Goodness, how did that bolt get torn off?"

Win and Owen stared at him as if mesmerised. Robin said brightly, "Someone been fighting?" Dead silence. "That's a joke," she added weakly. "This is a bad time, Dad. Give me a bowl, Owen, and we'll be on our way."

Win said, "It was like that when we came home last night – the cat-flap. Broken."

Bill frowned. "Who d'you think?"

"Well, a cat didn't do it."

"Dogs?" Robin asked, and looked frightened. She shouldn't have mentioned dogs. She looked around.

"The cats are in my bathroom," Win said. She was obviously uneasy. "Except for the new one," she added wildly, "he has to be separated." She began to gabble. "Owen has a kitten, isn't that neat? They can come out now, Owen. We have to keep the door closed—" she turned back to the Selhorsts "—of course we can have the screens – I mean, the *doors* can be open providing the screen doors are latched."

Bill thought he understood the problem. "You've seen the Shepherd."

79

"No." Panic flared. "Have you?"

"No." Something was very wrong here.

Owen came back to the living room accompanied by the cats and carrying the kitten. Robin forgot the tension and started to croon.

Bill drew Win to a sofa. "Sit down and tell me about it."

They had known each other for a long time and outside her work she was closer to him than to anyone else. Besides, she was terrified. Owen wasn't in much better shape, concerned for her and for the new kitten. He sat down beside Robin and let Win tell the story: the exchange of gunfire, the Stingray crashing, Win adamant that they should not stop. And then they'd arrived home to find the cat-flap smashed, obviously kicked in, and a *rib* inside on the floor, a dog's rib, they'd surmised: a message. Fortunately, Win said, sidetracked, the cats must have been too frightened to go out; they were all here unharmed.

"But," Robin put in, appalled, "the crash! He's still there in the car?"

"No!" Win and Owen spoke together then he deferred to her. They had discussed it, she went on. Owen had said he'd go back alone, she wouldn't let him; in the end they'd gone back together, Owen driving his car. They felt safer in a car they thought Hubbell – if he were alive, if he were conscious – wouldn't recognise. With hindsight they guessed that he would have seen the Volks in the garage, but by then it didn't matter.

They drove back, Win in the passenger seat with the rifle, and they went all the way to Angel's Camp but the Stingray had gone.

"I'll bet you were relieved," Robin began, and then checked. "Oh, I *see*." No wonder the two of them looked as if they were in a state of siege: expecting Hubbell to show at any minute, come to even the score.

"You'll have to report it," Bill said, "or did you do that already?"

Win shook her head. Owen said, "She thought she'd shot Hubbell, you see: killed him. She saw him jerk as she fired but he must have been trying to dodge, as if you can dodge a bullet. Whatever, he survived, but we didn't know that till we went back. And we – I did push him off the road, the Rolls is scraped where I nudged him. So if he died in the crash – or died, then crashed – we were responsible. We didn't dare report it."

"We should have done," Win confessed. "Oh dear." She sighed. "What do we do now?"

Everyone looked at Bill. "You report it," he said firmly. "And tell the truth. Best way; the only illegal thing you've done is failure to report an accident. I guess you can live with that."

"I fired at him."

"Self-defence. Is there a bullet hole in the Rolls?"

Owen said there was: in the boot – the trunk, he corrected.

"There you are. Call the sheriff now. We'll stay, lend moral support." But they all knew that with Hubbell on the loose more than moral support was going to be needed.

Virginia shut Henry in the house and, the gun on her hip, drove to the Selhorst place. Finding no one at home she went on to the Carver house where Owen pulled her unceremoniously inside the front door and slammed it behind her. "The cats," he explained. "We're keeping them in. Where's Henry?"

"He's shut in too. I guess you know." She was acknowledging their greetings. "I called last night but you were out, Win, and anyway, everyone was on their guard already, against the Shepherd."

"Hell!" Robin exclaimed. "He's in a different league from the Shepherd."

Virginia sat down. "I don't agree. I think he's scared of you. At least, he's—"

"Never!" Win grated. "Look what he did—" she pointed to the place where the cat-flap had been, "—and he fired at us three times."

Virginia was baffled. "What *are* you talking about?"

"We're at cross-purposes here," Bill said. "What are you talking about?"

"The hound. Hubbell's hound is loose again."

Robin collapsed against the back of the sofa. "That's all we need!"

Bill said thoughtfully, "So he came back and took it."

"No," Virginia said. "Misty released it. She did it deliberately. That was the other thing: Hubbell came home and he beat her terribly. The Nelsons met her on the road and she was in such a state Amy says she wasn't really fit to drive. Apparently he left her unconscious and went to the Dodges' place, and Misty managed to get away before he came back to the cabin. She let the hound go because she thought Hubbell would spend time looking for it instead of coming after her. And at the Dodges' he tried to . . ." She stopped and gulped.

They waited on tenterhooks, forgetting their own news. "Yes?" Robin prompted, "He tried to – what?"

"He threatened them," Virginia said, red-faced. "Because Constance had fired his mother, said she was a thief – but you know all that."

"How did he threaten them?" Bill asked. "What did he say?"

"Oh, I don't know. He's a loudmouth. Anyway they got rid of him,

and called the sheriff. Now what was this about someone firing—"
She gasped. "Hubbell?" She stared at Win. "He fired at you? Or . . ."
Her eyes slewed to the cats who had arranged themselves about
the room.

Win gestured to Owen. She couldn't tell the story again. He
took over and as he spoke emotions flitted across Virginia's large
plain face: astonishment, anger, sympathy for him and Win, finally
trepidation as she absorbed the possible repercussions. When Owen
mentioned the rib bone Bill stiffened and, glancing at Win, saw that
she hadn't missed his reaction. He looked away quickly.

It was Robin who asked curiously, "What was the point of that
bone? Something like the Mafia making their bones? A sign he meant
business of some sort?" She turned to Owen.

Bill said carefully, "Could it be that he found the body of the other
hound, the one that went missing back in the spring?"

"But what would that have to do with Win?" Robin asked, and then
she remembered the gunfire when she'd gone down the forest path to
find them. If Win made a habit of patrolling her land armed . . .

"Yes," Win said, watching her. "I shot it. I put the body in the
old cabin above the cove, under the floor, but that came down
in a mudslide. Owen found some bones when he was down there
exploring. I'd tried to keep him out of it, out of the cove, in fact;
I didn't want him involved." She smiled wryly. "Didn't trust him
completely. So I told him it was dangerous to go through the Hole
because of the tides, and I didn't let on that there was a way through
the forest. It didn't work. He found the bone so I told him everything."
She looked at him fondly. "But by then I'd trust him with my life.
Anyway, we went to the cove the day that whole pack was running
in the forest – I wanted to bury what was left of the carcass but the
eagles had taken it, them and the foxes. I guess the rib surfaced after
we were there."

"So you figure Hubbell knows – or suspects – you shot the dog,"
Virginia said. "And if he knows it killed . . ." She bit her lip, glancing
at the kitten asleep on Owen's lap. "I'd have shot it myself if it had
threatened Henry," she added stoutly.

"I shall tell the police," Win said.

"Loose dog," Bill pointed out. "Your pets, your land, you had every
right to shoot it. Don't give it another thought."

Virginia said suddenly, "You reported last night's shooting, and the
accident?" Win nodded. She went on, "He must have been looking for
Misty when he met you in the Rolls. So he'd have been in a filthy

mood. Having discovered his hound was loose too. I wonder where he was in the interval. Because the Nelsons came home in daylight but it must have been quite late when you met him."

"He'd have been searching for the hound," Bill said. "I thought I heard shots before dark but I couldn't pinpoint them. Didn't pay much heed actually, might have been someone on a boat, kids playing around. That could have been Hubbell in the cove, looking there for his hound because that's where the deer hang out, but why he should fire is beyond me. That would be when he found the bone: in the mudslide. Which explains why he kicked in the cat-flap, Win. It's possible someone – Myra most likely – told him a hound had killed one of your cats. And that would explain why he chased after you when he saw the Rolls." He turned to Virginia. "You should go back and tell Grady and Paul about all this. They need to know."

"They're away." She looked uncomfortable. "They've gone – on a spree to Seattle. They'll be back tonight."

"Did Constance go with them?"

"No. She's home. I'll visit with her, put her in the picture, warn her about the dog."

"And Hubbell," Robin said darkly. "The guy's a psychopath. Didn't he try to murder someone before and went to jail for it?"

Dale Sumner, in uniform this morning and accompanied by a younger colleague, new to the area, had experienced some difficulty in trying to explain the situation at Prosper to a townie. Steve Barclay was a keep-fit fanatic, all bone and muscle, creases in his spotless pants, who'd never had anything to do with loggers on their home ground, nor their dependents. He would assess situations in the light of his own experience. His initial comment on the shooting was 'road rage'. Sumner considered this, but Win Carver was known to Hubbell, and he'd know the Rolls. Sumner thought it more likely there was something personal going here.

At Angel's Camp they turned left. There was no light in the bar but it was only ten o'clock; Riessen could still be in bed.

"It could have been a class thing," Barclay said, harking back to the shooting, "if the Rolls crowded him off the road, or blinded him with those great big headlights."

"Could be." Sumner was wondering where it had happened. Hubbell had crashed his car, Win had said, but with the sun slanting through the trees, chequering the trunks with gold, it was impossible to tell whether the gold was sunshine or a fresh gash. It wasn't important anyway, it was the shooting that was the priority. And there was Misty; the firing hurt no one, but Amy Nelson had said Misty was in bad shape. He'd call at the Hubbell place and check her out.

He'd turned down the track before he had second thoughts. If Hubbell was at home . . . But no one was there. No cars, the hound's chain loose on the ground, the collar unbuckled, no one in the cabin when Sumner opened the door and called. And they'd left the place unlocked, whoever was last to leave.

They walked round the back but there was no sign of life. As they returned to the car Myra Hubbell approached from the direction of her own place. "They're away," she told Sumner without preamble. "Which one was it you was after?"

"Misty?" Sumner suggested.

Myra was studying Barclay. "You're new," she said, noting the fresh tanned features, the crisp uniform, unable to restrain a smile. "She's in town," she told Sumner carelessly.

"We didn't pass her."

That caught her attention. "What is this? I don't ask her which town she's going to. Maybe she went north. She said she were going to have her hair done."

"When was this?"

"'Bout an hour since. Why? Has something happened to her?"

"Where's Kent, Myra?"

She glared at him. "I asked you, Dale Sumner, what you're asking questions for. My son's a man and his wife's a grown woman. I don't come round asking them where they're going, what they're about, when they're coming back—"

Sumner lifted his hands in surrender, trying to halt the flow. "We heard he beat up Misty yesterday."

"Gossip! Folks got nothing better to do. Maybe she give him some cheek, you know Misty. He coulda give her a slap or two but they musta made it up. There wasn't a sound from them last night."

"They were here?" Sumner turned and stared at the cabin.

"Where else would they be? This is their home."

"They didn't lock up."

"Why should they? I'm next door."

Barclay decided it was time he played some part in what was

clearly an interview, of sorts. "How do you know they were here if they didn't make a sound?"

"I—" She hesitated. "She said they were. Why would she lie? She come across this morning, told me Kent had gone out and she were going to town to have her hair done. He'll be looking for his hound." Her eyes widened. "Has he – that car – I always said—"

"He's all right," Sumner said, "far as we know, and if Misty was here . . . How did she look?"

Myra was embarrassed. She muttered something, clenched her lips and glowered.

"Looked bad, did she?" Sumner prompted.

"Not too bad for her to go to the hairdresser," Barclay pointed out.

Myra glanced at him. "She'd got a lot of make-up on but then, she uses a lot . . ." She didn't finish. No doubt she was used to her son giving his wife 'a slap or two'.

They drove away. At the start of Opal Crane's track there was a cluster of small children and their older sister. Obviously they'd be aware that there was a police car at the neighbouring cabin: it was equally obvious that they wouldn't leave their own territory, not with this threat in the vicinity.

Sumner stopped. "I told you all to stay by the house," he shouted across his companion as the Doberman bayed in the background. "Don't you kids never listen to what you're told?"

Their eyes were on Barclay, eager and expectant. He returned their stares expressionlessly. "What were they after?" he asked as Sumner drove on. "I didn't like the look of the girl."

"Police is the enemy," Sumner said. He had enough on his plate without having to listen to the other's reaction if he knew Opal's kids expected men to give them money. "Funny," he mused, reverting to the subject of Misty, "like you said, she couldn't be that badly marked if she don't mind showing herself at the hairdresser's. I'll need to talk to Amy Nelson soon as we're done with Miss Carver.

Eleven

Coming from the city Steve Barclay thought himself sophisticated, and his initial impression of Prosper was one of revulsion. The squalid cabins, rusting car wrecks, the litter of snotty kids aroused the same contempt in him that he felt for low life in urban slums. So he was amazed when they came out of the trees and saw the large and opulent houses above the shore; nothing could have made a greater contrast with the dying community upriver. "Hell," he said, "these must all be millionaires."

"Maybe one or two," Sumner conceded, "but they'll all stick together."

"So? We're not investigating them."

Sumner looked surprised. "No more we are." He gave a derisive snort. "Like I said: we're the enemy. I guess that could go down here too. Everyone's got something to hide, right?"

Barclay shot him a puzzled glance. "You figure this shooting's suspect? Not road rage?"

"It was a joke, man. I don't make judgements before I meet people. I've met Miss Carver but that was just about environmental stuff, like when she come in to report a dead orca washed up. This is a crime; why didn't she report it last night when it's supposed to have happened?"

"Like I said—" Barclay began, but Sumner was pulling up on a gravel circle at the back of a rambling house. A Rolls Royce stood outside the double garage, a nasty scrape along the shining door panel on the driver's side.

A small dark fellow admitted them to the house, Sumner beaming good humour, Barclay expressionless, noting that the household was assembled in strength: an old fellow who, from his clothes, looked like the gardener, a woman of similar age – his wife? A striking girl who seemed to find him amusing. The little guy who had admitted them was nursing a tiny kitten.

Win introduced everyone. They sat down and Owen served coffee and cookies. Win told her story. Owen took Barclay outside to see the bullet hole in the Rolls. Bill told Sumner they were concerned about Hubbell's intentions, where he was at this moment.

Sumner turned to Win. "He seems to bear you a grudge, ma'am."

"I shot his dog."

"The first one," Bill put in. "One of the hounds was loose back in the spring and it killed Miss Carver's cat. It was on her land," he added pointedly.

"Hubbell knew this?"

"His mother will have told him. You see the door?" Bill got up and opened it so that Sumner could see the plank nailed across the hole. "He must have kicked it in, and then he threw a bone inside. A rib, presumably from his hound, the dead one. Hubbell was in the cove yesterday."

"I put the hound under the floor in the old cabin there," Win said. "It came down with a mudslide, and the body with it."

"So he knows," Bill said. "The bone was a message. Given his nature, we'd be a lot easier if we knew he'd left the area."

Sumner knew that all these people would be a sight happier if Hubbell had died in that crash, or even if Miss Carver's bullet had struck home. It was self-defence after all.

"He was at his cabin last night," he told them. "Not there now," he added quickly. "And we didn't see the Stingray on the road. It was his mother told us. His wife was home too."

"But –" Robin turned to her father, "– Virginia said—" She glanced at the deputy, hesitated, and took the plunge. "One of our neighbours met Hubbell's wife on the road and he'd beaten her so badly she could hardly drive. You're saying she went back to him? I don't believe it."

"Amy Nelson reported that meeting," he said. "But Misty must have gone home afterwards."

"You saw her this morning?"

"No, she'd gone to town."

"Then you must have passed her on the road," Bill put in. "Driving an old pickup?"

"No." Sumner regarded him thoughtfully as the door opened and Owen came in with Barclay. "Her mother-in-law said she'd probably gone north."

"To the hairdresser's," Barclay said, coming in on cue.

Robin stared at him then turned back to Sumner. "You have to talk to Amy Nelson," she said firmly. "If she said Misty was in such bad shape do you think she'd have gone back to the guy who did it to her?"

"They do, ma'am," Barclay said and, as she rounded on him, dug himself deeper. "You see it all the time," he assured them, seeing that they were all taken aback, all except Sumner who was observing them blandly. "They'll come to the police," Barclay continued, thinking that it was time these folks learned how the other half lived, "and when it comes to going to court they withdraw the charges. Next thing you know they're back with the same guy: out drinking, coming home drunk – and it starts all over again."

"You sound as if you approve." Robin was furious.

"He's a city boy," Sumner said, pouring oil on the water. "He's seen too much of it. But to get back to the shooting, ma'am" – addressing Win, but his gaze slipping casually to Owen – "why didn't you report it last night, when it happened?"

"I thought I'd killed him," Win said simply. "And I wouldn't let Mr Hughes go up there, but he persuaded me in the end. That is, we went back together and found Hubbell had driven away, so he was unhurt. Why report it?"

"A gunman on the loose and you weren't bothered, ma'am?"

"She wasn't thinking straight," Bill said. "In the relief of not having shot the fellow she forgot the legal requirement of reporting an accident. Owen too; they were both in shock."

Sumner hadn't taken his eyes off Win during this interruption and she knew he was waiting for her answer.

"I suppose," she said slowly, "that if I thought at all, I'd have imagined he'd come to his senses and, guessing I'd report it, he escaped before the police arrived." She eyed him doubtfully and blinked. She added, "And I'd be afraid of what would happen when you found out I'd fired at him."

"It hangs together," Sumner said as they drove away. "She was scared of her part in the shooting. And the Britisher isn't sure of the law in the strange country and he's her employee. He has to do what she says, so they did nothing until this morning, and then they asked Selhorst's advice. He told 'em to call us. I figure that's how it was – as far as it goes, but there's more to this situation than what we heard there. They're hiding something. Was there a hole in the Rolls?"

"Yeah, a big one. I'd say it was a magnum did that."

They came to a sign made of bleached driftwood neatly printed with the name, Nelson. A creek came down through a meadow of thin grass and before the bridge a track ran to the back of a house that was smaller and less impressive than its neighbours but, like all of them, looked out over the ocean. When Sumner cut the engine they could hear surf pounding on rocks below the bluff where the house perched like a limpet.

"Wind's rising," Sumner said, sniffing the salty air. "My, what a place this must be in a storm!"

Barclay was disappointed in Amy Nelson. After Robin Selhorst he'd been hoping for another beauty – perhaps a more amenable one – but the woman who opened the door was clearly an egghead: straight brown hair drawn back in a pony tail, big glasses, a man's T-shirt, baggy Levis. She told them that her husband was in the cove to the south hoping to come across the track of the loose hound, and he'd be on the lookout for the German Shepherd too, the dog the police had known about for days. Sumner acknowledged that and asked if Nelson was armed. He was known to the police through his work which occasionally brought him into contact with poachers – with their victims if not the criminals themselves. Amy said of course he was armed, he would shoot the dogs if he found them – but Sumner was concerned about Hubbell. He told her, choosing his words, that someone in a yellow Stingray had shot at Miss Carver last night.

"That's Hubbell!" She was shocked. "That's his car. Where did this happen?"

"On the road up to Angel's Camp. We don't know if he's still in the area, but we'll find him, don't worry. Now tell us about your meeting with Misty."

She did so, her fingers tracing the contours of her own face as she detailed the injuries, her eyes unfocused, recalling an image she found acutely painful ". . . and she said how he gripped her head and beat the back of her skull on the floor. I told her she must go and have it X-rayed in case there was a crack. She said it hurt too much to tell."

"What would you say if I told you she went back to him?"

She sat up straight, her eyes wide. She glanced at Barclay but instead of rushing to deny the possibility she said slowly, "Are you telling me she *did* go back?"

Sumner gave a faint nod.

"I'd say she has a death wish," she said firmly. "A masochist? God, I can't believe it!" The more she considered it the more amazed she became. Finally she said, "It makes me feel sick." There was a long pause during which she continued to review the situation without self-consciousness, until the obvious question presented itself. "How do you know?" she asked sharply.

"Myra – her mother-in-law – told us."

"Oh, so Misty's not home now?"

Sumner shook his head. "We didn't see her."

Barclay stiffened and stared at him.

"And Hubbell's there?" Amy asked.

"No. He's left. He was there – or so Myra said." Sumner added casually, "Misty's gone to the hairdresser this morning."

"Oh no." She was adamant. "No way. I can just about believe she might go back to Hubbell. Women do; they can be half-murdered and still they go back. But to show herself in public with a face like hers? Never."

"So where now?" Barclay asked as they went out to the car, adding, "You think Misty's in the cabin, don't you? You figure he came back and finished her off. And Myra – she knows?" But he ended on a tentative note.

Sumner was grim. "Amy Nelson's telling the truth. You felt it, didn't you? But Myra Hubbell? Someone has to be lying and my money's on her."

If she was lying he failed to break her. She amended her statement to admit that Misty had been marked, but no more than if she'd walked into a door. In fact, she said hastily, the girl could well have done it herself. It wouldn't be the first time.

"You're saying she injured herself?" Sumner was incredulous.

Myra shrugged. "I gotta tend to Seth," she said sullenly. "He's the real injured one here. He's crippled with a wasting disease," she told Barclay. "'Fact, he don't have much longer to live."

"Can he talk?" Barclay asked, surprising Sumner, but his reaction was nothing compared with Myra's astonishment. Immediately she was suspicious.

"What's that to do with you?"

"Did he see Misty after the fight?"

"They didn't – no. He's disabled. He watches TV all day, he couldn't get over there. He uses a walker round the house, days he *can* walk."

They were standing in front of her cabin. Barclay looked towards her door. "I'd like a word with him."

"Maybe we should take a look at Misty's place," Sumner said pleasantly.

Myra was torn between the two of them: Misty's cabin or Seth? Sumner was bringing all his presence to bear, needing an invitation to enter Misty's cabin, knowing this woman was lying in her teeth, wanting to discover the reason for it. He was aware that it could be a relatively innocent reason, although he doubted if anything were innocent where the Hubbells were concerned, kin or no kin.

She made up her mind. "Come on, both of you," she grunted. "I'm not having you bothering my man, he's having a bad day. He's got no control over his bodily functions." She bared her teeth at Barclay, who was embarrassed, as she'd intended. "You figure Misty's so badly beat up she's hiding in the cabin," she said as they followed a path through the trees and the other cabin came in view. It seemed a senseless remark when there was no vehicle in the yard. Sumner was trying to make sense of it as they entered the cabin and looked around.

"Have you touched anything?" he asked.

"I've not been in here. I got no call to come rooting around in another woman's home."

They ignored that and moved through the place: the main room, the bedroom, the bathroom. Sumner took the bedroom, shadowed by Myra.

The bed was made, covered by a cheap patchwork quilt. They'd brought flashlights with them and Myra registered amusement as Sumner went down on his knees to look under the bed. There was a lot of dust; Misty was tolerably neat but only where it showed. He stood up, dusting his knees and, ignoring Myra, proceeded as if he were alone. He glanced in the bathroom, came back and opened a big old clothes closet. As he studied the top of the dresser Barclay came to the doorway and watched him.

Sumner picked up the green box, still sealed, which he'd noticed two days ago. He moved back to the main room, the others retreating before him. Myra regarded the little box warily.

"What's this?" Sumner asked.

She shook her head. "Perfume?"

"It's Polo," Barclay said. "For men. No—" as Sumner stared at him, "I don't use it, not on my pay. It costs an arm and a leg."

"A present, would you say?" Sumner asked of Myra.

She nodded. "I guess."

"She makes that kinda money, does she?" Myra continued to stare at the box. "A present for Hubbell?" Sumner mused. "Or a present to *her*? Or it was stolen? Like the sweater."

"It were a present," she said quickly. "Her friends give her nice things. She knows some wealthy people." She clamped her lips shut as if she'd said more than she'd intended.

Barclay frowned and as quickly smoothed out his expression. Sumner looked at the cook-stove and the enamel coffee pot on its top. He felt the stove's fire-box with the back of his hand. The others watched him. His attention returned to Myra. "Your son drives a yellow Stingray?" Her hands jerked. "Last night someone in a yellow Stingray shot at Miss Carver coming home from Stagg."

"No!" She looked scared. "Miss Carver! What's he got against—" Her mouth hung open, her eyes went to the window, towards the place where the hounds had been chained. "Never!" she gasped, and then, unsure of herself, "You're kidding."

"We've seen the bullet hole in her car." She shook her head helplessly. "He didn't come home last night, did he?" She wouldn't look at him. "What else have you lied about? Misty?"

That brought her to life. "She were here! I said: she come home, come across to me this morning—"

"She didn't go to have her hair done. That dresser's been cleared of stuff." He made a gesture with a big hand, the other cupped as if sweeping tubes, jars, lipsticks into a bag. "She's run, and taken the pickup, holed up some place. And Kent wasn't here; he'd never dare come home after the shooting. First place we'd look for him."

"I didn't see him. She said he were here. I believed her."

"If you know where he is, you tell him to come in to Stagg. We need to talk to him."

"Is Miss Carver hurt bad?"

"No. And if Misty gets in touch with you, you tell her to keep away, you hear?"

"She was worried when you told her Hubbell shot at Miss Carver."

"Yes." Sumner manoeuvred the car round the tight turn to the road and headed upriver. "That came as a shock; it was something she didn't know, which was interesting. It meant he didn't come home last night, because he'd have told his mother about the shooting."

"The stove was cold."

"What? Oh yes, but if Misty got up early, made coffee, then the stove would be cold by now. But would she have stopped for coffee? Would she have come back at all? There was no purse lying around. No, she'd have taken that when she left yesterday. I don't think she was there last night. Myra's lying, but why?"

"Where are you going now?"

"Angel's Camp. Misty frequented bars, and Norm Riessen's a

92

well set up fella. She had to know him; maybe she called there after she ran into the Nelsons."

"Too close to home."

"We'll see. 'Sides, I could do with something to eat. It's getting late. Maybe he'll fix us a sandwich."

But the bar was still closed, the forecourt empty of cars. "He lives in a trailer at the back," Sumner said. "Let's find out what's keeping him."

"Misty?" Barclay was facetious.

"If Amy Nelson's to be believed Misty won't be in any shape to entertain guys for a while yet."

The trailer was pleasantly sited at the edge of the clearing, trees crowding behind it, but an effort had been made to present a homely appearance in front: stylised plastic birds on sticks rising out of beds of candytuft and lobelia. The door was locked and there was no movement inside when they shouted.

They turned their attention to the cabins but all of these were locked as well and where the ragged curtains allowed they could see the interiors were unoccupied. All the bathrooms had frosted glass in the windows. There were no insect screens. This was accommodation at the bottom end of the scale.

"Who's the pickup belong to?" Barclay asked. It stood at some distance from the buildings. They walked over and inspected it. There were empty oil drums in the back and a smell of garbage.

"This has to be Riessen's," Sumner said. "His good car is a white Bronco."

"Another one who's done a runner. Now what?"

Sumner was thinking. "Grady Dodge," he said slowly. "It was Constance Dodge's sweater that Myra stole – no, Miz Dodge *said* Myra took it, don't let's jump the gun. That box of scent, what was it called?"

"What scent?" Barclay was lost. "What are you on about?"

"I took it from Misty's dresser. You said it was too expensive for you."

"The Polo? Stuff for men. What's the rush?" Sumner was striding back to the car.

"We're going to call on the Dodges, find out where that stuff came from. What's the betting it came from the same place as the sweater?"

"So?"

"So Misty's a hooker, right? There's nothing to show she confines herself to guys she picks up in bars. There's men in Prosper would spend ten times on a meal what she charges for an hour."

"Man, you're reaching. And suppose they did screw her, where'd that leave us? What are we doing anyways? What's on your mind, Dale?"

Sumner checked as he was about to switch on the ignition. He stared at the pumps on the forecourt. "I don't know," he confessed. "But here we have three people missing—"

"Not really. There's nothing to say—"

"They're not around, and they should be. Here's Riessen closed his bar and left without warning. I was talking to him two days ago and he never mentioned he was planning on leaving. There's Hubbell shooting at folk and his wife badly beaten, and they've both gone missing. I want to know why."

"And some rich retiree in Prosper is going to tell you, huh?"

"There's a connection. Whatever happened, the Hubbells are involved, and Myra Hubbell is a maid in Prosper – or was till Constance Dodge accused her of stealing. Is that connection enough for you?"

"Polo?" Constance repeated, stunned. "The men's aftershave? What can you be talking about?"

Sumner appeared disconcerted and she took pity on him. "I did give my husband some Polo at Christmas. Why is that important?"

"I was wondering if he'd missed it," Sumner said mildly. "You lost a sweater."

"Of course I did." It was a sore point. "I came in and reported it. I've discovered since that there's a bottle of my Chanel missing – and for all I know, other items."

"Maybe the Polo went missing too, ma'am. Would your husband know?" Sumner looked round as if Grady were present or was elsewhere in the house.

"He's not home." She was frigid. "I'll see if it's among his things."

She left them mutely surveying the room: the Indian blankets, as wall hangings, old and subtly coloured, the tiled coffee tables, the telescope, the books. There were pictures the like of which Barclay had never seen before: a decrepit stone cottage in a menacing landscape; a rearing horse with a lion taking a bite out of its leg, the rider in a red cape and with a huge sword – how could anyone live with that on his wall?

Sumner was running his eye along the shelves of books: military, historical, warfare; the same field guides, blue and white, that Win Carver had on her shelves. Animals and flowers went down big with these folk.

Constance returned. "I can't find it," she told them. "I think the conclusion's obvious. And I don't think Myra would be buying Polo for her husband." Meaning she could never afford it.

Sumner nodded. "Actually it was in Misty's cabin."

"Yes." Constance swallowed. "Myra passed the sweater to Misty too. And Misty handed it on to Clarissa at the Schooner Hotel, and she sold it to a lady off a yacht. A chain of petty theft."

"Myra said the Polo was given to Misty by a friend."

"She would say that, wouldn't she?"

"Quite."

Barclay had to do all he could to remain deadpan. He was hugely amused by Sumner's imitation of some high-class English detective he'd seen on television. 'Quite'. One for the book. He looked away and caught a movement outside the window by the front door.

The door opened and a big plain woman came in: unsmiling, oozing confidence, hands flashing amazing rings.

"Hi!" She nodded perfunctorily at the police. "I've come to join the party."

Constance stood up and went to the kitchen. Virginia sat down. "I'm Mrs Manton," she told Sumner, and waited. He introduced himself and Barclay. She nodded approval – he called her 'ma'am' – and turned to accept a mug of coffee from Constance. "What's happening?" she demanded affably. "Is your business the sweater, the killer dogs, Misty Hubbell, or her grotesque husband?"

"Couldn't they be connected?" Sumner was the soul of diffidence.

"Well, now," Virginia glanced at her friend, "I never thought . . . Are they connected?" She grinned. "The Fassett sweater has to do with Hubbell shooting at Win Carver? How could that be?"

"Threads?" Sumner suggested, then, leaning forward, taking them into his confidence, "Isn't it strange that here we have several crimes inside – what is it? – four days, in a community where there hasn't been a crime for years and years—"

"That we know of," Virginia put in darkly.

He didn't take her up on that. "Is it likely," he asked ingenuously, "that there's no connection?" He leaned back. "Of course there's a connection: the Hubbells."

"Problem family," Virginia murmured, not looking at Constance.

"Did you or your husband have anything to do with her?" Sumner asked.

Virginia gaped, stared, and snapped her mouth shut. "Yes," she said shortly. "I fired her."

Sumner nodded. "Of course. No one would employ her after Mrs Dodge realised she was stealing."

Virginia said nothing but then he hadn't asked a question. Barclay was thinking about the use of pronouns and wondering whether he'd misinterpreted that 'her'.

"Misty never came here?" Sumner asked carelessly.

Both women jerked to attention and seemed to hold their breath. He looked from one to the other enquiringly. Constance shrugged, wide-eyed. "I don't remember. Why should she?"

Virginia said coldly. "No one down here would employ her."

"She has a poor reputation," Sumner said. "She's a prostitute. Hubbell beat her up. And now she's disappeared. I need to find her." The diffidence was gone, and the joviality. He was no longer the hick cop deferring to rich ladies, and they knew it, but they weren't about to knuckle under to him.

"So how can we help?" Virginia said coldly.

Constance said, as if it were an academic question, "You're implying something else has happened to her since Hubbell assaulted her. Why aren't you looking for Hubbell?"

"Meaning he could have attacked her twice? Could be." Sumner's eyes wandered, as if by accident, to his colleague.

"Perhaps we could have a word with Mr Dodge," Barclay ventured.

"He's in the city today," Constance said.

"Then maybe Mr Manton?" The polite gaze was transferred to Virginia.

"They went together," she told him. "They'll be back tonight."

Constance said firmly, "Tell us more about the connection between these events. I agree that the Hubbells are involved with all of them but how do we come into it except as Myra's employers?"

Sumner thought about it. "I don't think you need more than that, ma'am. I mean, you can't be directly involved, but you could throw some light on the situation—"

"What situation?" Virginia interrupted. "The fact that Myra worked down here has nothing to do with her son beating his wife. How can it? We never saw Misty, she wasn't employed – here . . ." She trailed off, the belligerence melting away.

"And never came here," Sumner said. There was no response. "And none of you went to her place," he added idly, as if closing a book.

There was silence. If he'd said 'bang!' they'd have jumped a foot in the air.

"Everyone, but *everyone* is lying," Barclay exploded. "And where are the men? You could be right: she fucked all of 'em."

"Did I say that? They certainly seem to have gotten out of the way." Sumner smiled grimly. "This is another two made 'emselves scarce when we arrived on the scene. Ain't that somep'n?"

"And now?" They were driving up the road, leaving Prosper.

Sumner didn't respond for a while. They passed the cabins and the forest closed in again: dark and quiet and impenetrable. "It's weird," he said at last. "All the menfolk disappearing . . . And yet, is it? Did they go because—"

"What in hell!" Barclay reached for his gun. A figure had burst on to the road – the only way to describe it as he freed himself from brambles to virtually fall on the tarmac. A man in a flotation jacket and a helmet. "What's he doing in a forest?" Barclay's voice verged on hysteria.

"The river's below the road," Sumner reminded him. "It's used by kayakers. Here's another of 'em."

A second helmeted figure appeared. Both were gesturing wildly to the police to stop. Since there was no sign of injury on either Sumner wasn't unduly alarmed. Not until he remembered the gorge on the river and realised that there could have been a third kayaker. This could be nasty.

Both fellows were out of breath, chests heaving. The one at Sumner's window pointed. "There's a car in the canyon," he gasped. "It's caught between two rocks. God knows how you're ever going to get it out."

"We leave 'em there." Sumner beamed with relief. "It's not the first time. What kind of car?"

"You can't tell. It's submerged, all but. You can only see its roof—"

"And the top of a window," his companion said. "You can see through a window like."

"There's a guy inside—"

Sumner and Barclay were immobile "What colour is the car?" Sumner grated.

"Yellow, bright yellow. You can see the guy, sort of washing around . . ."

Twelve

There was no proper access to the gorge except by water, no way of viewing the car except from the air. The rock walls of the chasm were not very high – about fifty feet – but they were sheer and only roped climbers could traverse to the place where the car was wedged. A fall into the water here could be fatal; the river foamed and boiled for a hundred yards, and halfway along the stretch of white water, under the big landslide, there was a cataract and a fall of some ten feet. Here the river formed two channels, both involving drops, and kayakers preferred to take the course that avoided a nasty rock in midstream below the fall. Today they'd had no choice; below the more hazardous drop the car had wedged so tightly that it didn't move under the pounding of the torrent.

All this was reported by the two men. Taking the throw-line which they carried for emergencies, they'd broken out of the main flow below the cataract, beached their craft and returned over the rocks. One fellow, roped and belayed by his mate, had managed to work his way to within a few yards of the car. It was then that he'd seen the body floating around inside, 'like a doll in a washing machine'.

They were too wet to sit in the police car but they were in need of hot food and dry clothing, and they'd had a shock. However, neither would hear of abandoning their kayaks. Since they insisted on returning to the river, Sumner sent Barclay down with them. He believed them when they said the car was virtually submerged, but recovery wasn't his problem. Viewing the body was – or rather, it was Barclay's. All they had to go on so far was hearsay.

They left, and were almost immediately lost to sight, though not ear-shot. Sumner had qualms, standing at the top of the precipitous slope, thinking he should have waited for reinforcements and more rope. Crashes and shouts came from below; Barclay would be descending too fast, but surely, with the trees so close together, a slip would be arrested before it became a fall? Which was why no one had considered going down by the great gash of the landslide; there were no trees, not even bushes to grab in the event of a fall, and the earth there was dry and smooth and excessively steep.

The bare slope was convex; he could see so far: maybe one, two hundred feet, then came a lip and nothing below that until the tops of the trees showed on the far side of the river. The car, the waterfalls, even the walls of the gorge were invisible. The voices of the men were no longer audible, lost in the snarl of the cataracts.

The Stingray must have gone down the slide, anywhere else it would have been caught and held by the trees. There was no parapet at the side of the road and, oddly, no skid marks, but now, knowing what to look for, Sumner could see faint gouges in earth like fawn cement and, about eighty feet below, something glinting in the sun. It could be litter but it could equally well be glass from a headlamp. There was no way he could find out, not without a rope from above.

He paced the tarmac looking for signs. Not prints, not here – but maybe where the guy had crashed? He didn't know whether that had happened west or east of the slide. He called Mrs Carver on his mobile. She wasn't sure, they had been so confused . . . He asked if Mr Hughes might remember.

There was a pause, presumably while they conferred. No, she said, he didn't know either, but it would have been soon after Angel's Camp because they'd said that if Hubbell had been chasing them before the junction they would have stopped there and asked Riessen to call the police.

About to thank her and sign off, Sumner did a double-take. "He was still open then?"

"I guess so." Win sounded puzzled. "It was only ten o'clock. The light was on in the bar. Why?"

"You're breaking up." Sumner shifted the mobile to make his own voice fluctuate. "Thank you, ma'am; I'll be in touch."

Riessen, he thought, Riessen was still at Angel's Camp when Hubbell crashed, indeed, when they were all shooting. A magnum and a rifle would have torn the night apart. He must have heard the shots.

Leaving the car he started to walk up the road studying every tree. It was mid-afternoon now, the sun behind him, again lighting the trunks at intervals but it wasn't their western aspects he was interested in; Hubbell had been coming west chasing the Rolls, the marks would be on the east side of a tree.

After he'd walked about a mile a van came along from the direction of the highway, two big tanned women in the cab. They stopped and asked if he needed a ride. They were the wives of the kayakers so he told them that the men had found a crashed car in the river and he'd sent his colleague back with them. If the girls went on to Prosper their husbands should arrive shortly. The men had a few miles to go to the sea but he imagined that the difficulties were over now that they had passed the gorge. He said nothing about the body; the fewer people who knew about that the better. Once the media and the public learned the details, this road would be blocked with traffic, and the thought of that slide – the top of it without so much as a guard-rail – made him shudder.

He must have been less than a mile from Angel's Camp when he found the tree, gashed on the side facing the road. The trunk was leaning drunkenly, though it could have been like that before last night. There was a low bank and it was this that had stopped the car after it struck the tree. There was a depression where the snout of the vehicle had ploughed into the soil, glass from a headlamp, yellow paint on bark, and marks in the dust that could have been footprints but were too scuffed to tell for certain.

Hubbell would still have been facing west when he reversed out of the bank. He must have continued in the same direction either going home – but surely not after shooting at Win Carver – or more likely looking for a place to turn. Was he concussed? He could have banged his head on the steering wheel. No one in his right senses would try to turn above the landslide. Perhaps the road widened a fraction at that point, or appeared wider in the light of one headlamp. Whatever, he turned, started to turn, and went straight over the edge. Sumner hoped, despite everything, that the fellow was dead, at least unconscious, before the Stingray sank.

He walked back to his car and drove to Angel's Camp but it was as abandoned as it had been earlier. He sat on the forecourt and reported the accident and then he returned to the landslide to wait for Barclay.

Myra sat down with a jolt on the top step. Sumner had suggested they go inside the cabin but she had refused.

He said diffidently, "You must have had some idea . . . You lied about him being home last night. You thought he'd gone after Misty, didn't you?"

She wasn't listening. She was seeing images. "He coulda jumped clear," she said.

"Myra! Barclay here, he went down to the river. He was *there*!"

"I need to . . ." She stood up, grabbing at the rail. "I need to see him."

"No way. Look at this guy!" Barclay was bleeding, his shirt torn, hat missing, covered with mud from his boots to his plastered skull. "And he was on a rope," Sumner pointed out, then, his voice dropping, "Kent had to be turning the car and he misjudged his space."

She stared at him with blank eyes. "This were after he shot at Miss Carver."

It didn't surprise Sumner; folk's minds were scrambled when they were in shock. "Yes, ma'am," he said gravely, "afterwards."

"Or Winnie Carver shot him and pushed him over the edge."

"We gotta consider all the possibilities."

"He could still be alive, like in an air pocket?"

"No, ma'am."

She looked at Barclay, ignoring the state of him. "It coulda been her inside the car? You could tell by the hair, it would come loose. Long, it were: blonde. It coulda been her."

"Misty." Sumner wasn't asking a question, he was reflecting.

"It's more likely it's her," Myra insisted. "And him still alive."

Sumner glanced at Barclay, who shook his head, not sure what was expected of him.

"It were Hubb – your son, ma'am."

She started to mumble. Sumner listened for a moment then, raising his voice, suggested that a neighbour might come over, keep her company, help with Seth. Her laughter was more of a screech.

"Who did you have in mind? Win Carver who shot him, or her toy boy? Connie Dodge? Ginny Manton?"

"There's Opal Crane."

"Now isn't that wild? Such a little place and so much carnal sin. Who's responsible for it all, huh?"

"You tell me, Myra."

"I have to tell Kent's daddy," she said with dignity, dismissing them.

The police arrived in droves, the main concern of each contingent being to offer suggestions as to how to recover the Stingray and the corpse. One look at the landslip, however, and even the younger men turned their attention to the timbered slopes. Two went down but, without experts to guide them, without ropes, they returned – not without difficulty – maintaining that no one could approach the fall where the car was lodged. The state these two were in when they crawled out to the road convinced any more potential heroes that the site was inaccessible.

The sheriff flew over in a helicopter but the wind was strong now and the combination of down-draughts, timber, and the constricting walls of the chasm ruled out the possibility of lowering a winchman. Privately the authorities prayed for rain and a surge that might move the car; otherwise it would appear that explosives were the only answer. No one said so publicly, not with a body in the vehicle, and his mother only a few miles downstream.

The media arrived, the local Press first, alerted by their monitoring of the police waveband. The Stagg paper being a weekly, the editor had his eye on the main chance, and summoned the big boys. By dusk there were three Press representatives on the scene, and two television crews, but no members of the public. A patrol car sat at the junction with the highway, turning back motorists who had no business on the Prosper road.

The fact that a yellow Stingray and its driver had plunged into the Blacktail River had been broadcast on the early evening news but not everyone had heard the item. Paul Manton and Grady Dodge, driving home from Seattle, were astonished to be stopped by police at Angel's Camp and asked their business.

Grady was too drained to speak, let alone to bluster, and it was Paul who answered for both of them, eliciting the information that Hubbell had run out of road and drowned. Allowed to proceed, they were silent for a few minutes until Grady said without emotion, "I would have expected it to be Misty."

"No, he'd never sacrifice his car."

"In the circumstances he would. It would be a small price to pay to finish her off."

"For God's sake, man! You'd be up there with Hubbell as chief suspects!"

"It's Hubbell drowned," Grady reminded him. "Not Misty."

When they reached the Dodge house they could see through the undraped windows that both wives were there. Virginia came to the door as Constance busied herself with drinks. She turned at their entrance and proffered large whiskies as if they were celebrating.

"You heard the news?" Paul asked, sparing Grady who, he thought, had had as much as he could take today, and that on top of the horror that hung over the poor guy.

"It was on television," Virginia said. "You heard it on the radio?"

"No. The police stopped us at Angel's Camp. They're keeping the public away, afraid someone else will go off the road and end up in the river. There were police cars at the scene and a lot of vans: TV, Press, you name it."

"Ghastly," Virginia said. "You weren't stopped?"

"I said—"

"I mean at the place where it happened. You didn't speak to the Press."

"No way!" Paul was horrified. He looked at Grady, who was paying no attention, sunk in gloom. "Nothing to do with us," Paul said loudly, trying to penetrate the black mood.

The women saw the problem, and were concerned. Virginia said pleasantly, "Well, supper time; we'll be getting along home I guess?" Raising her eyebrows, asking mutely if Constance needed support or to be left alone with her old man.

Constance nodded and the women stood up, followed obediently by Paul. They moved to the door, chatting politely and inanely about seeing each other tomorrow. Behind them Grady was oblivious; he could have been asleep but his eyes were open, staring at nothing. Constance glanced back at him, went outside and pulled the door to. "It went off all right?" she asked Paul anxiously.

He sketched a shrug. "No problem with the test. But now he has to wait. Nothing you can do except give him support. You're good at that, Con." He looked at his wife. "The bitch! I could kill her."

"Whoops!" Virginia held up her hands. "The police are everywhere, sweetie. You have to learn to watch what you say."

He snorted. "Like Grady said: it's not her that's been killed, it's her husband."

"Well maybe she did it," Virginia said comfortably, taking his arm, pulling him away. "And she'll be caught and hanged. All our problems solved."

"Not quite," Constance said. "There's my old man."

"We might as well pack it in." Sheriff Wendell Scott grimaced as the first drops of rain hit the roof of his car. "Nothing we can do here."

"It's a problem," Sumner said. "If the water level was lower a diver might force the door or break a window, get the body out that way."

"The level's going to rise with rain," Scott pointed out. "Maybe the car will free itself, float clear. It could stick again but from what Barclay said it couldn't be in a worse position than it is now."

Barclay had been sent home. The only thing left to do here was to keep the media and the public at bay. "The wife has to be found," Scott said. "That's your job. You'll know where she hangs out."

"She'll be holed up, her face the mess it's in."

"Why did Hubbell do that? Any idea?"

Sumner shrugged. "She played around: part-time hooker, probably full-time when he was away."

"So why'd he beat up on her this time?"

"I don't know." Sumner was puzzled. "You figure a guy like that needs an excuse?"

"If his wife's a hooker, he's used to it, isn't he? Brings more money into the home – or had she just started?"

"She'd been at it a while. She was part of the furniture in the bars in town, and at Angel's Camp no doubt. You must have seen her yourself." Scott's eyes narrowed. "No," Sumner amended, "you wouldn't take Mrs Scott in them places. Misty'll have gone to some friend until the bruises fade. She'll come back soon enough when she hears the news. Nothing for her to worry about now."

"The way he treated her she got cause for celebration."

"You're right there. Good thing – for her – she wasn't on this road last night."

They laughed carelessly: hard-bitten professionals who had seen more domestic violence in their working lives than they could remember.

"Stop treating me like an invalid," Win said.

"I'm not!" Owen protested. "I just asked you to go and sit down. You know I hate people in the kitchen when I'm cooking. Besides, Pip needs company and I don't want him under my feet."

Win sat down with the kitten on her lap. The tortoiseshell queen woke up, stretched and started to wash. Displacement activity.

"Such a relief to know we're safe again," Win said, her eyes going from the cats to the door. They were still waiting for the joiner and a new cat-flap.

"We won't be truly safe till those dogs are caught."

"Or shot." Win played with Pip's tiny paws. "He could have been shot."

Owen stopped grating orange peel. "You think he shot at the cats?"

"Not him, me. If I did hit Hubbell, even winged him, he would have had difficulty steering."

Owen's shoulders sagged. "He's dead," he said flatly. "Whether it was a bullet, or drunk driving or drowning, it's immaterial. You know you didn't kill him; he drove away."

"What happens when the body's recovered and they find a bullet track?"

"It'll be a flesh wound, that's what. The police won't be bothered." He came over to her, carrying a bottle of sherry. "Now this is what we're going to have with the mussels," he announced, determined to stem this flow of guilt. "And the claret should be just the right temperature for the venison. Let me finish the sauce and I'll be right with you."

"You've surpassed yourself this evening, dear boy."

"Why not?" He trotted back to the kitchen for his own drink and brought bowls heaped with mussels to the table.

Rain slashed the window, startling both of them. A mile away a white swathe marked the sand bar at the mouth of the river. Dusk had come early and lights were showing in the houses.

"We're in for a wet night," he said, relishing the warm comfort on this side of the streaming glass.

He went back to the kitchen and returned with finger bowls, geranium petals floating on the water. "This is perfection," Win said, "I hope . . ." She trailed off.

He looked wary. She went on, "I was about to say I hope everyone is as contented."

He looked out at the lights, so solitary in that wild place, so brave. "They should be. We're all fit and comfortably off, all have congenial partners – except Bill, and he has Robin short-term, his friends all the rest of the time."

"I was thinking of Myra actually."

"Don't. You start down that road and next thing you'll be saying we shouldn't eat good food when elsewhere people are starving." He added slyly, "They could go down to the shore and pick mussels. They're free."

"And delicious." Good manners and common sense prevailed, but the switch in mood had been an effort. They applied themselves to the food in silence, both thinking of Hubbell, the one with relief, the other wondering exactly how he had died.

"I hope Win isn't stewing over that bastard in the river," Robin said, tossing a green salad. "What will the cops do if they can't get the car out, Dad?"

"I don't know. Fortunately it's not my problem. Blow it up maybe?"

"Wouldn't Myra have to give permission?"

"Misty is next of kin. It's a tricky point. It's either explosives or leave him there till the level in the river drops. They might cut a hole in the roof, get the body out that way."

"It's a great relief." She hadn't been listening, had gone off on a track of her own.

"Why?" He gazed at her with concern. "Surely you didn't know the fellow, not closely."

"Are you kidding? I mean it'll be a relief for Misty. She can come home now. What are you frowning at?"

"I was wondering how those two will hit it off: Myra and Misty."

"How they always did, I imagine."

"Hubbell's death makes a difference."

"It certainly makes a difference to Misty – no more beatings – but how does that affect her relationship with Myra?"

"She could blame Misty."

"She wasn't there! She'd run by then. The Nelsons met her on the road in the early evening."

"I know that, but people who are bereaved don't think logically. And they have to blame someone. Myra will say things like he got drunk, was chasing after the girl, anything: time and place won't mean zilch to her. Hubbell was already in a rage when he came across Win. Misty had lost both his hounds, remember. Myra will say it's all Misty's fault."

Amy and David were watching an ancient version of *The Hound of the Baskervilles*, eating bean stew out of basins on their laps.

"The background isn't very realistic," Amy said. "And is the fog really as thick as that on an English moor?"

"I guess. They call them pea-soupers." David glanced at the window. "We don't do so bad ourselves in that line."

"Too windy for fog tonight. A good thing too. Virginia said there are police and media people parked all along the road above the slide. Paul and Grady passed them when they came home from Seattle."

"They'll go back to Stagg. No one wants to be on that road at night, least of all in a storm."

Amy stared moodily at the screen. "David, how are they going to get him out of the car?"

"I don't know and I don't care. All that I'm concerned about is finding that hound – and the Shepherd – and shooting the brutes. And now I won't have Hubbell stalking me afterwards. That guy was a menace to everyone in Prosper, one way or another. If he hadn't drowned someone would have taken the law into their own hands eventually."

"Like Misty you mean."

"Her or one of her lovers."

Which just showed how naive he was, she thought; prostitutes had clients, not lovers.

Thirteen

The storm blew itself out in the night and the wind dropped. By dawn the cloud had crept down from the mountains, fog rolled in from the ocean and at Angel's Camp visibility was virtually nil. The two cops in the patrol car could have been in a forest clearing or a shopping mall for all they could see of the cabins or even the side of the bar where they'd parked to escape the wind.

They were working a four-hour shift at the junction and this pair had agreed between themselves to do one hour on, one off. While one smoked and watched – ostensibly – the other tried to sleep in the back. The junction was invisible, first by virtue of clouds obscuring the moon, while at dawn there was the fog. They weren't worried, the crash would wake them, they said. There was a barrier across the Prosper road, not solid enough to damage a vehicle, but sufficient to make plenty of noise if someone tried to get through.

The cop who was called Larson suddenly came alive. "Heh, Paulie, look what's here. We got customers."

Diffused yellow light showed in the fog. Dimmed headlamps advanced slowly, creeping across the forecourt.

"Paulie! Wake up, man!"

"What? Who's that?"

Larson didn't answer, he was opening his door, climbing out, slamming it shut in alarm as the other vehicle came on. It stopped suddenly, the driver evidently having seen the black and white paintwork at the last moment. Larson moved forward, aiming his flashlight. He waited for the window to be wound down then, abruptly, he stepped back and drew his pistol.

"Drop it!" he shouted. "Drop it or I fire!" A pause. "Show me your hands – *now*!"

Paulie came running, dodged sideways and crouched, his gun drawn.

Larson stared at small hands with long fingers spread against the window glass. "See if she's alone," he told Paulie.

Of course she was alone; you can't hide a second person in the cab of a pickup. Larson had been frightened and said the first thing that came into his head.

Misty was unperturbed as she climbed out of the car, blinking in the light of the torch. Swelling showed under the heavy make-up. "I was going for my shades," she protested.

"We weren't to know that," Larson grunted. "It's early to be on the road. I guess you were looking for breakfast."

She tried to see past him but it was impossible given the lack of visibility. "Is he serving breakfast?"

"The place is closed, ma'am. No one's here." Her eyes moved. "No, he's not there neither —" Larson guessed she was thinking of the trailer "— and there ain't no one in the cabins. Place is deserted. So you'll need to get back on the road and try some place else." He was new to the area and had no knowledge of the locality and its inhabitants.

"I'm on my way home."

"Be as well to go home then . . ." He checked. Maybe she'd got those bruises at home. "You look as if you've been in a fight," he said, probing.

But she was known to Paulie and he'd heard the gossip at the station. "You're Mrs Hubbell," he said, and it sounded like an accusation.

Larson gaped. He hadn't heard about the violence but he knew the name of the drowned man.

"And I live at Prosper," she said. "So if Norm isn't here — to give me breakfast — guess I'll drive on."

Larson's mouth opened and closed. Paulie said, "There's a barrier. I'll shift it, let you by."

"What's the barrier for?"

"Stop people driving down who don't belong in Prosper. Sheriff's orders."

"What sort of people?"

"TV, reporters. Folk come to rubberneck. Sorry we had to stop you, ma'am." It was grudging; she was only a hooker but clearly she'd had a hard time. No doubt she deserved it, still . . .

She sighed and settled herself gingerly in the pickup, pausing as she reached for the ignition. "What happened to Norm?" she asked carelessly.

"No idea," Larson said. "Friend of yours?"

"No. I just wanted my breakfast, is all."

*   *   *

"Misty Hubbell's back," came the sheriff's voice on the phone.

Sumner stared. "When?"

"Five o'clock this morning. Drove into Angel's Camp looking for breakfast, is her story. Paulie says she's on first name terms with Riessen."

Sumner tensed. "Riessen's still not home?"

"No. I don't want to put out a call for him," the sheriff sounded as if he were talking to himself, "and why should I? He could be a perfectly innocent guy who was having it off with a neighbour's wife, and now he's decided to go fishing. No more'n a coincidence in timing. Adultery's no crime."

"He had to have heard the shooting."

"It'd be better if the media didn't start thinking along those lines. You go back to Prosper; you have good reason, far as any media people's concerned. You're there to acquaint the widow with the circumstances of her husband's death. You're kin to the Hubbells anyways, aren't you? And while you're consoling her find out how close she was to Riessen, and if that had anything to do with Hubbell assaulting her. What's her relationship with her mother-in-law?"

"If Myra Hubbell's had the same idea as you, I'd say Misty's still in trouble. We better hope old Seth don't have a shotgun lying around loaded."

"Confiscate it. You'll find some excuse. And find out where Misty was when the Stingray left the road. Did it fall or was it pushed? Get back there soon as you've had your breakfast. Don't take Barclay, you're in counsellor mode. Make like a pussy cat, think like a rat."

He stood on her porch looking embarrassed, even shy. "Thought you might like me to visit with you a whiles," he said when she opened the screen, her eyes hidden behind the dark shades. "Give you an explanation like, answer questions?"

She looked wary but she was related to him by marriage; she couldn't send him away. When there's a bereavement families stick together. She stood back and he stepped inside.

"How're you doing?" he asked awkwardly, parking himself on the old sofa.

She shrugged. "What d'you expect?" Her eyes wandered. There was a mobile phone on the table.

He touched his own temple, nodded at her. "He done that because of the hound?"

110

"I told you he'd kill me next time he was home." She made it sound as if it was Sumner's fault.

"In that case you might say you got off lightly. You're not dead." He peered at her. "My, girl, he beat you up proper though."

Her mouth twitched. "Last time," she said, almost smug. Her tone lightened. "I got no beer, Dale; he cleaned out the fridge. I'll need to buy in a fresh stock if you're gonna make a habit of dropping by."

"Jesus, Misty! You don't have him to reckon with no longer, but you got his mom next door!"

"So? Cops have a right to go anywhere, and you were his cousin—"

"Several times removed. You don't seem upset; still, I guess a woman that's been through what you have couldn't be expected to have much feeling left for the guy what done it."

"Hell, battered wives stay with a man what beats up on 'em, it don't mean they have to spend the rest of their lives in mourning once he's dead."

"If you felt like that why did you give him presents?"

"Like what?"

"Like that Polo stuff in your bedroom that you said you'd give him before you told him about the hound went missing."

"He never give me the chance. He come home, saw one hound where there shoulda been two, and he laid into me like a pile driver."

"It wouldn't be that you did give him the Polo and he asked how you come by it?"

"No, he never saw it. Leastways, not that I know of. When I come round – did you know I were knocked out cold? – he'd gone. I didn't waste time getting out of here myself, I can tell you."

"Did you come back that night?"

"After what he done to me? Come *on*, Dale!"

"You didn't?"

"No! Someone says I did, they're lying."

"Myra says you both were here." She stared at him, the picture of bewilderment. "Then," he went on, "she says she saw you, next morning, and it was you said Kent was here."

"She's having you on. Why would she say something like that?"

"I can think of one good reason. Kent beat you up once, you released the other hound, Kent came after you again, Myra thinks he caught up with you, and the second time he coulda done worse. So she claimed you both spent the night, all friendly like, in this cabin when all the time she thought you was in a shallow grave in the forest. Or drowned in the river."

Gwen Moffat

"Yeah. She'd do anything to protect her boy." Misty didn't seem concerned. "'Course," she went on, "most mothers are like that with only sons, which is why the guys turn out like they do." Her eyes went to the mobile. "Some of 'em do."

"Who give you the phone? Another present from a millionaire?"

"Why on earth d'you say that?"

"Because they cost, is why. And you said as Paul Manton were generous."

She regarded the phone thoughtfully. "He is."

"And?"

"And what?"

The screen door crashed open. Myra stood on the threshold, eyes black holes in a white face, her hair uncombed, looking as if she'd just got out of bed. For all the notice she took of Sumner he might not have been there. She focused on Misty and snarled.

"You think you're safe!"

The girl had been leaning against the sink. She'd stiffened at sight of the visitor but her only overt action was to remove her glasses. Sumner looked from the bruised eyes to Myra who said conversationally, "I thought he'd killed you." Her smile was mad.

Sumner stood up. Sitting he felt intimidated but as long as he could look down on her, on both of them, he could put his trust in brawn and quick reactions. At least neither of them was armed, not to his knowledge.

"I'd like a word, Myra," he said in his cop's voice.

"What makes him special?" she asked of Misty.

The girl blinked, then said slowly, "He's a cop. And he's family, so he got a right to come here, asking questions, like wanting to know where presents come from."

"That weren't what I meant—"

"It'd better be." Misty raised her voice. "I guess he thinks something funny's going on, like I got stolen property here, right, Dale?"

Myra's gasp turned to a hiss. She rounded on Sumner. "You don't know the half of it. Whoring, blackmail – and now she's outdone herself," she was shouting, "now she's murdered my son!"

Misty raised eloquent eyebrows at Sumner. He moved round Myra, watching her hands, placing himself between her and the table drawer where there could be knives.

"We're going over to your place," he said, and there was no doubt it was an order. "I need to have a few words with you."

Myra stepped back. In the doorway she turned, Sumner crowding

112

behind her. She couldn't see Misty for his bulk but she said loudly, "Kent was more important to me than anything else. Think about it."

"That's no way to talk," he said as they walked past the dogs' chains, mute reminders of their dead owner. She stopped and stared at them. "Slipped its collar again," she murmured, and he realised she didn't know that the hound had been released deliberately. He wasn't about to tell her.

"She was never home," she said. "She didn't care about the hounds but they was his pride and joy."

He didn't respond, thinking that a fellow who put his dogs before his wife deserved all that was coming to him, although his own opinion was that the Stingray's plunge to the river had been divine justice, not human. All the same, he was intrigued by a side-issue. "What was that about blackmail?" he asked. "Who blackmailed who?"

She ignored the question. They came to her yard. "You're not going inside," she said. "You'll disturb Seth."

"Seth and me's related. I'm going in."

She glared, considered protest but abandoned it in favour of a better move. "I haven't told him yet."

He looked from her to the cabin and saw Seth at a window, leaning on his walker. "That's your decision, I guess." But he sounded doubtful.

"I'd rather you didn't come in." The tone was pleading but he wasn't fooled. However there was no need to go in the cabin, and this way he might do a deal. "All I wanted was his rifle," he said.

"Why?" On guard immediately.

"Because he has no need of it any more, and you don't have a license." That was guesswork but she didn't deny it.

"He don't have one." She was sullen.

"Come on, Myra. All the Hubbells hunt. They have *armouries!*" He paused, astonished at his own words. Where were Kent Hubbell's weapons? He looked towards Misty's cabin.

"Where's his rifle?" Myra asked, guessing the thought. "You've took it?"

"I'm about to, when I have Seth's."

"Kent had a magnum too, but he kept that in his car." She caught her breath as if she would have said more but had thought better of it.

"What were you driving at when you said Misty was involved in blackmail?"

She was silent, biting her lips. Considering options? He didn't trust her an inch. She glanced up slyly. "Ask Norm Riessen."

"I shall when I can find him."

She started at that, stared, then frowned. "He's missing?"

He nodded towards the other cabin. "Friendly, were they?"

"Where'd she get that phone?"

"You tell me. Could Riessen have given it her?"

She was staring into the trees but she nodded faintly. "That'll be it," she said, as if to herself. "And now he's disappeared."

"He's not at Angel's Camp."

"And her sitting in there waiting for the phone to ring, waiting for word to join him."

"I couldn't get any more out of her." Sumner laid Seth's rifle on the sheriff's desk. "But I left her in a good mood after she accused Misty and Riessen of murdering Hubbell. Incidentally she wants to know about recovery of the body."

"What did you tell her?"

"That it was too dangerous for divers to go in there, that we were hoping the river would rise and float the car free. She said, 'June, the river's at its highest level now'."

"She's right too. Best thing is to wait for it to drop, then we can cut a hole in the roof, get him out that way."

"Could be weeks before the water goes down."

The sheriff wasn't getting any support here. "Did you mention explosives to her?"

"I wouldn't dare. She's in shock. But I think she'll come to accept there's nothing can be done at the moment."

Scott studied the rifle morosely. "Where's Hubbell's weapons? Don't tell me he doesn't have any."

"No rifle, no ammo. Misty says it was kept in the bedroom. Both women say he has – had a magnum, and that he kept it in his car."

"So he took the rifle when he went chasing after Misty – if that was what he was doing when he met Miss Carver?" Scott was silent, thinking about it. He looked up sharply. "Why'd he beat Misty?"

"She said because of her losing one of the hounds back in the spring. She'd told me that he'd kill her when he found out about it."

"And instead of that it was him got killed. And his mom says Misty murdered him. Or the two of 'em: Riessen and Misty? What's the girl say about her relationship with Riessen?"

"I went back and asked. Just friends, she said. I pointed out that a friend wouldn't take kindly to what Hubbell done to her, but she said Riessen didn't know. She didn't go to Angel's Camp after she met the

Nelsons on the road, too embarrassed to show her face there. She went straight to a friend in Ocean Shores."

"But she didn't mind him seeing her this morning, except he wasn't there. And she didn't know that – unless she *did* know, and wanted us to think she didn't." Scott shuffled papers on his desk. "It could have been an *assisted* accident," he mused, "like if Riessen was directing Hubbell to turn round above the landslide and told him he still had yards of room when his rear wheels was only an inch from the drop . . ."

"Would you allow your wife's friend to help you turn above a precipice?" Sumner was amused. "A more likely scenario would be that Riessen found Hubbell concussed and he sent the Stingray over the edge with the guy inside."

"In which case there'll be no marks of foul play on the body and we'll never prove murder. I think we'll put out a call for Riessen. We need him to tell us did he hear all the shooting that night."

"I don't think he's gone far," Sumner said. "I'll swear Misty's expecting a call."

"Of course she is." Scott was testy. "She's a hooker."

"True, but she won't be working for a while. It's a friend she's expecting to phone. I wonder – could he have done a runner and left her to face the heat?"

"What heat?"

Sumner ignored the direct question. "I'd give a lot to see Hubbell's body, find out if there's a bullet wound."

"Riessen needn't have put it there. Miss Carver was firing, remember. Maybe Hubbell managed to drive as far as the slide and then fainted from loss of blood."

"That wouldn't be murder."

"Could be, but it needn't have happened that way neither. She, they – she had the Britisher with her – they could have driven on a ways, following Hubbell, and when he stopped from weakness, they coulda finished him off – as Riessen could have." He paused. "Presumably how Myra thinks he did it," he amended. "We have to watch our backs on this one, we should at least make a show of investigating before the body's recovered. Is the slide on Carver land?"

"I doubt it, that far inland. It would have been at one time."

"So go to her and find out. Talk about permission to go on her property to recover the body. Not that we need it but she won't know that."

"What else am I supposed to be asking?"

"Did you think about the blackmail angle? OK, so it's a demented woman mentioned it, that and murder, but – smoke and fire, you know. Ask questions. Take Barclay, divide the families between you—"

"Ask who's being blackmailed?"

Scott exhaled heavily. "Don't you feel there's something wrong? Look at it: petty thefts, hounds running loose, wife beaten by a husband who's found drowned a few hours later, wife's friend disappears—"

"Wait a minute." Sumner held up a big hand. "I can see him beating his wife, because she was responsible for the hounds, but how does that relate to thefts from rich folk miles away?"

"That's for you to find out."

Fourteen

Virginia was vacuuming when the doorbell chimed. A police car was parked outside. Paul was walking Henry; she had to face this on her own. She opened the door to the younger of the two deputies, the good-looking one. She relaxed a little. "Now what's this about?" she asked bossily, looking round for the other one. "Where's your partner?"

"He's with your neighbours," Barclay said, and saw her throat work. She should have asked which neighbours, but the atmosphere had tightened, as it does when the interviewee realises that words have to be watched. He entered and removed his hat.

"My husband's walking the dog," she said brightly, gesturing towards the shore.

The fog had lifted. There was a heavy swell running after the storm, surf breaking on the rocks. There was no sign of a man or a dog.

She brought coffee and sat down opposite him. "Now," she said, in the tone she would have used to a student nurse with a problem, "how can I help you?"

Sumner and Barclay had discussed how these interviews might go, what questions to ask initially, how much information should be released. They'd come to the conclusion that since they had no idea what they might uncover, the shape of an interview couldn't be envisaged, so they'd have to play it off the cuff.

"We're trying to understand the circumstances of the accident," Barclay explained. "There'll be an autopsy of course."

"You're talking about Hubbell?" She was amazed. "What can we possibly know—"

"It's his mother." He was apologetic. "She maintains it's murder."

She laughed. "She would." Her face changed and she was unable to hide – more than fear – terror? He watched her steel herself, regaining equilibrium as obviously as she had lost it. "Who is she accusing?"

"Norm Riessen."

Her shoulders dropped. Barclay was thrilled, he could read her like a book, betrayed by her body language. "Although tomorrow it could be someone else," he added, smiling, taking her into his confidence. "Why did you fire her?"

"I didn't employ her. It was Mrs Dodge, and she caught the woman stealing."

"Yes, Mrs Dodge is another one that Myra has it in for, but you employed her at one time, ma'am."

She stared at him. Her eyes wandered and came to rest on a decorative pitcher. "Actually," she admitted, "I block out that episode. Yes, I did employ her for a short time but small things disappeared, the kind you couldn't be sure you hadn't mislaid, or lost outside the home: lipsticks, a rather gaudy scarf; she took bright things, like a magpie, you know? And she drank; my husband said she was always at his Scotch."

She was talking too much, and she'd missed the point that if she'd suspected Myra of stealing she would have warned her friend, but Constance had continued to employ the woman until last week. "Did you employ Misty?" Barclay asked.

"Never! Who would – I told you yesterday—"

"You employed the mother-in-law. Before the thefts started, or you were made aware of them, you could have asked the girl to come in for parties and stuff. You'd need extra hands; those folk in the woods, they need the cash."

"Even so. No one in Prosper would have Misty in the house."

Barclay nodded as if she confirmed his own opinion. "No more would my wife, not that I'd be interested . . ." He spread his hands, leaving the rest to her imagination.

"I didn't mean – you can't think . . ." She stopped, gathered her wits and said intensely, "I was a nurse, Mr Barclay; no way would I allow that woman anywhere near my kitchen. All prostitutes are suspect nowadays, surely you realise that. You're a policeman."

"Suspect, ma'am?"

"Health-wise." She spat it out.

He nodded slowly. Manton was – had been a surgeon. The nurse had married her boss. Come up in the world. Status-conscious. He pressed his advantage. "Are you missing a mobile phone, ma'am?"

"No. Why?"

"Misty has one."

"She needs it for her job. You mean she had one before she ran away."

"She's brought it back with her."

"Brought . . . She's not up there now? She came *back*?"

"It's her home, ma'am."

"She dared!"

"Why shouldn't she come home?"

"With Hubbell a few miles upstream, drowned inside his car?"

"Go on."

"Why, it's obvious to anyone who knew the bitch. She killed him, of course."

"On her own?" He was sceptical.

The rings flashed as she spread her hands. "She had so many men . . ." she hesitated, "but Riessen was the closest."

"She confided in you?"

"I told you . . ." Anger flared and died. "Almost certainly she drank at Angel's Camp – and this is why Myra's saying Riessen killed her son! Misty and Riessen would have been in it together."

"How did you make out?" Sumner asked, when Barclay picked him up outside the Dodges' place. From inside the house the colonel stared out at them, reminding Barclay of a goldfish in a glass bowl. "Manton wasn't there," he said absently. "And his wife's rattled."

"She's not the only one. What made her rattle most?"

Barclay was recalled to the present. He tore his gaze away from Dodge in his glass cocoon, started the car and related the exchange with Virginia. "She protested too much, insisting she'd never allow the girl in the house. She was so fierce it made me think the girl had to be there, at least once, and you can guess what that suggested. And she was terrified when I mentioned murder, but she relaxed when I explained that it was Myra accusing Riessen of killing Hubbell. And she said the same as Myra: Misty and Riessen were in it together. But if the doctor was screwing Misty . . ." Barclay trod on the brake and the car stopped. They were at the bridge over the little creek.

"It gives us another suspect," Sumner said. "You realise we've switched from accident to murder."

"That's because other people are assuming it's murder. And there's the blackmail angle."

"Did you touch on that?"

"No. I figured I had enough for the present: something going between Manton and Misty, Virginia wondering if he'd—" Barclay stopped, startled.

Sumner nodded. "If the girl was blackmailing Manton, he'd have killed *her*, not her husband. All the same, you done well; you got more than I did."

Barclay had been about to drive on. He checked and turned to Sumner. "The Dodges were cagey?"

"Cool, is how I'd describe her, and she's the dominant one. As for him, he hardly spoke, tried to give the impression he was bored. There was a newspaper beside him; he didn't pick it up but his eyes kept coming back to it. Unnatural behaviour – everyone's interested when there's a violent death in the neighbourhood – but Constance had an excuse for the lack of interest: said that apart from employing Myra as a maid there was no contact between the two communities – naturally, she said."

"Trying to distance herself. What about unnatural contact?" Barclay leered.

"I asked about the mobile. They showed no surprise. They hadn't lost one and I had the impression they knew already that Misty had one. Now how would that be? Maybe Misty's had it a while but I didn't see one when I was in her cabin on Sunday. If the Dodges do know that she has one then either they've seen her with it, or she told 'em she had one. Either way one of 'em has been in contact with her very recently, yet Constance swears they haven't seen the girl for so long she can't remember."

"But what about the colonel?"

"He said he might have seen her in Stagg but since he's not sure he'd recognise her – and at that point Constance cut in and said they didn't move in the same circles. Her face said it was a joke but she was giving me to understand that the Hubbells are low life, not fit to be discussed."

"You're reading too much into it. They're snobs, that's all."

"There was more to it than snobbery," Sumner insisted. "There was hatred."

"Fear," Barclay corrected. "It's the upper class thing. In a place like this money's no defence against armed psychopaths."

"Except he's gone now. He's dead. No, the hatred wasn't for him, it was for Misty – worst when I said she'd come back. It was the only time Dodge came out of the boredom mode. Jumped like I'd touched him with a cattle prod."

"Well, well." Barclay looked up the flowery meadow to the Selhorst place. "Selhorst too? And the Britisher? "*And* the guy doing the cougar count?"

"Maybe. Misty played the field. So what? We're not sex police.

We're here because Scott figures there's something wrong with Hubbell's death, but we opened a can of worms – needn't have anything to do with Hubbell." But he sounded uncertain.

"Something had to lead to the blackmail."

"You're right." Sumner stretched his legs. "C'mon, I'll take Miss Carver, you go and visit with old Bill and his daughter. She might tell you something. He won't."

Sumner was to have a wasted journey. Barclay set him down at the start of Miss Carver's track and he walked the few hundred yards to the house, thinking that, arriving without a car, he might surprise them in some revealing behaviour. Surprise them anyway.

In the event the house was inhabited only by cats and the double garage was empty. He walked round the building, finding the cat-flaps secured on the inside (the damaged one still nailed up) which puzzled him until he remembered the loose dogs.

He peered through windows, stalked on the inside by occupants as alert as coyotes. He glanced at the bedroom floor but, this being a two-storey house, there was no way he could satisfy his curiosity and discover whether they shared a room, whether Hughes was toy boy, houseman or secretary. He smiled at the kitten, traversing awkwardly from a velvet curtain to a window sill, opening miniature jaws in a soundless mew. He doubted that Hughes' status here had anything to do with Hubbell's death.

He moved away from the house and looked for Bill Selhorst's place but it faced north, its view westward blocked by a craggy knoll. The ground this side of the rock was drifted with orange poppies and yellow hawkweed. There were also brambles. After one attempt to climb the slope he retreated to the track which was lined with blue-eyed grass. The profusion of wildflowers could be the result of people sowing seed. A nice thought.

He plodded along the track, observing the houses above the shore: Nelsons', Dodges', Mantons'. What did they find to do here apart from walking the dog, planting wildflower seeds, picking up the groceries, trips to the waste disposal unit?

He found part of the answer at the Selhorst place where Robin was entertaining Barclay. Her father and David Nelson were searching for traces of dogs in Stack Cove while Win Carver and Owen had gone to Seattle to have the Rolls repaired. They'd all be back by nightfall, Robin assured him, meanwhile he'd have to make do with her. "Although," she added ingenuously, "I can't tell you anything you don't know. As I was telling Steve." First names already, and

Barclay hadn't been here above a quarter hour. A warning bell rang. Was she as ingenuous as she appeared?

"Anyway," she was saying, "I don't live here. I'm just visiting."

"But you know everyone," Sumner insisted.

"I suppose. The Nelsons haven't been here long but I visit with Amy. I don't know David very well. He's not highly sociable."

"And Owen Hughes?"

"He's better. Good manners – but then I only just met him."

"And Hubbell." No change of tone. The name was dropped and the silence stretched.

"Yes, I know him," she said at last. "Unfortunately."

"Your father's had problems with him?"

"My father doesn't have problems, they pass him by. But if you ask me, the whole Hubbell family's a mess of problems – although Kent's the worst. Of course, Myra's a thief but if you lock your doors and windows your possessions should be safe. Dad says he has nothing worth stealing but his cameras would fetch a bit providing Myra knew where to find a fence." She seemed to consider the possibility of finding a dealer in stolen goods in Stagg. "Have to be Seattle," she said.

"And Hubbell?" Sumner prompted.

She shrugged. "I don't think he's a paedophile. He's probably no more than a flasher and a groper. Can you be both – sorry, can *one*? Though on second thoughts Hubbell could be all of those," she added darkly.

"Kent Hubbell?"

She giggled and as quickly stifled it. "I was talking about *Seth*! Of course he's past it now, thank God, so Opal Crane's kids aren't at risk or someone would have shot him. But me – I've seen more of Seth's private parts than I care for, although only the once. A long time ago." She stopped suddenly.

"How did you deal with him?" Sumner was fascinated.

She sniffed. "I was sixteen and into psychology in a big way. I told him what was wrong with him, and I found Myra and told her where to get help because what he was doing – flashing – could get him a jail sentence, particularly if he was targeting little kids. There were more around then when the timber company was still logging up by the junction." She grinned engagingly. "Myra's never forgiven me. Calls me 'madam', would you believe. Her idea of sarcasm."

"She works here."

122

"She did, when I wasn't home. She doesn't now."

"Where did old Hubbell – er – expose himself to you?"

"There, at their cabin."

"What were you doing there?"

She blinked. "I guess I'd gone there to deliver some message: tell Myra not to come here because I was home from school, something like that."

"Kent wouldn't have been married at the time."

"Right." She was very still.

"A charmer, everyone says."

"They do?" She stroked her chin in a curiously masculine gesture. "He can be," she admitted. "Violent men often are. That's how women get sucked into their orbit." Her eyes flashed.

"Like Misty."

"Well, Misty's stupid. And a masochist."

Barclay wished he could take his notebook out but it was more than his job was worth with Sumner into his stride.

"And yourself?" Sumner said softly.

She gasped. "Who've you been talking to?"

He beamed and was suddenly avuncular. "Did I say something?"

"You can't believe a word Misty says," she was fierce, "or her mother for that matter—"

"Neither of them said a word against you."

"Oh. Well, anyway," she was floundering, "he was the only presentable male around at the time so naturally I – he was noticeable, you know, and he is – was quite a looker when he was younger – the bastard."

"The charm and the looks were a front?"

"Of course."

"What was your father's attitude?"

"To what?"

"Your relationship with Hubbell."

"There was *no* relationship! And Dad didn't know. It was nothing really, less than a one-night stand, kids' stuff."

"You don't seem to have much time for him."

"I loathed him; he was a vicious, depraved brute." There was the slightest pause. "Don't you agree? Look how he treated Misty."

"So you're another who's not about to mourn him." Sumner stood up and Barclay followed suit.

"I'd dance on his grave. That's going to be a bit difficult for a while, isn't it?"

She seemed happy as a meadow lark as she saw them out. "Gloating," Barclay suggested as they walked to the car.

"More like triumph, I'd say."

"You figure they were an item, her and Kent Hubbell?"

"I'm not sure I know what that means, but she's sore about something and I'm willing to bet it isn't only because he beat his wife. Maybe when the Selhorst woman was a kid Kent came on too heavy; maybe *she* made the running and he was scared – but I don't think so, somehow. Wasn't much would scare Kent. Funny thing, he were my kin but I never heard a whisper to connect him and her."

"You wouldn't. You in Stagg, them way out here."

"All the same, it's a big country but not many folk in it. I heard enough about him womanising: girls in Stagg, and such, an' fights – he were always fighting, probably over women. And there was that wounding charge . . ." Sumner ruminated, gnawing his lip, his eyes on the mouth of the river and the roof of the Mantons' house. "Did you tell Robin Misty was back?"

"No."

"She knew. I'll swear she knew."

"Virginia or Miz Dodge coulda phoned her. They had time."

"Why should they? To warn her? Warn her about what, to say what? She came clean about her and Hubbell."

"Smokescreen."

"Smokescreen for what?"

Fifteen

Requests for information on Norm Riessen's movements bore fruit. Three days after he disappeared Scott received word that he'd been in Portland, Oregon, using his credit cards to buy gasolene and a new tyre for his Bronco. The vehicle's registration had been noted in the latter case. Of more significance was the fact that he'd visited a sporting goods store and bought camping equipment: a rucksack and sleeping bag, a tent. He was going into the back country.

The sheriff had suffered a sea change, having realised the extent of the hassle involved if it turned out that Hubbell's death had not been an accident. The influx of police and media had produced enough problems but the last straw came when kids evaded the police guard at Angel's Camp. They slipped by in the darkness and actually reached the river. They couldn't have seen anything of the Stingray, which was completely submerged since the rain, and how they escaped drowning was a mystery. The sheriff doubted that they'd traversed the rockface anyway. When they returned to the road they looked like victims of a hit-and-run, according to Bill Selhorst, who was passing, and who took them to their car on the highway. No one else tried to reach the river, not to Scott's knowledge, although maybe some had and were still down there, he thought grimly. He prayed that the Stingray would break up under the incessant pounding of the water and the body be washed out to sea and disappear, food for crabs.

When Riessen surfaced in Oregon attention shifted and the last of the media people left the area. Most had been recalled already, editors and readers no longer interested in photographs of white water. The incident was last week's news and although one or two imaginative reporters might have been tempted to follow Riessen's trail, they were diverted almost immediately by a teenage shooting at a school way down in the opposite corner of the state.

Sheriff Scott was vastly relieved that Riessen had left the area. He was rid of police and media and, and if there had been any possibility of foul play, he was rid of the most likely suspect as well. Publicly he accepted that it was no more than a coincidence that Hubbell should have died violently when his wife was having an affair with a neighbour. And another coincidence that the neighbour should have run? The question niggled but it wasn't this sheriff's problem. Riessen was in someone else's jurisdiction now.

Then Misty disappeared again.

Opal Crane reported it, and although both Scott and Sumner guessed that the girl had gone to join Riessen they had to admit it was odd. She hadn't taken her pickup. Resigned and only faintly curious, Sumner returned to Prosper.

"I met that fat deputy on the road," Robin said, coming up the steps, jostled by Henry. She ran her hand over his elegant head. "A white Afro: I love it! Hi, Gin! Sumner says Misty's gone again."

"She's in and out of that cabin like a gopher," Virginia said. "According to the police."

"She walked this time. She didn't take the pickup."

"Really?" Bill was interested. "Maybe it wouldn't start."

"Sumner says it's running fine. He says Myra told him Misty called someone to fetch her. She has a mobile."

"She's gone to join Riessen," Virginia said. "He's her pimp; they got rid of Kent, Riessen did a runner, Misty went . . ." She stopped.

"But Misty came back," Bill pointed out. "That's not logical if she was an accomplice in Hubbell's murder."

"There was a breakdown in communication," Virginia suggested. "They went separately after the murder, and couldn't make contact again. So Misty returned home to wait for Riessen to call her, and he did, and she's gone."

"Why didn't she take her truck?" Bill mused. "It wasn't Riessen who picked her up; he's hundreds of miles away. You're saying she had another man give her a ride, to take her to Riessen? That sounds remarkably exploitive."

"Oh, come on, Dad! She's a hooker, exploitation's the job. She had it off with everyone—"

"*Everyone?*" Virginia was suddenly outraged.

"No, no! Not everyone. I meant all the guys that – of her type – class – you know what I mean!"

Bill was amused. "She means everyone with the exception of Paul – and Grady, Owen, David and myself. Right, my dear?"

*   *   *

126

Robin and Owen sat on the top step of Win's deck, gossiping cosily. Win was having her nap and the kitten and the marmalade tom were competing for attention, fondled absently by Owen who was absorbed and fascinated by the latest development.

"You don't think," Robin breathed, "that when I said Misty had it off with everyone and Ginny blew up – that Paul—?"

"Why not?"

She giggled. "Would you dare, if you were married to Ginny?"

"Win says Paul has the money."

"Why, you old cynic!" There was no response. He was looking down the spine of South Point. "See something?" she asked.

He came back to her. "Just a large bird."

"Do you have time for a walk? We could go to the cove. The tide's in so we'll have to go by the woods. Bring Win's gun. Best to be on the safe side. Bill says he's seen no sign of the dogs, however. Him and David have been visiting the cove at low tide and they haven't seen any tracks."

"Both of them?"

"Both what?"

"They visit the cove every day?"

"I guess. Why?"

"Oh, nothing."

The forest was quiet. It was a grey day with splashes of sunlight on the water but once they were in the trees they moved in a green twilight where their feet made no sound on the mat of dead needles. An owl called – strange in the daytime – and not a breath of wind stirred the fronds of the sword ferns and the hanging mosses. Owen's shirt clung to his back but it wasn't a warm afternoon, merely heavy and humid. This was a world away from the bright woods of Snowdonia: all silver birches and wildflowers. Nothing bloomed under these trees, only fungi clustered on downed timber, and a plant like skeletal hands protruded from the spongey floor.

The gloom didn't last long. There was a lightening of the air, a taste of salt, and the path dropped gently until there was a glint between the trunks that wasn't sky. They came down through the belt of red alders and the cove revealed itself. It was high tide and the water leaden, every stack inverted in its mirror image. The thin line of a dying wavelet ran along the shore, and the water retreated leaving only a narrow strand below the jumble of bleached logs.

They started to stroll south on the damp sand, Robin quizzing her companion on the plot of Win's current book, Owen parrying her curiosity with the reminder that he was only the secretary, she must go to Win for details. "I do believe you're producing porn," she declared, but his reaction was to turn the tables and demand an exposé of her lifestyle. She obliged to some extent, tacitly acknowledging that he wasn't going to come clean about his relationship with Win. Obviously he was hiding something and she didn't think it was the plot of a book. They strolled and chatted, pausing to study flotsam left behind by the summer storm. Occasionally a seal popped up and followed their progress with limpid eyes.

The belt of wet sand widened perceptibly. "Oh, Lor'," Owen exclaimed. "She'll wonder what's happened to me, and I'm doing Chicken Catalan for dinner."

They turned back, talking food. The trees marched beside them on their right, first the alders and their lush green understorey, then the firs crowning the slope, itself gouged and gashed with slides where the unstable ground had slipped in the winter rains. Owen remarked how ghastly it would be if you missed the exit path and the tide was too high to return through the Hole, and the light was fading. Robin stared at him.

"You'd just wait for low tide. You do have a dark mind. Is that the Celtic blood?"

"That's not the worst of it; there are wild beasts in the forest. Imagine!"

"You should be a writer yourself. You're wasted. Did you never think of that?"

"Never." He was quite snappy. "What's that seal doing on the beach? Doesn't it know there are predators about?"

They were approaching the headland of South Point. Owen, not trusting his companion as a navigator, had been looking anxiously for the start of the path. "It ought to be marked," he muttered crossly. "One could miss it, you know."

"That seal's dead," Robin said. "The eagles have been at it."

"We haven't seen any eagles."

"Well, something's been feeding on it; the back-end's skinned."

He looked reluctantly, terrified that they would walk right past the path. Robin pushed ahead and then stopped. She turned to him, her mouth and eyes wide, one hand at her throat. He looked from her to the thing on the tide-line and saw that it was no seal but a human body, and what she had taken for flesh was a shiny red skirt. Where the sprawling legs were not lacerated they were the colour of the fungus on the forest floor. The wet hair was tangled with weed, the face invisible.

"But she left!" Robin said. "She went to join Norm. What happened? Owen, don't stand there, say something! Oh, I'm sorry, I – it's shock. I haven't seen a body before. It looks so dead, doesn't it? I mean, you wouldn't think this was Misty, would you?"

Saturday evening in the middle of June was the worst time for a body to surface, and that when the sheriff had been congratulating himself on losing Norm Riessen to someone else's jurisdiction. A second death at Prosper revived the sensation of being crowded. The problem of the body in the Stingray might be shifted to the recovery teams (except for the paperwork) but the body in Stack Cove he must deal with himself. Except that this was Saturday evening and in one way that gave him an out. He must keep men in Stagg: for the streets, as despatcher and co-ordinator. Two men could not be spared for Prosper, one must suffice, and only one knew the ground. Simple when the problem was confronted; he sent Sumner to Prosper.

Although it was his second trip that day, this one made a welcome change from bar brawls and drunks throwing up in the back of the car. So, unlike his harassed superior, Sumner was in a benign mood when he arrived at Bill Selhorst's house. Since Bill had reported the body the police were under the impression that he'd discovered it. No sweat, he told Sumner, it was his daughter and young Hughes who'd come on it in Stack Cove; Robin was now visiting with Win Carver but he knew where the body was, they'd said you couldn't miss it. The tide was on the ebb and it should be possible to reach the cove by way of the Hole instead of trekking through the forest.

There was rather more water in the passage than Sumner had anticipated. Bill said that in the normal way he'd have waited until it was dryer; he'd been in the cove quite a bit recently, in fact he'd been here yesterday morning but then there was no body.

They saw it immediately as they stepped up the sand slope beyond the Hole. "No way could it have been here," Bill repeated. "Even if we'd thought it was a seal carcass, we'd have investigated, looking for tracks. I was with David Nelson and we were after those dogs."

"No dogs were here." Sumner stood back from the body, eyeing the ground. Two sets of footprints approached from the south and left at a tangent. "No animals have been here at all, not even eagles. Yet."

Bill glanced from the body to the rampart of the forest. "I don't reckon the dogs are about. We found old tracks in one place below a slide, but so far as fresh prints went, we figured they'd moved to another area."

Sumner wasn't listening, he was studying the rocks of the headland. "This wasn't where she fell; she's too far out from the cliff."

"Fell?"

"What else?" The deputy was surprised. "You're saying she walked into the water from the beach?"

"You're thinking suicide."

"And you're thinking murder. That's my department."

"No." Bill was serious. "I'd assumed it was an accident – of course." The pause was marginal. He went on more firmly, "Obviously she fell; look at those gashes." He squinted at the cliff. "She fell – on to rocks – so it had to be low water, then the tide came in and took her away on the ebb – and the next tide brought her back." He raised his eyebrows at Sumner.

"Which would explain why you didn't see the body yesterday. She'd have been floating. And you wouldn't see her out there in the weed."

Offshore a raft of kelp lay immobile on the surface, dark globular heads reflecting the light like skulls. Amongst the weed the body would have been just another piece of flotsam.

They turned her over and winced at sight of the battered face. She was wearing a reddish scarf, darkened by the water. "Suicide or accident," Sumner said heavily. "Not our job, thank God, but we have to move her, stop her floating away again. We'll take her through the Hole and then she'll be handy to pick up in the morning. Too late now to call the chopper out."

Splashing alerted them to the approach of Paul Manton and David Nelson who emerged, dripping, from the wet passage. Neither seemed troubled by the body but then both were professionally interested. Paul nodded a greeting and glanced up at the rock face. David looked along the beach. "No sign of the dogs," he murmured.

"How long d'you think she was in the water, Doctor?" Sumner asked.

Paul grimaced. "I'm a surgeon. You might as well ask me how long's she been dead. She was alive yesterday, wasn't she? Didn't Myra see her?"

With the trees blocking out the light the interior of the cabin was dim except for the television screen. Seth sat in front of it, propped up by cushions, drooling a little but watching Sumner's face intently. Myra had turned the sound down but the images and the flashing lights gave the illusion of a fourth presence in the room, and one more active than the others. The people were almost immobile, eyes bright points in the gloom.

The couple's reaction to the news was virtually a non-reaction. Seth's eyes flickered; Sumner wondered how far the old man could turn his head, whether he would have glanced at his wife had his neck been flexible. As for Myra, she had stiffened certainly, but now she was still, waiting for more.

"It's a shock," Sumner observed, pushing for comment. "Your own daughter-in-law."

Seth snuffled. Was it his version of a laugh?

"She were nothing to you," Myra told him sharply. Her hand traced the neck of her blouse. "Did she jump off of the cliff then?" she asked politely, as if Sumner were a stranger.

He shrugged. "Who knows?" His eyes strayed. "When did you see her last?"

"Never," Seth said clearly.

Sumner stared. He didn't know the guy could still speak.

"Don't take no notice of him," Myra said. "She come over sometimes if I were away a whiles, keep him company." She glanced at her husband with contempt. He grinned.

"When did you see her last?" Sumner persisted.

"Thursday." She was prompt and firm.

"She was gone yesterday?"

"I told you this morning."

"Spell it out. It wasn't important this morning and I've forgotten the details."

"I went across, see if the hound come back, see if she were feeding it. She'd gone. Took the rifle. I looked." She nodded at his surprise. "Forgot to tell you that. It were her took Kent's rifle, brought it back with her. I saw her take it out the pickup. You know what? You'll find my son were shot with that rifle."

"Why didn't you report her missing this morning?"

"Who cares? She were a whore – a murdering whore. I thought some man had picked her up."

"So Misty left yesterday morning or the day before," Sumner told Scott on his return to Stagg. "More likely at night or someone would have seen her go down to the point. What I can't understand is why she didn't take the pickup."

"How far is it?" Scott was doodling on a pad at his desk. "From her place to South Point?"

"It's around three miles, and I never saw her but she was wearing heels all of three inches high. No shoes now, of course, they'll have come off in the water. I can't see Misty walking even one mile when she's got serviceable wheels out front. And she took the rifle. Unless she threw it off the point . . ."

"So someone gave her a ride." They stared at each other. "You moved the body," Scott said heavily.

Sumner wasn't having that. "If I didn't, the next tide would have taken her out to sea and the fishes would have got her."

Scott nodded glumly, hoping that would serve when his superiors came to accuse him of slovenly procedure.

"I think it's terribly sad." Amy lay on her side in bed, staring at the moonlight on the water. "She had all her life ahead of her, with that brute dead. She could start over."

"You don't know how her mind was working," David pointed out. "She must have been unstable."

"If she was it didn't show. She had to have been scared but only of *him*. Like I said, there was nothing to be afraid of any longer – and there was Norm Riessen waiting for her in Oregon. She had it all – and she goes and throws it away."

"Forget it." He turned towards her, raising his head to see the bright path on the water. Down on the shore a fox barked. He smiled. "I reckon those dogs have gone," he said with deep satisfaction.

"How do you know?"

"They hadn't touched the body."

"Oh, Dave! You think more of animals than you do of people. All she meant to you was a kind of bait, a pointer as to whether predators were in the vicinity."

He didn't respond. She hadn't asked a question. And she was right.

Paul scratched Henry's woolly skull and focused on the mouth of the river. The tide had turned and the strip of sand would start to fine down shortly. Something small and dark was moving fast along the water's edge to slip smoothly into the river. He could see the broad arrow of its wake heading for the shadows under the far bank: a river otter.

"What are you thinking?" Virginia asked.

He stretched his legs and the wicker chair creaked. "I'm wondering why we don't have a boat."

"Because I'm a bad sailor, that's why." She thought about that, and about him. "No reason why you shouldn't buy one. Where would you keep it?"

"That's the problem. I wouldn't like to own something as valuable as a yacht and have to berth it miles away at Stagg."

They were silent again. She knew he wouldn't buy a boat, he was too lazy to learn to sail. "You could keep a horse," she said.

"Why on earth do you suggest that?"

"Because you're bored." A long pause. "That's why you had to find yourself some amusement."

"I didn't go searching, Gin."

"Maybe not. You didn't run when she came looking though, did you?"

"Jesus, Gin! She's dead. Can't you give it a rest *now*?"

Virginia sighed. "Her death brought it all back. One blocks it out – Constance will be trying to do that too. When the bitch was alive she poisoned relationships, and now she's dead she's done it again—"

He gave a snort of astonishment. "She kills herself just to claim attention? Is that what you're saying? You're crazy."

"That's what suicides do."

"But she wasn't that sort of a woman—"

"So what kind of a woman was she? You tell me that. You tell me what she was like, you're the one—"

"Gin! Shut up! We've had this for weeks and I'm sick of it. It's over, it was over the next day. The focus has shifted and the spotlight's on Grady. My friend Grady, remember? And he's in far worse shape than ever I was. I was lucky. And Constance is your friend. Just bear in mind how they're feeling at this moment and thank God things turned out how they did for us."

"You go to bed, hon," Grady said. "I'll stay up a while. I shouldn't have slept this afternoon."

"One more drink. We'll make it a nightcap. How are you feeling?"

"All I'm feeling is relief. Overwhelming relief. I'm not even worried about the result of that test. There's something I never told you. I'm wondering if it was a scam from start to finish."

"You know it was. Riessen spiked your drink."

"Not that. It was when I woke in that awful cabin. There was a condom on the floor. It was that that suggested to me what had happened. Now I wonder if that – that object – had nothing to do with me, that she brought it over from Riessen's trailer. I'm sorry, I've disgusted you."

"No. It's a technical point. I was thinking . . . So she need never have been in bed with you at all. Could it be that she isn't – wasn't – HIV either, that that was part of the blackmail, to stop you telling me? And then she told Hubbell that you'd raped her and he turned blackmailer . . ." Constance's eyes widened, the moonlight reflected in them.

"And now both blackmailers are dead." He was smug, and then he caught her expression. "What is it, hon?"

"For God's sake," she whispered, "don't . . ."

"Don't what?"

She closed her eyes and breathed deeply. "Don't forget Myra. She was in it too. But there, you can forget her. I'll deal with Myra."

He nodded, happy to relinquish problems. She wondered whether his lack of imagination was an asset or a disadvantage, but then it shouldn't have to be put to the test. There would be no more police interviews. Misty had fallen from South Point. In any event Grady had never been out of his wife's sight since his return from Seattle.

The preliminary report on the body was available the following day, Sunday. Apart from the pathologist and his assistant the sheriff was the first to know and he felt as if he'd been kicked in the stomach.

Under the red scarf there was bruising, and the hyoid was broken. Misty had been strangled.

Sixteen

For a short time that Monday morning Prosper was divided into two camps with the people on the coast ignorant of the fact that a major investigation had started at the cabins in the forest. However, total ignorance lasted for only as long as it took detectives – or rather one detective under Sumner's guidance – to arrive at the shore. The police cars parked before the Carver place and approached the headland on foot. Win and Owen came out on the deck to observe the proceedings and wait to be approached. The newcomers were on Win's land. The group comprised the man in plain clothes and two in uniform in addition to Sumner.

"What are they after?" Win asked. Owen said nothing. "Owen?" Her voice rose.

"Presumably they've found something suspicious."

"Should we go down?"

"No. Let them come to you."

By now the other households knew something was afoot, the unmarked car and the black-and-white having been observed by Virginia. The telephone lines came alive. It was obvious that Misty's death was the focal point, the strangers having waded through the Hole. Their movements were viewed by everyone except Bill and Robin with concern; even David was considering the effect a police presence might have on the wildlife. When the body was removed yesterday Prosper had assumed that the affair was over, apart from the funeral, and that would be a family matter. That the police had returned was surprising, that they should be accompanied by a man in plain-clothes was puzzling to say the least. People awaited a knock on the door with mixed feelings.

There was no knock. The uniformed strangers remained out of sight, presumably in the cove, while Sumner and the plain-clothes man returned to the unmarked car and drove away. The black-and-white remained on the track below Win's house; even unoccupied it suggested, as in some sci-fi drama, that the settlement was under surveillance.

"They've left it there deliberately," Amy said. "They're trying to intimidate us."

"Rubbish. They have to leave it somewhere." But David was uneasy. "I'm going to find out what those guys are doing in the cove. If they're proposing to bring dogs in, the wildlife's going to be disturbed."

"Why would they want to bring in dogs?"

"They're tracing Misty's movements."

Amy stared at him. "I don't get it."

"You think she walked down here on her own, all the way from her cabin? How d'you think she reached the point?"

"I never gave it a thought. But we all go down on the shore: fishing, collecting mussels, clams in season."

"When did you ever see Misty on the shore? Or any of the loggers come to that?"

Amy's hand went to her mouth as she realised the implication. She doubted if he did. He was expressionless. "At least I know where you were every night," she said, trying to make a joke of it. "And that goes for all of us," she added quickly. "I mean, no one down here lives alone even if they don't share a bed. Everyone has an alibi, right?" Her laugh was strident.

David didn't react, didn't turn a hair. Taking his rifle he went down to the Hole, only to be stopped on the other side by the police who asked him his business and suggested that if he had to patrol the forest he should do so from another access point. They also asked about the rifle and he warned them that there were two large dogs loose. They pointed out that feral dogs would have attacked the body and insisted that he return through the Hole before he confused old tracks with his own. In fact there were no old tracks about the place where the body had lain; subsequent high tides had smoothed the sand and no print showed other than those of this morning.

"What are you looking for?" he asked, reasonably enough.

Traces, they said, something to show how the accident had happened.

David retreated and, because the forest path started at the back of Win's place, stopped to relay the sparse information.

"They said 'accident'," Owen observed. "Not suicide?"

"Suicide wasn't mentioned."

"She didn't kill herself," Win said. "Those women are tough."

"Suppose she found she had something incurable," Owen said. "Like cancer or AIDS."

"She wouldn't believe it. Tough and stupid, that was Misty Hubbell."

"I'm going in the forest," David told them, not interested in the exchange. "I'm worried about the deer. They've not come back since that pack of dogs were around. I haven't seen a deer for ages. And that means the cougars have gone too."

"Where did Sumner go?" Owen asked. "And the detective – if that's what he was – the one in plain-clothes?"

"I have no idea. I didn't ask."

"That guy's inhuman," Owen declared when he was out of earshot. "He thinks more of animals than he does of people."

"So do we, my dear, present company excepted. After all, Misty was no great loss."

He glowered at her. "Just don't say that when the police come, that's all."

"Why should they come here? They might ask permission to go on my land but it's a bit late in the day for that."

"This place is the nearest house to where the body was found." His eyes glazed. "Of course they'll come here. We have to watch our step."

"Owen! Her death can't have anything to do with us. Or are you thinking that there's some connection with what happened to Hubbell?"

"Not really. It's just – don't *give* the police anything, don't volunteer information."

"The reason I'm not bothered is because I lost my son, is why! It don't matter to me *how* she died, whether she fell or were pushed. Who murdered my boy? You tell me that!"

For what had seemed like hours but which had been no more than forty-five minutes (much of it across at what had been Kent's cabin) Myra had parried questions. No, she hadn't heard an engine on Friday, nor on Thursday, hadn't seen a strange car at any time until now, and no, she couldn't say how her daughter-in-law had reached the cove if she hadn't walked there. She didn't know who were the girl's friends – except that one from Angel's Camp, him that had gone to Oregon: Norm Riessen. As for the others, Misty had friends everywhere and yes, of course she knew all the men in Prosper, lived here since she married, hadn't she: four years. What had she done since Riessen left? Myra couldn't say; she wasn't the girl's keeper.

The first questioner was middle-aged with the look of a bird of prey about him: a strong hooked nose and wide eyes in deep sockets. His mouth was small and prim, not a generous mouth. He made her feel uncomfortable. She thought he must be a high-flyer although she hadn't caught his rank, if he'd given it, only the name: Powell. Nevertheless, she had coped with him so far quite competently, while Seth dribbled and scratched himself and said nothing. Having one of his bad days, she'd told Powell.

It was when the other one arrived, the bald fat one with a face like a clown and dressed like a bum, with his pants soaked to the knees, who'd listened a while and then remarked that she didn't seem bothered by the manner of Misty's death – it was then that Myra cracked.

"I'd have thought she'd be a comfort to you," the fat man said, making like he was puzzled. "You're all family. She'd lost her husband."

Myra snorted and glanced at Sumner who had sidled into the cabin and was leaning against the door jamb. The place seemed crowded with big men. Sumner stared at her. If he wasn't about to acknowledge kinship in front of these strangers then no more would she.

"Not a loving wife?" Fatty suggested.

She looked from him to Powell, trying to determine their relationship, confused as to how much they knew. "She had friends," she muttered.

"So we've heard."

"Lots of friends," Powell said quietly.

Fatty raised eyebrows like furry grubs. "In Prosper? Down in those big houses on the shore?"

"I wouldn't know." She was lofty and her look at Sumner dared him to speak.

Fatty seemed to come to a decision and, pulling out a chair, sat down cater-cornered to her at the table. She stared at the meaty thighs straining his chinos. "We're presented with two scenarios here," he told her chattily, while she tried to understand why he was taking the initiative in front of his boss. "She was killed in her cabin or in the cove. Either way she went down there in someone else's vehicle. So who was the driver?"

"She coulda been dead," Myra said stupidly.

He was patient. "The body had to be taken away. A guy don't walk three miles carrying a body."

"Or a woman," Powell said in his quiet, insinuating voice.

Myra gaped. "A woman done it?" she whispered.

Powell said, "A woman's even less likely to carry a body three miles."

"But," she looked wildly from him to Fatty, "who . . ." Her eyes closed, as if, open, they would betray her thoughts. "You figure a jealous wife, like? Some woman come out from Stagg and throttled her?"

"A heavy woman with big strong hands," Powell suggested. "Misty was small, she wouldn't put up much of a fight."

Myra stared at him, dumb as an ox. Seth snuffled among his cushions.

"What happened to her shoes?" Fatty asked.

Her head turned slowly. "How would I know?"

"And the mobile? And the rifle?"

"She took 'em with her." There was a stiffening on the part of the police. "She had to," Myra elaborated, recovering, not troubling to conceal a smile. "They're not there so someone took 'em. Not me." She gestured widely. "Search the place. They're not here."

"She don't have them." The fat man was called Jake Dineen. They stood by his car as he told them how he saw it. "If the girl walked out to the road she could have taken the mobile, if she was expecting Riessen to get in touch, but she wouldn't take the rifle. On the other hand, if she was killed in the cabin, the killer could have stole both the rifle and the mobile." He turned to Sumner, his clown's face amused but curious. "What d'you think, Sumner?"

The deputy was diffident in the face of the city men; all the same, he was the local authority and he appreciated that Dineen wasn't treating him like a hick cop but appealing to his superior knowledge. "I'm thinking," he said carefully, "that your two scenarios as to where she was killed, means two different men, different *kinds* of men. If she was taken to Prosper alive, the killer could be one of those residents, and that's one of five men just. But if she were killed here, I don't see any of those five visiting her in her own cabin, and the in-laws within screaming distance."

"You figure she had time to scream?" Powell asked.

"The killer wasn't about to risk it."

"Five men," Dineen repeated. "And their women? Are they big and powerful, with strong hands?"

Sumner's jaw dropped. Dineen beamed at him. "Let's have a look at 'em, shall we?"

"Strangled?" Grady repeated. "I don't believe it."

139

Constance brought a platter of angel slices to the coffee table between the two detectives and glanced at their cups. "More coffee?" she asked, adding in the same tone, "We understood she'd fallen from the headland. Our neighbour's a doctor. He saw the body."

"Oh yes, ma'am; the body fell but she was strangled first."

Grady's jaw was clenched. Constance shook her head. "How ghastly," she said, handing them napkins.

"We have to talk to all her contacts," Dineen told her gravely. Powell lifted his cup and eyed the husband over the rim.

They had dropped Sumner at the Mantons' house with instructions to sit tight, make innocuous inquiries and listen hard to his end of any telephone conversation. By now, briefed by the deputy, the detectives knew that these people on the shore were all of a class: professionals, active or retired, and if they weren't all rich, all mixed comfortably together. They could be expected to present a united front. Dineen assumed that if he were to elicit anything even approaching the truth from them it was essential to keep them from communicating with each other, at least at the outset. Which was why Sumner was now with the Mantons.

The detectives found the Dodges in their greenhouse. Constance was immediately recognisable from Sumner's description: a robust woman in a cotton shirt and well-cut pants. Evidently she was treating pests because she had a spray in one hand, a pot containing a knobbly cactus in the other. Behind her a large fellow peered over her shoulder with an expression of wary concern. As Dineen approached she put down the spray and pot and came forward, not exactly welcoming – they were an interruption – but polite.

"Good morning!" She made an announcement of it.

Dineen was on his best behaviour, introducing himself and his partner, explaining that there were a few questions, background material . . . glancing towards the house suggestively. Unlike Myra, the Dodges were under no illusion concerning which was the senior man. They moved indoors, Powell and Grady in the rear, sizing each other up. Powell was expressionless, Grady looked as if he were confronted by a large and unpredictable animal.

Over the coffee Dineen dropped his bomb, wondering if they knew already that Misty had been murdered. Someone did.

"She wouldn't have had any contacts here," Constance told him, her eyes passing over her husband and fastening on the telescope. "No one employed her of course. Her mother-in-law worked for us but from

140

what she said, Misty wasn't keen on housework, so no, I doubt if she knew any of us."

"Myra says she knew everyone."

"Figure of speech." She was quite sharp. "By 'everyone' she would have meant people she met in bars in Stagg – and at Angel's Camp."

"We don't go in bars," Grady informed them stiffly.

"Not to say *frequent* them." Constance sounded as if she were reproving a small boy who had spoken out of turn. "We do go in bars occasionally: an aperitif before lunch, that kind of thing, but so far as serious drinking's concerned," she smiled to show it was a joke, "we entertain at home."

"Too early to offer you a Scotch?" Grady seemed to remember his duties as a host.

Dineen declined. No one referred to Powell who appeared intent on the furnishings, on the pictures and ornaments, his eye coming to rest on the massive telescope. "May I?" he asked.

Grady nodded, surprised. "Don't move it," he said quickly, "The tripod, I mean. It's a very delicate instrument," he added with pride. Powell, who had mentally priced it in the thousands, restrained a grin, remembering Sumner's contention that the money was all on the wife's side of the family.

Through the huge expanse of glass he could see that, southward, the whole of the point was visible. A house was perched on a bluff about a couple of hundred yards away, and beyond that, another, a large white clapboard affair, stood closer to the point. In the other direction, to the north, was the Mantons' house and beyond that, the mouth of the river with a sand bar exposed. It was low tide.

He swivelled the telescope carefully. The crest of the headland leapt into his vision, friezed with pink flowers. A gull almost filled the frame. If you wanted to be private in this place you'd need to stay inside your house and – he glanced at the sides of the glass – if the neighbours followed the Dodges' example, no one had drapes. Blinds yes, but if you lowered your blinds, wouldn't that imply you were up to no good?

Behind him the conversation was centred on Myra Hubbell, Constance saying that she had fired the woman recently, the sheriff had the details. Myra had been caught stealing.

Powell turned to see the boss's eyebrows raised in his direction. "You were talking to Sumner," Dineen prompted.

Powell came and sat down. "Myra says that the items that ended up with Misty were in fact presents to her," he said. "Myra had nothing to do with it."

"Of course." Constance was dismissive. "It's what she would say."

"They weren't presents?" Dineen asked.

"Oh really! A designer sweater! Some toilet water – for men? Now why would I give Myra those?"

"Misty," Dineen corrected. "They were alleged to be presents to Misty."

"That's even more ridiculous. I didn't know the girl – that is, I knew her by sight, one could scarcely miss – but I don't remember that I ever spoke to her."

Dineen turned to the husband, smiling broadly and without exposing his teeth. Grady's nostrils expanded and he blinked rapidly. "Loggers," he blurted. "It's a distressed area, you know? You can't blame 'em: picking up trifles here and there. After all, a fellow don't need toilet water." He gave a harsh bark, caught his wife's eye and looked embarrassed. "The sweater's a different matter. Valuable item, and she was fond of it. Nasty, stealing clothes, but then how else could they acquire decent things, eh? You have to make allowances."

"Possibly." Dineen sat up straight, as straight as a fat man can sit on a soft sofa. His tone changed: no innuendoes, no chatty asides, but the smile was still there. It was unnerving. "Now," he began, "last Thursday night: a vehicle came past here. You're – what? – a hundred yards from the track. Did you see it pass?"

Grady stared at him. His wife was facing the ocean. She turned and considered the windows flanking the door. "We would have seen lights, but only if we'd been looking – and, of course, if we were in here. What time would this be?"

"We don't know – yet." Dineen looked annoyed as if his research were at fault. "Any time after dark, I'd say. No? Well, they could have driven past without lights."

"They?" Constance repeated. "There was more than one of them?"

"I was using it to suit either sex, ma'am. I should have said 'he or she'."

"'She'. You mean Misty."

"No. I mean her killer."

Grady snorted in disbelief. "A woman killed her?"

"Why not?"

"Why not indeed." Constance seemed genuinely amused. "There

must have been a number of ladies from Stagg gunning for her. But to get back to Thursday night: I wasn't aware of anything on the track, neither a strange vehicle nor any of the neighbours. I'm sure we'd have remarked on it, it would be so unusual." There was a pause. "But if she didn't come in a vehicle, how did she come?"

"You don't think she'd walk here?"

"No, not Misty."

"Someone brought her," Grady said. "Someone came in from outside. If Riessen wasn't in Oregon—" He stopped suddenly.

"Yes?" Dineen pounced. "If he wasn't there—?"

Grady shrugged. "She drank at Angel's, everyone knew that. They could have been . . ." He glanced at his wife.

"But it's public knowledge," she said. "Why, someone – could it have been Myra? – suggested that Norm Riessen was Misty's pimp. No love lost between Myra and her daughter-in-law, I'm afraid, but then you see, Myra is certain her son didn't die in an accident. You know about her son drowning in the river?" Dineen nodded. "Still there as a matter of fact. Well, Myra says that Riessen had a hand in that – that he murdered Kent, and Misty was involved as well."

"How do you know all this?" Dineen asked.

"Jungle drums, the grapevine." She smiled. "We're a tiny community, more like an island; whatever one person does or says, everyone knows in a very short time. No one can have secrets in Prosper."

"I see that." His eyes were on the telescope. "A pity that isn't equipped for night vision or you might have seen what was happening on the point on Thursday night."

"We wouldn't be looking." She wasn't fazed by this harping on Thursday night. "I can't remember what we were doing. Could that have been the evening we watched *A Passage to India*, honey? Yes, I do believe it was. I remember now: Virginia – our neighbour – brought the video over that morning. There! That's why we didn't see any lights or hear anything; we were absorbed in the movie."

Seventeen

In the car, slowly negotiating the potholes between the two houses, Dineen said, "So what did you make of the Dodges?"

"I'd like to get him on his own." Powell was grim. "Away from her. She monopolised the conversation." He came to a halt outside the Mantons' house. "They'll be on the phone right now; I'd give a month's pay to know what she's saying."

"She won't have much time. And Sumner's listening to this end." Dineen's eyes gleamed at sight of the second large lady of the morning. She stood at the opened door but, unlike Constance Dodge, this one had no finesse. "I know who you are," she grated as he pronounced names. "And I'm waiting for an explanation. Sumner here says you're questioning us. Why?"

The doctor was on the telephone as they entered the house. Sumner, standing in front of a huge stone fireplace, nodded to Dineen, his eyes going pointedly to Manton. It was pretty obvious that one of the Dodges was on the other end of the wire.

Paul said, "I have to go now; I'll call you back." He put down the phone and shook hands with Dineen, courteous but concerned. "Our neighbours say Misty was strangled. Is that right?"

Dineen blinked. "You didn't notice, sir?"

"I didn't see her throat. She was wearing a scarf and I didn't move it. I'm a surgeon – or was – not a physician, and I've never seen a case of strangulation." He frowned. "So that's the result of the autopsy, strangulation?"

"The preliminary report. Bruising on the throat is superficial *and* deep-seated, and the hyoid is broke."

Paul moved to sit down, remembered his manners and gestured to the others to be seated. Virginia started at his glance and turned to the kitchen and the coffee pot.

"What we need to find now is witnesses," Dineen confided.

Paul stared in disbelief. "You can't believe someone saw it happen!"

"She had to be brought here, either alive or dead. Could a vehicle approach the shore without someone seeing? There are ten people living down here and you're all surrounded by glass." Dineen gestured at the west wall of the living room and the vast panorama of the ocean.

"You've only seen the Dodges' house and this one," Paul pointed out. "The Nelsons don't have much glass facing the track, and Miss Carver's house is old with smallish windows. . ." His voice died away and when he didn't resume Dineen's eyes slid to Sumner.

"She's nearest to the point," the deputy said. "And she has a fair-sized window on the deck facing the ocean. The killer couldn't go behind her house to reach the headland because the brush is too thick; he had to pass by the front."

Virginia approached with a tray. She said harshly, "It's staring you in the face: he put the body in the cove to throw suspicion on someone in Prosper! Like Win, or her young secretary. It had to be someone who knew—"

"Oh, shit!" Henry had pushed past Paul's knees and made him spill his coffee as he picked up a mug. "This damn dog! Put him out, Gin."

She glared at him. "We haven't been letting him out—"

"Those dogs are gone." Paul was dabbing at his slacks with a handkerchief. "Sorry about this," he addressed Dineen, grinning shamefacedly. "Large poodles aren't exactly noted for grace, and this one is the world's clumsiest."

"I like standard poodles," Dineen confessed. "Always thought I'd like to have one. Apparently they make good gun dogs."

"Oh, yes." Paul was enthusiastic. "Henry loves retrieving."

"We'll excuse you while you change your slacks." Dineen was benign. "That coffee's going to stain unless you put them in water right away."

"That's all right. They're old."

"Go and change," Virginia snapped. "I'm going to put Henry on the leash."

The police were left alone, staring at each other, then Dineen's lips thinned. He rose and followed his hostess outside.

She had gone down the steps and was calling to the dog. "What are you afraid of?" Dineen asked.

"Me!" She turned on him angrily. "Why – what makes you think that?"

"Mrs Manton! You're obviously upset."

"I think – I think – oh, Henry, there you are! Here boy!"

The poodle came reluctantly. She grasped his collar and led him up to the deck where a length of rope was fastened to an iron ring. She clipped it to his collar and stood up to glower at the headland. "Yes," she said tightly, "I am bothered. Not scared. Just for a moment there, I was thinking what could happen if the dog didn't come back. There was a pack of them running free in the forest. The Rottweilers have gone home, they were guard dogs from Stagg, but there's still a German Shepherd loose and they think he'll have met up with one of Hubbell's hounds. I adore my old boy here." She rubbed Henry's head. "Can you imagine what two wild dogs would have done to him? He's no fighter, he wouldn't stand a chance."

"You know who the killer is," Dineen said.

Her hand went out to the wall of the house for support. She mouthed at him but no words came.

"You know who he is," he amended.

"No." It was all but inaudible. "How could I?"

"Because if he's trying to fasten suspicion on you or one of your neighbours, *he* knows *you*."

"It's a reasonable theory." Paul stepped over the door sill. Dineen wondered how long he'd been there. "What you're suggesting is that the killer had it in for one of us – but why?"

"That's what we have to find out," Dineen said. "I think you know him – or her. A strong woman could have done it. But you may not know the killer very well. If you're right, ma'am, and he is trying to pin the murder on you, it could be that you've done someone an injury without realising it. What about Myra Hubbell for instance?"

"What about her?" Virginia was hostile.

"You employed her once."

"And I fired her. She's a thief."

"But Constance Dodge continued to employ her after you fired her."

"Who told you that?"

"My wife only suspected Myra was stealing," Paul put in quickly. "She didn't broadcast her suspicions."

Dineen studied the man's face, noting the chin lift a fraction, the tightening of the facial muscles. "I wonder if Myra has friends," he mused. "We've been concentrating on the men who were Misty's clients," his eyes came round to Virginia, "but if Myra knew men who owed her a favour, then they could have acted for her: brought the body here on her orders. I don't think Myra could have done it herself, you know, not powerful enough. You need a big strong guy – or woman, like we said before."

As the police drove away Paul slipped the lock on the door and pulled Virginia along the passage to their bedroom. "Extension," he hissed as if they could be overheard. "Can't be seen phoning from the living room if they come back."

Constance must have been waiting for his call because she picked up the phone immediately. She had been in a breathless rush the first time, telling him that Misty had been strangled, that the Dodges maintained they didn't know her – and then the police had arrived. She would have taken stock during the interval and now she was calm, asking what questions Dineen had asked, whether Paul thought the police were motivated in one direction or they were just fishing.

"Fishing," he said, wondering if Grady were close to her, hanging on every word as Virginia was. He would have preferred to speak to Constance without his wife in the room; she was too excited even to sit down, demanding to speak to the woman who was, after all, her friend, not his, furious that he should actually be holding her off, demanding she keep quiet.

"What was curious," he said now, addressing Constance, glaring at Virginia, "is that they didn't push it, follow up an advantage, I mean. Like when Gin lost her cool and told them the killer was trying to throw suspicion on us—"

As Constance interrupted he noted with satisfaction that at last something had sunk in; Virginia had collapsed on the bed as if she'd been punched. "No," he said grimly, seeing fear replace his wife's hostility, "I spilled some coffee, created a diversion at that point. Not that it did any good in the long run; Dineen came back to the same point – and yet he never realised that Gin was about to imply that someone down here had something to hide. He went off on another tack, seemed to think one of us had done the killer an injury, and that the guy was getting his own back. He even suggested it could have been Myra . . . I *know*, but Dineen's like that, isn't he? Friendly, confiding . . . well, *I* didn't think it was an act . . . He said Myra could have a friend, a guy who she'd convinced to kill Misty . . . No, he said she wasn't strong enough." He laughed, his eyes narrowed at Virginia. "Actually he suspects Gin; he said a strong woman could have done it—"

He'd overstepped the line. "Give me that phone!" Virginia shouted, lunging at him. He relinquished it and retreated to the living room, wondering how he might get her out of the way so that he could go next door and have a sensible but uninterrupted discussion with Constance.

Not with Grady, a loose cannon if ever there was one. There was only one worse. He grimaced at the sound of his wife's raised voice from the bedroom.

Constance replaced the phone. "Paul says Dineen suspects a woman. That is, he said a woman could have done it."

"I have to tell them." Grady said thickly. He was sprawled on a sofa, a tumbler of whisky doing duty for the drowning man's straw. Reaction and alcohol were at work.

"You don't tell him anything," Constance said. "Paul won't." Providing he can keep Virginia muzzled, she thought. "You're in the clear. Myra won't talk either." And that was wishful thinking. Why shouldn't the woman talk? She had nothing to lose . . . or had she? There might be a way of silencing her. "I could have heard her," she said: "heard her go by in that old Subaru. There's a hole in the muffler, it makes one hell of a noise."

"No one else will have heard it. I have to tell him. For God's sake, Con, it's only a – a condition – that I probably don't have. You think I don't, Paul too, and all of it based on a trick anyway. All I did was go in a bar. The crimes were on their side, they're the perpetrators, not me: spiking my drink, fraud, blackmail."

Constance was stiff with frustration. "That's why you have to keep quiet! You have a motive. You're the most likely suspect: the desperate victim turning on the extortioner."

"No, it's not like that!" He sat up sharply. "I'd told you! Paul and Ginny knew, it wasn't a secret any longer. I couldn't be blackmailed: not by Misty or Hubbell. Don't forget him, he tried it too and the same thing applied. We called his bluff, sent him away with a flea in his ear."

"Don't you remember why? Because I told him Misty was HIV positive. And there's another motive for you killing her: revenge."

"So? You know I didn't do it. What night was it? Thursday. You said we watched *A Passage to India*. That was true, we did. I was never out of your sight except to go to the bathroom."

"Try convincing Dineen of that."

"No need. You're my alibi."

"Oh, honey! Everyone else in Prosper has the same alibi, more or less."

He gulped the rest of his drink and fell back. "Why Prosper?" he pleaded. "Why us?"

"Why not? Five men living within three miles of the victim. There are no others. Seth's immobilised."

"Do we look like clients for a hooker? I ask you."

"So far we've met five people and any one of 'em could have killed her," Dineen said.

"Three were women," Powell pointed out. "Two were big enough. Or it could have been collusion."

"Which of those two guys was sleeping with her, Sumner?"

"When I talked to her she virtually told me it was Manton. She said Dodge would never dare."

"You didn't tell us this before!" Powell turned on the deputy, snarling.

"She's – she was a liar. You didn't ask me for gossip."

"And you didn't have time to give us any," Dineen put in. The local man's experience was too valuable to risk crossing him. "Stop here, Powell. What's the gossip on these?" He indicated the modest house perched on its bluff above the shore.

"The Nelsons," Sumner said. "He's the naturalist: counting lions and deer to find out if there's enough deer to introduce wolves in the forest. Got no interest in anything human, outside of his wife, that is. She's a plain little thing, speaks her mind."

"That'll make a nice change," Dineen murmured, but he gave no order to turn down the Nelsons' track. "And the old house, the one nearest the point, that'll be Miss Carver, the authoress? What's the gossip on her?"

"There's a Britisher living with her, supposed to be her secretary, maybe the housekeeper. I don't know."

"Ah. Lesbians?"

Sumner was flabbergasted. "That was a joke," Powell told him.

"Not really," Dineen said. "If they're an item, there could be jealousy involved, like if Misty was Carver's lover and the secretary, so-called, was jealous."

"He could be gay," Sumner said stiffly. "That's the secretary, so he wouldn't be interested in hookers. He does the cooking. And he's got a kitten. House swarms with cats," he added. "They hated Hubbell – but not Misty. They wouldn't have had anything to do with her."

Dineen was intrigued. "Why did they hate Hubbell?"

"Because of the cats, and his hounds always running loose." Sumner gaped as a thought struck him. "That were Misty, of course: she looked

149

after the hounds, so it was her was responsible for them slipping their collars." He stopped, side-tracked and lost.

Dineen asked, serious now but puzzled, "You're suggesting this Carver woman and her – fellow – could have had a grudge against Misty because she didn't control her hounds?"

"Hubbell's hounds," Sumner corrected. "No, of course not. Anyways it was Kent what smashed in the door."

They were mystified. "What door?" Powell asked.

"It's nothing to do with—"

"I'll be the judge of that." Dineen was harsh. Sumner thought better of protesting that this was an unconnected crime; the man had asked, right, he could have it all. Accordingly he related the events of a week ago when Hubbell came home to find his hound missing, had beaten Misty, smashed Miss Carver's door, been shot – and shot at – by her, had run out of road and ended in the river. "But you knew that part already," he said. "It was front page news."

"For you maybe," Powell said, glancing at Dineen who was staring at the Carver place. "We have three murders on our case-load at the moment, not to speak of armed robberies and a coupla rapes. You had a road-rage attack and an auto accident is all."

"I didn't know about him smashing the door," Dineen murmured. "What else did he do? I'm intrigued by this Miss Carver."

Eighteen

"It's more than my life's worth to interrupt her." Owen shelled a prawn and arranged it with its fellows in a sunburst of Chinese leaves. He surveyed the result critically and Dineen wondered how much of this was a pose. "I assure you," the Welshman went on, "she only had one paragraph to do, but there you are." He moved a prawn a quarter of an inch. "Authors! They're all the same."

"You've worked for them before?" Dineen asked politely.

"Never. I'm a chef. And I don't work for Miss Carver."

"You're doing the cooking."

"Naturally. I like it. Don't you cook?" There was no response. He opened the refrigerator and placed the salad on a shelf. It was 12.30 p.m.; was he anticipating a protracted session with the detectives or did he always chill salads? He didn't close the fridge. "Beer?" he asked brightly. "I'm having one."

They drank Hefeweizen and, to an outsider, they would have appeared a convivial trio seated on the slightly shabby sofa and chairs, a kitten on Hughes' lap purring like a toy engine. He focused on Powell. "You're Welsh," he said.

"How d'you know that?" Powell was taken aback.

"The name of course, but the features too. Typical Welsh cast. Your people are from the Valleys?"

Powell nodded, glowering. Dineen turned to him with interest. "What's that mean: the valleys?"

"My folk came from the Rhondda," Powell said, mispronouncing it.

Hughes nodded. "South Walian. I'm from the north."

"What are you doing here?" Dineen asked, pushing for the high ground.

"Seeing the country. Meeting people. Showing my friend how to get the best out of her computer."

"Employed."

"No. I don't have a green card." He'd seen that one coming.

"You know Misty Hubbell."

"Never met her." He didn't turn a hair at the sudden switch. "I don't – didn't know any of the Hubbells as a matter of fact. Of course I know all about them."

"Gossip."

"No, there were facts too. The trouble is, you can't tell the difference, can you? Another beer?"

"Ah, we have guests!" An old woman, white-haired, wearing Levis and a crumpled blue shirt, entered the room, attended by what seemed a crowd of cats. They stood up and Hughes introduced the police. Dineen apologised for the intrusion but Powell concentrated on the little Welshman, seeing that the guy appeared always to be concerned with trivialities: fussing with food, serving beer, not treading on cats . . . toy boy or gay? It had to show one way or another.

"What happened to the door?" Dineen asked, shattering his partner's thoughts; they'd been engaged in small talk – for Christ's sake, Dineen had been talking *cats*. The door? Everyone was looking at it but, since it was open and end-on to them, Powell could see nothing wrong with it.

"We're waiting for a man to come and fix a new cat-flap," Miss Carver said. "We found it broken when we came home that night . . ." She looked at Hughes.

He nodded eagerly. "It had to be Hubbell," he told Dineen. "It seemed to tie in with the shooting. You know about that of course."

"Only at third hand. Why don't you tell us how it happened?"

He seemed only too willing. "We'd been to a lecture in Stagg and we met Hubbell at the junction, there by Angel's Camp. He passed us, turned round and followed us down the Prosper road. When he caught up he started firing. As he was passing Miss Carver fired, and he crashed." He stopped as if that was all there was to it.

"You stopped?" Dineen was diffident. He glanced at Win but her eyes were closed. She could have been asleep.

"No, I didn't stop," Hughes said. "It wasn't a dramatic crash and I had no intention of walking back and being shot. I drove home but eventually Miss Carver persuaded me to go back – and he'd gone! Disappeared. No sign of the Stingray. I was so relieved."

"Relieved?" Dineen was incredulous. "Didn't it occur to you that there was a vicious gunman on the loose, that he'd be more than anxious to even the score? After all, if he'd driven away then he was fit."

"We were in shock." Miss Carver sounded wide awake.

Hughes ignored her. "All we could feel at the time was relief," he repeated. "I'd sort of nudged him as he passed, and she fired at the same time – missed him of course but we weren't to know that at the time. We thought we were responsible for him crashing, and until we discovered that he'd driven off, just like that, we thought we could have killed him."

"I still think so," Miss Carver said. "That I was responsible, I mean."

Dineen looked as if he were having difficulty following this. "So he just glanced off of the tree and then went further, into the canyon?"

The old lady seemed to crumple. Powell wondered how old she was, thinking that there could be no sex in this house, not in the house. Outside it then? The Welshman and Misty?

"What we think happened," Hughes was saying, "was that he drove on in order to turn round and tried to turn above the landslide, and misjudged it. Perhaps he was concussed, or the crash had damaged the steering, even the brakes."

Dineen nodded as if he agreed with one of the hypotheses. "Why did he come after you?" He didn't sound particularly curious.

"Class envy?" Hughes suggested. "We were in a Rolls."

"When did he smash the door?"

"Class?" Miss Carver repeated. She gave a delicate shrug. "I shot his hound."

Hughes' leg jerked. The kitten woke and stretched. The tortoise-shell, who had been day-dreaming on the arm of the sofa, stiffened and hissed.

"When was this?" Dineen asked.

"Back in the spring." There was no emotion in the tone.

"But isn't the hound still alive, and loose in the forest?"

"That's the other one," Hughes put in quickly. "Hubbell had two. She shot the first one because it killed one of the cats."

Her eyes closed tightly, the lined old face full of pain. Dineen nodded, knowing now why she hadn't stopped after Hubbell crashed into the tree, wondering if the two of them could have pushed the car over the edge. No, impossible. He needed to talk to Sumner. The deputy was waiting in the police car; three of them descending on an old person could have been intimidating. "So there was a deal of hostility between you and the Hubbells," he said.

"Not really—" Hughes began, to be overridden by Miss Carver.

"Owen didn't know them," she said. "At one time I employed Myra Hubbell but I have no need of her now."

"Things went missing," Hughes put in.

"You do know her then." Dineen sounded tired.

"No." Miss Carver was sharp. "Myra left here before he arrived."

Hughes' mouth twitched. "You're interviewing all the men. It's the obvious thing to do, of course. I didn't know Misty; to my knowledge I never saw her. I know about her but that's a different matter, isn't it?"

Dineen sighed and looked at his partner.

"What were you doing last Thursday night?" Powell asked, like a terrier let off the leash.

Hughes looked at his companion. Both seemed at a loss. "We don't work in the evening," Miss Carver told Dineen, who showed no surprise at her use of the pronoun. "We eat early, at seven, and then we talk." Her eyes went to the door. "We used to sit out on the deck but not now, not even armed."

Powell's jaw dropped and Hughes caught the reaction. "Because of the loose dogs," he explained. "The cats used to come out with us or, more to the point, they'd be hunting down there in the rocks. It's too risky now. Why, feral dogs have attacked people! We've been taking guns with us wherever we go for over a week now. There was a whole pack of the brutes at one time. There are still two unaccounted for: Hubbell's surviving hound and a German Shepherd."

"Thursday night?" Powell repeated heavily.

Hughes spread his hands, looked towards the television set, shrugged. "One evening's much like another. We'd be in here: talking, watching the news, a documentary perhaps. If we look at the schedules we'd remember what we watched."

"You didn't go out?" Powell felt the energy draining out of him.

"We haven't been out since the night that Hubbell died," Miss Carver said calmly. "Not at night. There's been nothing we wanted to do in Stagg, and there were no parties here."

"Would the door have been open that night?" Powell asked, desperation creeping into his voice. "The night that Misty died?"

"Oh, I'm sure it was," Miss Carver said. "The screen would be closed of course."

"So you'd have heard a vehicle pass."

"No," Hughes said. "This is a dead end. Nothing passes."

"That's right." Dineen came in on cue, revitalised. "You're the last house, the one up against the point." Heads turned to the doorway but the view through the screen and the wide window at the side was of the ocean. "You'd have to be out on the deck to see the point," Dineen mused. "Or in a room with a window at the side of the house?" A look of enquiry directed to each in turn. They nodded. "And neither of you saw anyone on the headland?"

Hughes blinked. "In the dark? That's expecting a bit much." He thought about it. "The moon's waning now; you're right, it had to be full last week."

Powell stood up and walked outside. They watched him in silence. He came back. "A man on the point would've been clearly visible from the deck," he said.

"Oh yes." Hughes was boyish. "We watch the eagles; they sit there most mornings."

"But you wouldn't see anyone there at night unless you were looking." It wasn't a question. Dineen was merely echoing Constance Dodge.

"Dead loss," was Powell's comment as they walked to the Selhorst place.

"Not at all. They know more than they're saying, and they're lying."

Powell stopped and stared at him. Dineen halted and looked down the slope at the other three houses: the Nelsons', the Dodges' and the Mantons'.

"Right," Powell said savagely, "but is what they're concealing anything to do with the murder?"

"Or murders," Dineen murmured. "If the two deaths were connected you might wonder if someone had it in for the Hubbell family."

"Him?" Powell made a movement towards the house they'd just left.

"*She* had every reason to kill Hubbell – from her point of view. Handy with firearms too: shot his hound, shot at him, maybe hit him. Never mind Myra persuading some fellow to kill Misty, what about Miss Carver ordering Hughes to push Hubbell over the edge? And then Misty? But what could Carver have against Misty?"

Powell shook his head, exasperated. "Maybe she was killed for some reason we don't know about," Dineen went on, "or even suspect."

"Back to square one: two unconnected murders – if Hubbell's was murder, and not just him running out of road."

They resumed walking, Powell watching his feet, Dineen studying the lie of the land in its relation to the houses below the track. On their right the poppies made a spectacular show among the rocks of a little bluff, and the vivid blooms of the blue-eyed grass surprised even Powell, who cared nothing for wildflowers, or any flowers for that matter. "All the same, I could never live here," he said, following his own thoughts. "Imagine not going out for a week!"

"So they say."

They didn't pursue that because they rounded the bluff and a cabin came into view: extensive, with a raised deck and a fine stone chimney breast, but still a log cabin. Two people sat on the deck as if waiting for them: an old man and a girl. They stood up as the detectives came to the steps and Powell was suddenly aware that since they arrived in Prosper they had seen no one who was either young or pretty. Quite the reverse; apart from Hughes who, in Powell's opinion, wouldn't see forty again, everyone had been overweight, decrepit or, like old Hubbell, sick. In contrast Robin Selhorst was young and stunning.

On closer inspection she wasn't all that young, in her thirties maybe, but she was gorgeous; a little on the thin side but then, built the way she was, she'd be able to wear anything, and Powell loved to see women well dressed. Furs, she'd look great in furs: bronze maybe, and a low-cut ball gown like movie stars wore at premières. He was grinning as Dineen introduced him, unaware that with his looks he resembled a cartoon predator. Reluctantly he turned his attention to the man, disconcerted to find himself the subject of close inspection from this ancient guy with clothes that looked like they came out of a skip, and the confidence of a supreme court judge.

The visitors were seated on the deck and Robin brought beer, Canadian this time. Powell was consumed by embarrassment, thinking more of the need for a leak than the fact that he hadn't eaten since breakfast. Dineen solved the problem by asking for the bathroom.

"Sure," Robin said. "Come on, I'll show you."

Dineen looked meaningly at Powell who blundered to his feet and followed her indoors. Blinded by the transition from sunlight to gloom he kicked furniture, apologised, knocked something tall, clattering crockery . . .

"Sorry," she said. "Let me . . ." She reached round him, pressed against him. There was a delicious scent, a yellow light, an open door, and she was gone. He closed the door, breathing hard.

He took his time recovering. There was no sign of a woman here; there had to be two bathrooms, unusual in a log cabin. This was obviously Selhorst's territory but there wasn't much of him in evidence either: towels, a razor, soap, toothbrush – and a poster-size photograph of a sand dune, shadowed on one side, a mountain range in the background. Everything was in focus, from ripples in the sand and some animal's track, to the distant peaks.

He went back to the deck and Dineen left in his turn. "That photograph," Powell said. "What made the track?"

"Sidewinder," Selhorst told him. "I got the snake too, and you'd expect that to make the better picture but when I came to print it I saw that it was better with just the track. Show you the uncut version if I can find—"

"Dad!" It was a warning. "They're here on business. They want background on Misty. Isn't that right?" She smiled sweetly at Powell.

"You knew her?" he asked, cursing Dineen for leaving him to start this on his own.

"Not really; neither of us did."

"Her mother-in-law then?"

She glanced at her father. "Myra did clean here but not when I was home."

"Did you suspect she was stealing?"

Selhorst shook his head slowly, holding eye contact.

Dineen returned. He sat down and regarded Robin hopefully. She said, "I think it started when Mrs Dodge realised what was happening about ten days ago. Virginia Manton saw a woman in Stagg wearing Mrs Dodge's sweater: a one-off item costing an arm and a leg. You couldn't mistake it apparently. So everyone fired Myra, including Dad. I insisted on it; he's got some valuable cameras."

"She'd been stealing from Mrs Manton before that."

"Oh yes? I didn't know. Why didn't Virginia say?"

"She didn't want to alarm you."

"I don't believe it. If Virginia fired Myra it would have to do with—" She checked and threw a wild glance at her father.

"Myra is rather too fond of Scotch." Selhorst sounded apologetic. "And Paul Manton is something of a connoisseur. Malt whisky's far too costly to tolerate the maid helping herself to it. A pity but there you are."

"Not much to do here except drink," Robin put in cheerfully.

"Like mother, like son," Dineen intoned. "Hubbell drank too." He turned to Selhorst. "Is that why he drove into the river?"

"Had to be. Obviously he was drunk: chasing Win Carver and firing at her."

"Yes, why did he do that?" Dineen was curious. "She said she'd shot his hound . . ." He tailed off.

"That's enough." Selhorst was grim. "You didn't know Hubbell. He was a violent man, done time for wounding. And those hounds were his children."

Robin gave an angry laugh. "If he'd had kids he'd have beaten them same as he did Misty. But he treated those hounds like Win treats her cats."

"I can understand Miss Carver shooting a loose dog," Dineen said, "but how did Hubbell know she'd done it?"

"The bone, of course." Selhorst was surprised at his ignorance. "That's why he kicked the cat-flap in. It was bolted to stop the cats getting out, so Hubbell smashed it open and threw the bone inside. It was a warning, and it scared those two stiff."

The detectives didn't look at each other. "What time was he there, at Miss Carver's place?" Dineen asked. "Neither of them's good on times."

"I heard a shot in the evening," the old man said, "from the direction of the cove. With hindsight that could have been Hubbell loosing off . . . after he found the bone maybe? Temper? Intimidation directed at us? Anyhow it was daylight." He looked at his daughter.

"I didn't hear it," she said. "I was indoors, cooking supper. But Kent Hubbell was in a raging temper from the moment he arrived home. Had to be. He'd have found one hound missing; that was when he beat Misty. Did you know about that?" Dineen nodded. "Yes, well, the way he was driving in the daytime I'm surprised he didn't have an accident long before he did. He left rubber on the Dodges' drive, or would have done if it was cement; as it was I could hear the gravel flying from here and he went up their track like a bat out of hell."

Powell sat motionless, his drink inches from his lips.

"And where did he go from there?" Dineen asked himself, his eyes abstracted but his head turned towards the Dodges' house.

"He raced up the valley," Robin supplied, "back to his cabin, I guess. Poor Misty." She paused. "Or Myra," she added weakly. "Constance would have told him about Myra stealing the sweater, that's what he was so mad about."

"He went to Stagg and got drunk," Dineen said. "He was seen in the bars there, looking for Misty."

They were silent. Powell held his breath, waiting for a signal, for Dineen's next question.

"Did you see anything unusual last Thursday night?"

They had seen and heard nothing, had no idea who might have

strangled Misty and were too well bred to suggest that, in her case, violent death was an occupational hazard.

The detectives weren't interested. Adrenalin was pumping and they couldn't wait to get away.

Nineteen

At the foot of the steps Dineen sent Powell back to stop the Selhorsts using the telephone.

Grady Dodge opened his door and stared. "I didn't hear a car!"

Dineen was almost overwhelmed by whisky fumes but his expression was all happy innocence. "Thank you," he beamed, stepping inside as if invited. "Mrs Dodge around?"

"She's out." Dodge closed the door, apparently accepting the inevitable.

Dineen had to act quickly before the wife returned. "We're tracing Hubbell's movements," he said. "How much did he drink when he was here?"

"Hubbell?"

"Kent Hubbell. Did you give him your good Scotch?"

Dodge was fighting to orientate himself, his mouth slack, shaking his head.

Dineen tried again. "How long was he here?"

"Not long. He was just in and out . . . he broke a vase." His eyes wandered, looking for something that wasn't there. "We couldn't stop him . . . I couldn't . . . not frightened of the pistol. She sent him away, you know, my wife. Constance." Belligerence surfaced. "What's it to do with you? I was within my rights, I wasn't having that: threatening me in my own home! I told her: 'Call the police', I said." He grinned fiercely. "Didn't need to, she had the drop on him."

"Mrs Dodge shot him?" Dineen couldn't keep the surprise out of his voice but Dodge was too far gone to notice.

"No, no, no! 'Course she didn't. He drove off, didn't he? He took off as if—" Dodge stared at the detective and was suddenly terrified. He looked as if he were about to faint.

"He left here alive," Dineen said slowly and clearly. Dodge nodded. "You followed him?" A shake of the head, the starting eyes mesmerised by the other's stare. Rabbit in the headlamps, Dineen thought, then, "Mrs Dodge followed him."

"Never! We never saw him again."

"So how did you get him to leave?"

Dodge studied the rug at his feet. His face started to work. "Misty!" he exclaimed. He looked up and now there was life in the eyes, and relief. "Mrs Dodge told him that Norm Riessen – at Angel's Camp, you know? You had to pass it at the junction, where you turn off the highway. She told him Riessen was a pimp: her pimp, Misty's. She was a prostitute; well, you know that of course. What Hubbell didn't know was that Riessen was her pimp, d'you see? She'd be turning a very high percentage of her earnings over to another man and Hubbell thought it should all be his. He was livid when he left here. I thought he'd kill Misty."

"How did you know Riessen was a pimp?"

"What?" The room seemed to be still ringing with the tirade; its cessation came as a small shock. "Everyone knew," Dodge whispered.

"Everyone?" It was insinuating and it seemed to spur Dodge to the breach.

"Everyone." He was defiant. "How could she hope to hide it? She flaunted it in the bar, you could tell by the body language—"

The back door – the sliding glass panel that opened on the deck – slid aside and Dodge's wife entered with Paul Manton, quiet in their trainers, and both expressionless. Dineen could feel the tension. He would have preferred an outburst from them, but he had what he wanted. A door was ajar, he had only to push. "We've been discussing Kent Hubbell's visit with you," he said chattily. "On the afternoon before he died."

"I didn't—" Dodge began, his eyes pleading with his wife. He was interrupted by Manton.

"You don't look too good, Grady." He came and sat beside Dodge, taking his wrist in his fingers.

"He has to be careful of his heart," the wife whispered to Dineen, who didn't so much rise to the occasion as seize his opportunity.

"Come out on the deck, ma'am. I'd like a word. He'll be all right there with the doctor."

They went outside, he slid the panel closed and indicated a chair, waiting until she was seated before sitting himself. She didn't open the conversation but waited for him to take the initiative. He appreciated the significance of that. "You should have told me," he said sadly.

"Told what?" It was weak: the ritual response.

"About Hubbell coming here, and how you got rid of him."

She stared at the ocean. He watched her and saw her seize on

161

something as clearly as he'd seen Dodge galvanised when he'd grasped at the diversion of Riessen as pimp. Now the wife was going to go for the same story but she'd be more adroit. He waited, full of confidence.

"What was the result of the autopsy?" she asked.

His smile remained as if applied with greasepaint. Her eyes followed an eagle as it flew low along the shore, the white head startling against the grey water. She hadn't noticed his silence. Before she could do so he rallied, trying to sound firm. "We're waiting for a print-out, but would you hazard a guess as to the findings?"

She nodded and turned to him, labouring under an emotion he couldn't identify. "She was negative. The whole episode was a lie. It would kill him otherwise." She paused. "But then it would kill him anyway if she were positive."

"I'm sorry." That slipped out, basically he had to harden himself to contain his triumph. He'd been here only a few hours. "It was an open and shut case," he said.

"You're ahead of yourself." Her tone was sardonic now. "He didn't kill her."

"He had every reason to."

"No. We – Paul Manton and I, Grady too, we'd all tumbled to it that it was a trick, that she was never even in bed with him. I know what you're thinking: that even if she'd lied about being HIV positive, that he killed her in a fury because of the hell he'd gone through. Because he believed her originally, and of course he was devastated, suicidal. Oh yes, he could have strangled her, but he was with me all that evening, and night; he never left the house."

This time he wasn't bothered about her noticing his silence. Elation had left him as suddenly as it arrived. He felt drained. "What will you do now?" she asked, and he knew that she thought she had the upper hand.

"I have to ask him to come into Stagg to make a statement." And to answer a raft of questions, he thought with satisfaction.

"You can't do that. He's sick."

"He's drunk," he said.

"But he doesn't drink!" Robin exclaimed. "The whole affair is based on the premise that he was so drunk he didn't know what happened at Angel's Camp. Are you trying to tell me that Norm Riessen drugged him, like a Mickey Finn?"

"Constance said they were drinking Screwdrivers." Virginia said.

"Riessen had told Grady that a Screwdriver was orange juice with a dash of vodka. I guess it was mostly vodka; Grady wouldn't know the difference. Like you said, he didn't drink. Hell, he's made up for it since though. He's drunk now – and Dineen has taken him to Stagg to make a statement. Constance is climbing the wall. She can't find Nat; he's on his yacht some place and out of touch."

"Who's Nat?" Owen asked.

"Their son. He's a lawyer."

"Grady doesn't need a lawyer," Bill said. "He didn't kill Misty."

They stared at him, all except Owen who seemed to have found something unexpected on the kitten's neck.

The news had spread like a flame in brush. Dineen had collected his men and, along with the tottery Grady, had left Prosper. Those residents who hadn't witnessed the departure quickly learned of it by telephone and now that they'd seen Grady leave with the police, Constance had gone public. It wasn't only that Win and Bill were old friends but that, being old, and still having influential contacts, they might be able to help. Constance was well aware that, so far as the police were concerned, a wife's value as an alibi was questionable.

Virginia had found the Selhorsts at Win's place and had blurted out the story. The immediate reaction might have been predictable; Robin and Owen wryly amused, Win shocked. Bill was intrigued, like a naturalist learning of the abnormal behaviour of a familiar animal. It wasn't until they made the connection between Misty as blackmailer and her being strangled that Grady stopped being a pitiful figure and they realised his danger. Washington had capital punishment for first degree murder.

Bill amended his statement. "I don't believe he did it," he said firmly.

The kitten, taking exception to being examined so minutely, escaped to find a lap that was more accommodating. Owen wiped his hands on his thighs and regarded Bill intently. "Do you know something we don't?"

"I'd like to say Grady isn't the type to kill, but then who is?"

"I'm afraid Grady is," Win said. "He's repressed, neurotic, obsessed by status."

"Control freak," Robin contributed. "The kind of guy could erupt at the slightest provocation."

"Not first degree murder then," Bill said. "Manslaughter just."

"Constance swears he was never out of her sight that evening – and night," Virginia protested.

"Naturally." Robin was dismissive. "Anyone would." Her attention was caught by her father. "Where are you off to, Dad?"

Bill smiled gently and she was plunged into confusion, then puzzled. Owen had preceded the old man outside.

"Men's stuff." Virginia was contemptuous. "Too delicate for our ears."

"I take it the police are not concerned with Paul," Win said.

Virginia was suddenly still. Robin looked from her to Win, her eyes wide.

"There's no reason why they should be," Virginia said coldly.

"He had a stronger motive," Win said. "But then he wouldn't care, so she couldn't blackmail him." They stared at her in consternation. "*You* would care," she told Virginia, "but Paul's not frightened of you." She turned to Robin. "Constance has the money there," she said serenely.

Robin looked at Virginia. "Is she saying what I think she's saying?"

Virginia glowered. "You pick your moments," she told Win. "If you're accusing Paul of having an affair with that dirty little hooker, where's your proof?"

"I asked you if the police were concerned with Paul," Win pointed out.

"No, they're not!" Virginia stood up and addressed Robin. "We'll talk again," she said tightly, "When Win feels more like her normal self."

She stalked out. Owen and Bill were deep in conversation some distance from the steps. She unclipped Henry's leash from the rail and stamped past the men. I'm leaving," she threw at them. "Win's gone crazy." She was too angry to notice that they looked more resigned than surprised.

Back in the house Robin turned on Win. "Whatever made you say that about Paul?"

"It's probably true. That will be why she fired Myra, because Misty had seduced Paul and she couldn't bear to have a Hubbell in the house. I'm fond of Paul but he always had a wandering eye."

"We all know that but why say it?"

"Because Paul had a stronger motive than Grady."

Robin sighed, defeated, and stood up.

The men stopped talking as she came down the steps. "Win says Paul had a strong motive for killing Misty," she told them. "She said so to Ginny's face." Owen and Bill exchanged looks. "Well," she exploded, "what is this? Is she going senile?"

Owen nodded unhappily. "I hope it's no more than that; I'm praying it's not Alzheimer's."

Bill regarded him sadly but Robin was astonished. "Really?" She was full of contrition. "I thought she was just being stupid – or malicious. It never occurred to me – Oh, my God!"

"Don't worry about it." Owen made a passable attempt at reassurance. "Your reaction wouldn't have bothered her; part of the brain seems to be switched off. I'll put it right with Virginia."

"But the books! How can she write like she does? I mean, she's not a genius, but she's got all her wits about her there."

"Most of the time," Owen agreed. "It's just the occasional flash, you know? When she forgets manners, or etiquette."

"It's fortunate she has you," Bill said comfortably.

Owen looked away, embarrassed. Robin frowned. "What were you two talking about?" she asked, working on the residue of her anger.

Again the men exchanged glances. "You're keeping something from us," she exclaimed. "Come on, out with it." She was relieved to find a new subject, to forget old age and fading powers.

Bill said slowly, "Owen saw a man on the point on Thursday night, around the time Misty was killed. He thought it was me."

Robin laughed stridently. "How many more shocks are you going to spring on me?" Ignoring the fact that this was the first that he had produced. "So," looking from one to the other, "who was it?"

"The killer." Owen couldn't resist the drama of that.

"That's *what* it was. *Who* was it?"

"How would I know? I thought it was Bill because his house is nearest—"

"No, David Nelson is marginally nearer. Why didn't you think it was David?"

"I've seen Bill on the point quite often, I *associate* it with Bill. But it was only a glimpse, Robin, by moonlight, and then the moon went behind a cloud. When it was clear again the figure had gone."

"Are you going to tell the police?"

"Not now, it's too late. They'd want to know why I hadn't told them before. I couldn't say that it was because I thought it was Bill. It would draw attention to him."

"So who was it?" She went on, itemising, "If it wasn't Grady, or Paul, or either of you two, *could* it have been David?"

They thought about David Nelson and agreed that he was the last person likely to be involved in a sex murder.

"A woman?" Robin suggested, and thoughts flew to the powerful women in the community.

"No," Owen said, "it was a man; the shape's different. A man is a triangle with wide shoulders and narrow hips. Virginia and Constance would be more of a broad pillar-shape – glimpsed quickly in a flash of moonlight." No one smiled.

"Then who?" Robin begged.

Bill sighed. "If only Riessen were here."

"You'd fasten it on Riessen?"

"It could be him. Why not? He was the man who was closest to her. Not Grady or Paul but Riessen. Hubbell of course, but Hubbell was dead long before."

"Not all that long," Owen reminded him. "Only three days."

"I mean she was seen alive after Hubbell died." Bill turned to Robin. "I'm going to take a run into town, my dear. I'll leave you with Owen here, he'll look after you." She glared at him. "The dogs," he explained. "Don't forget the hound and the Shepherd. Don't go in the forest."

Stagg Harbor was humming, a forecast of fog having sent the little yachts running for shelter, while the whale-watching boats hadn't even troubled to put to sea. The sheriff's cramped quarters were populated by strange men in civilian clothes, by others in uniform drafted in from a distance.

There wasn't room for so much as a motor bike in the police car park. Bill put his pickup in a slot reserved for disabled drivers outside the post office and went in search of Wendell Scott. Shunted from pillar to post, eventually he ran his man to earth at the diving shack on the pier where he was talking to one of the local divers.

"You're thinking of raising the Stingray?" Bill asked, surprised. Melting snow in the mountains was keeping the rivers high.

"Just preparing the ground." The sheriff moved away from the shack and they started to stroll towards the end of the pier. "That's what they think I'm doing," he told Bill. "I come out here to escape that lot." Jerking his head in the direction of his own building. "Dineen's taken over my office to interview Grady Dodge, and every place is swarming with guys I don't even know their names, and half of 'em running around like chickens with their heads cut off."

"Why? What happened?"

166

"You mean, apart from Grady Dodge being the suspect for Misty's murder? They're pulling out. You didn't hear about Riessen? No, Dineen wouldn't say; he's obsessed with the murder; he's going to wind this case up in one day. All set for promotion, is Dineen."

"What about Riessen? They found him?"

"Not exactly. Someone found his Bronco." Bill's brain reeled. The Bronco abandoned? Burned out? "In Cicero, Oregon," Scott was saying. "Some hick town upstream from Portland. The local people had been watching some fellow out there in the forest, figure he's been changing identification on stolen cars. They raided him and found him spraying a white Bronco, among other things. No plates around but they traced the Bronco by its VIN. It was registered to Riessen. They went back to the garage a second time and found the owner had gone missing. He'd left a hand in charge and although the guy hadn't been there when the Bronco was brought in, he did know the driver did a deal: exchanged it for a '92 Renegade. And that wasn't all; Riessen went to the nearest gas station and filled the tank on his credit card."

"He got a poor deal. That Bronco was worth two old Jeeps."

"He wanted shot of the Bronco quick."

"Why?"

"We won't know the whole truth till we raise the Stingray. My guess is there's a bullet in Hubbell's skull will match Riessen's weapon – when we find Riessen, if he still has the gun."

"Lot of ifs there. I don't envy you your job."

"And this guy says we have to wait till well into July for the water level to drop." Scott looked back morosely at the diving shack. "And if there's rain to come we're back where we started."

The fog was creeping shoreward, grey tentacles sliding into the harbour, the fog horn moaning from Desolation Island. The port itself was still in brilliant sunshine but the sight of that advancing bank sent a shiver down the spine. "Riessen bought camping gear in Portland," Bill recalled. "Is he heading for the deserts or staying in the coastal ranges? Where's this place that he acquired the Jeep?"

"Upriver some twenty miles from Portland. He's staying in the forests. He's less visible there if choppers are looking for him."

"The Sierras?"

"He'd have to cross the river again. If he was going to California he'd have stayed on that side of the river when he was in Portland."

"When did this happen – that he changed his car?"

"A week ago. The day after he left here in fact."

"He didn't lose any time." Bill took a few steps down the pier, turned and came back, staring at the planks at his feet. Below the timbers the tide sucked and gurgled. Voices on the shore sounded distant, as if absorbed by the shining air as they would soon be muffled by the fog. "He could be here," Bill said. "He could be in Prosper."

Scott shook his head. "You're same as me, Bill Selhorst; you passed your sell-by date."

Twenty

B ill drove out of Stagg ahead of the fog. He had tried to find out
what was happening with Grady, on the pretext that he could
provide a ride back to Prosper, but he'd met with a brick wall in the
person of Powell. The police would bring Mr Dodge home, the man
said carelessly. Bill didn't push it, thinking that this was neither the
time nor the place to stand on his rights. Not that he knew what those
were in this situation any more than he knew who had killed Misty.
He thought he knew who hadn't.

Owen was marinating a leg of lamb. Seeing his neighbour emerge
from the fog and approach the steps, he dived for the door, wiping his
hands on a dish towel. "She's asleep," he said, grinning like a Cheshire
cat. "We're going to celebrate. Come over for dinner with Robin."

"Fine." Bill was wary. "What are you celebrating?"

"She sold the last book. Isn't that splendid?"

"She always sells her books."

"Yes, well." Owen was flustered.

Bill said, "I'm delighted, dear boy. I hope she is too."

"She doesn't know," Owen said weakly, staring at him. "She was
asleep when I took the call from her agent."

"All credit to yourself." Bill seemed unaware of any tension. "She
needs friends. Now, what I want to know is, have you been up to the
dam recently?"

Owen was lost, unable to switch from Win and the book, from Bill
and what he might know – or suspect – to the *dam*? "What dam?"

"Where our water supply comes from. There's a lake above us, in
the woods—"

"I knew that – vaguely."

"—and a dam. The access road starts at the plank bridge: the big
bridge over the river."

"I've never been up there. What's this got to do with me – or
anything?"

"No, your tyres aren't the right size anyway. No one else has been

169

to the dam recently; I've checked. I'm going up there. D'you feel like coming?"

"Why, of course." Owen was puzzled but polite. If the old chap wanted company he was willing to supply it, and he had nothing to do for an hour or so. He put the lamb in the fridge, wrote a note for Win, and followed Bill across to his cabin and the pickup. "What makes it important?" he asked, climbing into the passenger seat, noting that there was a rifle on its rack, assuming that Bill had the dogs in mind. "What's all this about?" he asked. "And why ask me to come?"

Bill eased down his drive and turned onto the track. "I'm not sure of the others," he confessed. "Paul that is – and David's not at home. It's like this: I was crossing the bridge, dipped headlamps because of the fog and the trees – it's black as the pit in there – and the lights picked up vehicle tracks turning off the road, going up to the dam. No one goes there unless there's something wrong with the water supply. My mind was on Grady's predicament and I didn't think anything to the tracks until I reached home, and then it clicked. I called people and no one's been up there. That is, Amy said David didn't, and Constance said Grady wasn't up there." He sounded doubtful, as if the wives could have been lying.

He swung the wheel. Owen could see nothing in the fog but he guessed that they'd turned on to the public road and were now running parallel with the river. "Who made the tracks then?" he asked, mystified. Bill was silent. "You think you know. What d'you mean: 'it clicked'?"

Bill sighed. "Maybe I *am* past my sell-by date. Win's heading for senility, why not me?"

God, Owen thought, I don't deserve this; I shouldn't be here.

"I think Riessen came back," Bill said, his voice suddenly hard.

"*Riessen?* What makes you . . . Who were you talking to in Stagg?"

Bill told him what he'd learned from Wendell Scott. They arrived at the big bridge and he cut the engine. The river could be heard below the road. Owen was trying to make sense of the story: fact or the fantasy of an old man? Owen knew all about fantasy, and with the fog thick in the depths, shrouding all but the nearest trunks, with the torrent below and his companion possibly on the verge of senility, he was acutely uneasy. He had never liked the forest; in these circumstances he loathed it.

They left the truck. "You see!" Bill had a torch. Owen saw what he had never noticed before: a trail that left the road at this point but which was so crowded by vegetation that a vehicle would be forced to push the undergrowth aside in order to make any progress. The mud was marked by wide tyre tracks: many tracks, but all made by the same vehicle. "Jeep," Bill said. "Jeep-type anyway." He walked back to the pickup.

Owen followed him with relief, his mind switching to Win and the kitten, to the lamb for tonight, the cat-flap and the need to phone the joiner again, find out what was keeping him . . . The truck advanced for the three-point turn – and turned up the overgrown track. "No!" he gasped. "Where are you going?"

"No panic. We'll go up to the dam, make sure he hasn't put poison in the well." Bill glanced sideways. "Joke," he said.

Owen sat tight, staring at the plants that brushed the closed windows. The track forked. Bill turned up the left branch.

"Where does the other branch go?"

"To the dam."

"Then why are we coming this way?" As if he needed to ask. They were following the tracks of the other vehicle; they showed clear in the headlights.

"He can't have gone far," Bill said. "This is an old trail: used to go to the cabin that came down in the landslide. It'll give out quite soon."

Owen surrendered himself to an experience which bore some resemblance to a dream or drunkenness or being under an anaesthetic. The alternative was force: to overpower his companion, turn the pickup and drive back to Prosper. The drawback to that was that the old man was driving as if he'd been born to off-road work, and now Owen couldn't even see the trail. They advanced, the vegetation parted and let them through; he was convinced that, were he behind the wheel, he would have plunged over a cliff, or into a swamp, or just stalled, stuck between tree trunks.

The air was damp. Moisture was condensed on broad leaves, scintillating in the headlights. Then came a brighter, more extensive reflection. Glass shone gold; there were closed windows, wheels, bodywork. A little Jeep stood solid on the trail. The pickup stopped. Nothing moved. "Thank God," Bill breathed, "it *is* Riessen."

"Who did you expect it to be? I *see*! You mean this lets Grady – and everyone else – off the hook." Owen climbed down and followed the old man to the Jeep. The ground was littered with beer cans and an empty whisky bottle. "I thought we were following Riessen all the time," he said.

"I couldn't be sure." Bill was shining the torch in the back of the Jeep. There was the usual clutter to be found in working vehicles: plastic bags, a shovel, a tool-box. There was no camping gear and no gun but there was a mobile phone part-hidden by small empty cardboard boxes. "Rifle and magnum rounds," Bill murmured. "That's a lot of ammunition for a walk in the woods."

"He killed Misty," Owen stated, trying the doors. They were locked. "Her mobile was missing from the cabin."

"This could be a different one." Bill stood back. "This truck's been standing here for days." There were leaves plastered to the flat surfaces and caught behind the wipers.

"It had to be him." Owen cast a wary eye at the forest but all he could see was the matt grey wall buttressed by the nearest tree trunks.

"Not necessarily. He could have come back looking for her."

"If they both had mobiles they could communicate."

"Mobiles don't work in the forest. Look at it this way: he came back, meaning to contact her, but someone else got to her first."

"Then he'd leave, wouldn't he? No point in staying when she was dead."

Bill didn't answer. "Maybe he has left," Owen went on. "He abandoned the Jeep days ago. He walked out, hitched a ride, and now he's hundreds of miles away." He was hoping that this was true.

"Or he could have come up against the same person that Misty did." Bill walked to the pickup and reached inside. When he turned he was loading his rifle, filling his pockets with ammo. Owen watched in dawning awareness.

"You think it's one of us! That's why you chose me to come with you, because you don't trust anyone else. You reckon one of the men—"

"Or women." He wasn't smiling. Jokes were over.

"Which one, Bill?"

The old fellow returned his stare grimly. "We'll know soon enough. If Riessen's in here, something's prevented him from coming back to his truck. If he's dead the police will trace his killer. For my money it's the same one as killed Misty."

Owen had a sudden image of the figure on the headland whom he'd thought was Bill. He considered dementia again and he gave the consideration benefit of the doubt. "I'm not armed," he pointed out, with as much firmness as he could muster. "I'll stay here and wait for you." Once Bill was gone he'd double back to the road as fast as possible; he had the pickup's track to follow now. If Bill came after him, he'd dive into the undergrowth; the old guy would never find him in the fog.

"You're coming with me," Bill said, and the rifle barrel shifted a fraction so that it pointed at Owen's ankles – but it could have been accidental. "You're not thinking straight," the old chap went on kindly. "The safest place for you now is with me. I'm an excellent shot." He closed the pickup's door and glanced at the Jeep, then at the ground. Owen watched and knew the old guy was looking for a track. He moved away. Owen stood stubbornly, resentful and scared of so many elements that he could no longer distinguish between real and imaginary hazards.

Bill checked, a ghostly figure now. He gestured with the rifle. "Come on, man!"

Owen moved with a rush, not wanting to lose sight of the only human being other than himself in this alien place. He was unaware of incongruity or if he was, it was part of the dream; a moment ago he'd been visualising Bill chasing him back to the road . . . now, as he caught up, almost treading on the other's heels, he realised that, whether the guy was a killer or merely senile, that he could turn his back. Trust produced trust and Owen crowded close, his eyes searching the forest jumpily, but seeing nothing. Moss brushed his face like cobwebs and he turned a scream to a gasp.

Bill was following a trail which, although it would have been reclaimed by the forest years ago, must be there still, under the trampled plants, plants which had been squashed by the man ahead of them. Here and there ancient blazes showed on trunks. At one point Bill stopped and Owen bumped into him. "Fog's lifting," the old man said, and sniffed. "There must be a breeze. Listen."

"What?"

"Water."

"There's water everywhere." He realised that this wasn't strictly true. The huge trees and the mosses, the sword ferns and vines, every twig and frond and leaf was bedewed with fog moisture. Already their trousers were soaked to the crotch. However, so far there had been no evidence of running water.

"He'll be close by," Bill whispered.

"But would he—"

"Quiet!"

They went on, now hearing the faint splash of a fall, Owen trying to see past the other man, thinking of rocks and precipices, seeing instead a large and alien object in the air. He grabbed Bill's arm. "What's that?"

Bill lifted his rifle, then lowered it, flicking his eyes everywhere but up. Owen was focused on what he now saw was a trash bag,

173

full to capacity and suspended by rope from a second line slung between trees. The remains of a deer carcass were wedged in a forked spruce. "Camp," Bill whispered, and then Owen saw more litter: torn plastic, cans, tangled rope, and something metallic protruding from the stamped ground.

"Go and look at that," Bill ordered in a normal tone. "I'll cover you, although I'm pretty sure he's not here."

With difficulty Owen prised a camping stove out of the soil. "Someone stood on this," he said. There was a small saucepan, empty and dented, the lid nowhere to be seen, there were the remains of another trash bag. Bill picked up a book of matches: open, muddied, half the contents missing. Under the mud the printing said it came from Angel's Camp.

"He was disturbed," the old man said. "He'd lowered his food – that'll be his sleeping bag and stuff still up there."

"Why did he suspend it? What kind of animal—?"

"Raccoons, bear, cougar: anything that would steal food. Is that what happened? A bear came after the food? Surely not, he was armed to the teeth, and yet – doesn't it look as if there's been a fight here?" Bill moved to the edge of the cleared site and looked down a miniature waterfall. The drop was only some eight feet or so but the ground on both banks was steep and rocky. "There's something—" he began.

"Oh, my God!" Owen whispered. "Is that him?"

"Unlikely." But the Welshman had gone: out to the side where the angle eased, crashing through the undergrowth, coming round under the drop to the skeletal remains below. Bill didn't follow. He stood on the edge, paying less attention to his companion than to the surroundings, the rifle levelled as he turned, trying to pierce the fog.

"It looks like a dog," came Owen's call. Bill made a flattening gesture with one hand, demanding silence. After a moment he descended to join Owen in contemplation of the bones: fresh bones, but the lighter ones, such as ribs and skull, broken or crushed as if by heavy jaws. Skin and hair adhered to parts. There were flies and beetles but very little smell.

"Is it the hound or the Shepherd?" Owen asked.

"The hide's pretty uniform in shade and the hair's short. I'd say it's the hound. So where's the other one?"

"Something's been eating this – what's that over there?" Owen couldn't see the line of a trail but his eyesight was sharp enough for familiar objects. It was the gleam that attracted him: a small wet button, and it was attached to a ragged piece of material, originally blue but now stained brown. It was the cuff and part of a sleeve torn from a shirt.

"Whatever killed the hound attacked Riessen too," Owen said.

"That's blood all right." Bill looked up. "If it doesn't clear we'll have a hard job finding him."

"There's his track. He has to be wounded; won't he have left a blood trail?"

"Blood will have washed away. I think he's dead. If he'd been mobile, he'd have gone back to the Jeep."

Owen opened his mouth to respond when they both heard a muffled thud. They stared at each other, questioning, waiting for another sound. Owen looked at the waterfall. "How did we hear anything through the noise of that?"

"Because it was loud; it had to be a rifle shot." They thought about it. "Could be David Nelson, of course. Shooting at the Shepherd?"

Their eyes came back to the bloodied remnants of shirt. "Or it could be someone signalling for help," Owen suggested.

"We can't be far from the shore. We can get back to Prosper by way of South Point."

"The Hole will be flooded."

"Then we'll take the trail over the back of the headland to Win's place. We should investigate that shot. Let's see if we can find his trail."

It was there but extraordinarily difficult to follow. The angle didn't relent below the level of the fall but descended in steps: drops of a few feet, screened by vegetation and the ever-present fog. Even the slopes between the drops were so steep that the men virtually fell from tree to tree. They went down separately, each following his own line but only a few yards apart, Owen determined not to lose sight of his guide. Riessen's trail hadn't been made by a man picking his way but plunging downhill as if allowing gravity to provide all his impetus.

Bill stopped, leaning against the upside of a tree, his hand up, palm out. Owen came to rest behind his own tree trunk and followed the other's gesture downwards. He could see nothing but now he could hear a fog horn and the susurrus of the tide stroking a sandy shore. The sound seemed to come from under their feet. "He reached the shore then," he said. "Why didn't he go on to Prosper?"

Bill shook his head but before he could speak the cloud below them parted, and they looked down past the crowns of hardwoods to a slice of silver water and a stack like a ragged fin with a scarecrow cormorant silhouetted against the light.

"Oh, great!" Owen breathed. "I thought I'd never see the sun again. Where do we get down?"

"Hang on. Let me find my bearings."

Mist streamers drifted in, veiling the stack, but another window appeared and hints of beige showed through the alders. Cliffs, thought Owen. "The slide," Bill said. "Now I wonder if we can get down that."

"It can't be more than a hundred feet to the beach."

"Yes, but if it's waterlogged you could be trapped in the mud worse than in quicksand. But we'll look at it."

They moved sideways, progress made even more laborious by the fact that they were now contouring the slope instead of descending it. Owen kept falling as his lower foot failed to find a purchase; he had no time to wonder how Bill was coping because he was concentrating on trying to stay upright. Then one foot sank, he grabbed at the air, the other foot foundered and, in a panic, he threw himself forward to distribute his weight, and his outstretched hand clasped something hairy and warm. It moved towards him and he screamed.

Above him Bill stopped, took a moment to stabilize himself and aimed his rifle. All he could see was Owen, kneeling, staring at the ground. Rattler, Bill thought, and dismissed it immediately, but then – snake: the man had touched a harmless garter snake. He descended carefully.

Owen looked up. "It's the Shepherd," he whispered. "It's *warm!*"

The dog was dead, and it had been shot through the chest. They stood looking down at it, then Bill transferred his attention to the landslide. It appeared to start at this spot but to vanish into shifting mist wraiths below. The surface was marked by a long indentation like a shallow trough. He considered it, frowning.

"What are we waiting for?" Owen asked. "He's down there, he's just shot the dog, so he's making for Prosper, right?"

"What's that mark in the mud?"

"He slid down on his arse, so his feet wouldn't stick. Or maybe his leg's broken."

"I guess." Bill moved out on to the mud. It was deep, but with horrid suction sounds he managed to hoist his feet clear.

"The fog's lifting," Owen hissed, hesitating before he followed. Below, the great bleached logs shone in the sudden light, and beyond them the surf lay along the wet sand.

A rifle boomed.

Bill lunged sideways with an exclamation. Owen flung himself backwards, then dived like a bird into the lush plants that were now a sanctuary. He crouched there, listening. There was no sound but the sigh of the long waves. His brain started to function again.

The shot had come from below and it had been directed at them. He had heard the passage of the bullet: leaves shattering but no impact, not even on wood, let alone flesh. He dared not call to Bill; to do so could betray his own position, and imply that there were two of them, if Riessen didn't know that already.

Peering through leaves, he saw only the top of the slide; then, looking up, he saw low clouds moving against blue sky. The blessed fog was back. Shortly he became aware of movement and heard creeping noises as if mice were scrambling towards him.

A brown head appeared, hatless, the gleam of a rifle. Owen cast about for a weapon: a stone, a branch. "It's me," Bill whispered. "Keep quiet."

He had plastered mud over his face and skull, even his hands. He said that Riessen must be holed up among the logs at the foot of the slide. He'd been waiting for them.

"Why?" Owen mouthed. "Why us?" Pointing to his chest.

"Misty," Bill whispered. "And Hubbell. He killed them both, what's a couple more? Maybe he's mad. You go back to Prosper and call the sheriff. I'll hold him here. He can't get away."

"But . . ." Owen looked up the slope, visualising the miles of forest between here and the highway.

"Not that way," Bill chided. "Down to the shore and back over the headland. Or you might swim through the Hole."

"I can't go down *here*!"

"You continue along the slope, past the top of the slide, and after a few hundred yards you can drop down to the shore. The fog will give you cover."

"Suppose it clears." Bill looked at him. "OK!" He grinned weakly. "I'm just an author – a chef, I mean – and I'm scared stiff." He looked away, feeling the blood rush to his face.

Bill grinned and patted his arm. "I won't tell a soul," he promised. "Now off you go – I'll keep Riessen occupied. You hear shooting, that's me drawing his fire."

Owen pulled back his wandering wits and concentrated on the immediate job. The distance from here to Win's house was less than a mile but distance in the forest had to be calculated by the state of the ground rather than how the crow flew, and of ground in the sense of *terra firma* there was none.

At the top of the landslide, where it had parted from the slope, there was an overhanging bank so unstable that small stones were trickling down it, set off by nothing more than moisture dripping from bushes impending over the edge. Owen traversed below this crazy cornice following what his desperate eye hoped was a deer track, or even a track made by one deer, but the slide was wide, and halfway across the track gave out. Stones appeared, embedded in the mud, then a kind of earthy shale that shifted under his weight. He dislodged a stone and its clatter was lost in the boom of the rifle. He swallowed a cry and plunged forward, but the scree shifted, taking him downwards. Darkness loomed; he threw himself into it and wet brambles enveloped him like a shroud.

When he recovered his breath he found that he was on such steep ground that he could reach his original line only by climbing. He pulled himself up the incline by grabbing small bushes and clutching at the base of ferns. When these gave way he clawed into the rotting vegetation, using his fingers like grapnels. He was appalled by the noise he was making but no one fired. He regained the lost height and stopped, amazed and suspicious because Riessen hadn't fired again. Had the man guessed his intention and was even now walking along the beach below, waiting for him to descend? He decided to stay high and strike the path to Win's place without going down. It couldn't be far away.

Now he had no trail at all. No one had gone ahead trampling the juicy plants, no deer had passed. He realised that the fog had the effect of muffling, if not stifling the sound of his progress. There was no possibility of moving quietly when he could never see where his foot was going to come down. The green jungle's hazards varied and here, close above the shore, it was as if a twister had struck at some time and the ground was a maze of fallen trees. Some, untouched since they fell, shifted alarmingly and he was terrified of trapping a leg. Others were rotten and sank with him, the vegetation that impeded him when he was upright, parting like a malevolent force, offering no more support than weeds.

He could see that there were big conifers on a level above him but here he was trying to work his way through the belt of red alders. There was more growth under the hardwoods than in the shadow of the forest proper. Now, despite his earlier experiences, he envisaged a soft path of pine needles under the firs that would lead him within a few hundred yards to the headland.

Intent on reaching the conifers, he stumbled, the ground opened in front of him and he was rolling, sliding down a log, dropping, falling. He stopped with a sensation of wet and cold and something sharp digging into his spine. He was lying in a stream. For the moment he could see no way out and then he remembered that in this place you made your own escape route. On hands and knees he started to crawl up the bank, telling himself it could have been worse; it could be raining, he could be wounded – and there were the cougars . . . Something had been eating that hound. At least he was alive, and fit.

He came to the down-timber again and was forced sideways. He guessed that there was rock under some of the fallen trees but the drops were masked. He reminded himself that half a mile is only eight hundred yards and a bit. He must be half a mile from the headland now but even the bit could defeat him. He was terribly tired. He wanted to give up. This is madness, he thought, I am alive and fit.

He went on. He came to a fallen tree that slanted at head-level. He couldn't go underneath because the space was filled with more timber. He thought he had no strength left but he managed to lever himself onto the inclined trunk and to drop down the other side. Too late he realised that a second tree was lying parallel, with timber below that. Slowly, inexorably, he sank between the two and the canopy closed gently over his head like the lid of a coffin.

He was trapped. He was going to die here. He didn't care. He remembered the bears and cougars and wondered if there was a way he could kill himself before they started to eat him alive.

He didn't know how long he was there; it was probably no more than a few minutes before he renewed the struggle and escaped by going down – probably into the final trap but at least moving, not waiting, even though he was only sliding, letting gravity take over.

He came to the stream, or another stream, and now, appreciating that the forest was a more powerful force than a man with a rifle, he made for the shore, crawling down the bed of the stream like a raccoon through tunnels of greenery until he came to a bare slope which he slid down to come to rest on dry sand against a solid log.

He pressed his face and hands against the lovely clean wood and swore he would never enter a forest again. Then, with the fog covering his movements, he walked along the tideline, grateful that it wasn't a spring tide which would have forced him back to the logs. Not that he'd have minded negotiating a stretch of logs, he thought jauntily; what were bare logs compared with the horrors a few yards inland?

He came to the end of the sand and encountered rocks. The sea was louder now, rushing and withdrawing, then quiet for a few moments, and the sequence would start again. He had to be under the headland and he had walked past the path.

There were few logs here. Unhappily he edged sideways, close to the incipient bank immediately below the trees. Darkness loomed – an overhanging juniper – and he shrank back. But he had to approach the trees in order to find the path. He could see nothing of it. He prayed for the fog to lift just a little, enough to show some sign of the escape route, not enough to reveal him to Riessen. He must still be within rifle range.

The path eluded all his efforts to find it. It must be the Hole then. They said it was impassable at high tide but they meant only that it was too deep to wade – surely? He was already soaked and so filthy that a swim was just what he needed.

As he stumbled over the rocks under the loose cliff he realised that the sound of the surf came from the Hole and when he reached the entrance he saw that the swell – slight except at this place – was piling into the passage from the north, against his projected swim.

The distance was about two hundred feet, too far to make it between waves. If he could find a ledge, even a couple of good handholds inside, he might be able to cling there and wait for the water to recede and suck him through with it.

He was waiting for a big wave when the fog was swept aside and all the stacks appeared. He looked back along the shore and the landslide was so close that he would have seen a deer on the slope. No man was in sight. He slipped into the water on a receding wave and swam as fast as he could, looking for a ledge on the walls, but the passage was dark and he was in a hurry. He hadn't gone halfway before the next wave came surging through. He saw it coming, knew he didn't stand a chance, turned and tried to ride it, anticipating impacts but not, strangely, expecting to drown.

He did hit rock at the end but only when the wave had lost its momentum and thrown him out where he started on the shore of the cove. He crawled over weedy humps, stood up and staggered to the tide-line before the next wave could catch him. Then the firing started and he dived for the nearest log.

The sand was deep and dry and but for the discomfort of his wet clothes he would have gone to sleep. He had escaped from the forest, from drowning, from being shot. As he lay there shivering he became aware of time, a factor unnoticed until now. The beach in front of him was full in the sun but the light was golden and shadows were long. Soon it would be dark and, with the tide on the ebb, he'd be able to wade through the Hole. However it occurred to him that now, with the fog dispersing, he might find the start of the path. The disadvantage here was that the log that concealed him was isolated; there was a stretch of sand between it and the trees where he would be in full view of Riessen. Which would be why the man had fired when he was washed out of the Hole and stood up. But there had been a lot of firing . . . echoes? Or Bill firing too? "You hear shooting, that's me drawing his fire." Had Bill seen him at the Hole and fired in order to distract Riessen, maybe to kill him? He would put his faith in that. Definitely two people firing.

He felt sick with the cold. The skin of his legs, showing through rents in his chinos, looked like dead chicken, scored and streaked with cuts and deep scratches, still bleeding. His teeth chattered horribly; after all that had happened was he to die of hypothermia? People survived in water after hours of immersion – but water would be warmer than this shadowed air. If he stood up to exercise he would present a target, so he tried to move his limbs while lying on his back but the pain of gritty sand on raw flesh was excruciating. He was overcome by self-pity and despair.

His sense of judgement slipped. He compared the distance to the first trees with that to the nearest log. The log was further. Grimly, trying to ignore the pain, he flexed his knees and ankles. He peered round the end of the log. Nothing moved in the cove, nothing showed on the landslide. Like Owen, Riessen must be hunkered down behind a log. He raised himself on all-fours like a runner and took off. An ankle gave way, he stumbled – and the rifles spoke almost simultaneously, one louder than the other.

The firing continued, not a fusillade but with deliberation, as if the antagonists were taking each other's measure. When it stopped he had reached the cover of some shrubby junipers and he was sure Riessen hadn't seen him. No bullet had come his way. Now all he had to do was find the path.

The hideous business began again: fighting the sappy green abomination – but as suddenly the ground sloped, he gave a faint moan of misery and allowed the gradient to take him downward, to the top of the bank above the smooth sweet sand. Hypothermia was forgotten; he would wait for darkness and low tide.

He paused in the head-high junipers as the arc of the sun slipped below the horizon, and by its last gleam he saw a figure prone on the landslide. Bill had been hit.

He jumped down and was stumbling south, back to the slide, before he remembered the rifle. He veered to the shelter of the logs, walking cautiously, peering ahead, wincing as he saw a flash but it was only a glint of metal, not the flash of fire. Now the slide showed only as a faint break in the vegetated slope and Bill's body was no longer visible.

He began to wonder what he should do when he encountered Riessen and then he wondered if those two had killed each other. He stopped to think about it, leaning against a log, and was overcome by a wave of exhaustion. He tore his eyes away from the slide to where wet sand was reflecting opal shades of the afterglow. The ebb had left snakes of kelp and a long mound that was probably a seal's carcass. Then it moved.

Of course it would move, drawn back by the suction of a receding wave. It moved again, was moving parallel with the shore: a humpy progress like a monstrous caterpillar.

Owen dropped flat and, raising his head, watched the thing drag itself along the sand. The movement struck a chord of memory: Special Services, men trained to approach an enemy prone, inching themselves forward on their elbows.

Back on the landslide a stone fell. The creeping figure stopped. A flash of fire came from it, and a crack, different from those before. Then there was silence again except for the wash of the waves. Then, unbelievably, there were shouts which Owen, shocked and disorientated, was unable to pin-point. The sounds could be a figment of his imagination. Probably there was a stream nearby, voices were often heard in water.

Owl-light now and the crawler was moving. Owen walked down the beach and followed. He heard the voices again and thought he saw sparks at the edge of the forest. They dipped and jibbed like glow-worms among the logs.

In front of him Riessen started to fire. There were wild shouts and Owen was racing forward to fling himself on the man's back as he turned at the last moment, firing but firing wide.

They were in shallow water, the bottom dissolving under their combined weight. For Owen all the discomfort and the pain, the terrors and the humiliations, were channelled into one last surge of adrenalin. He didn't attack in a frenzy but, finding Riessen a more powerful man than he'd expected, he was going to subdue him or be shot in the attempt.

Bill arrived first, limping and using a rifle as a crutch, carrying another. The rest converged: David Nelson, Paul, Grady and Sumner. Owen was still on his opponent's back, holding him face downwards in the shallow channel.

"Where's his pistol?" Bill asked.

"I threw it away," Owen said. He stood up, staggered out of the water and collapsed.

"Who the hell is it?" Grady asked, playing his torch on the prone figure. Paul and Sumner lifted him out of the water.

"It's Riessen," Owen said. "Is he dead?"

They turned him over and four torches were trained on the face as Paul felt for the pulse. "He's dead," he said, "but it's not Riessen. It's Kent Hubbell."

Twenty-One

After he had drowned Kent Hubbell, Owen was subdued, even morose. Bill remarked on it to Win and she said that Owen was questioning whether his action had been justified.

Bill looked her in the eye and said, "I'm holding a watching brief; you know where I am." He waited, but he left her to do the watching.

A week after Hubbell died the water level dropped sufficiently for divers to recover the body from the Stingray. It was Riessen's, and he had been shot in the back of the head. There was an exit wound but if the bullet was still in the Stingray there was no way of recovering it unless they raised the car. There were no plans to do so; the police assuming that the gun used was the magnum that Owen had wrenched from Hubbell when the man was firing at the search party. They, of course, had been alerted by the sound of rifle fire and had approached the cave by way of the trail from Win's place, the one that Owen couldn't find.

"Owen saved us from a third murder," Grady said cheerfully, having walked up to Win's on the evening after they had the news of the autopsy on Riessen's body. "If I hadn't fallen off that log as Hubbell was firing, I could have been the next victim."

"I doubt it," Owen said, bringing him a beer. "The range would be too far, and he could never have taken steady aim with those wounds. He must have killed the Shepherd by luck."

It was Hubbell's left arm and side that had taken the brunt of the Shepherd's attack but it was the fractured hip that had disabled him, probably sustained in falling over the drop below his camp as he grappled with the dog. That attack must have occurred shortly after he killed Misty; four days later his wounds were alive with maggots.

Dineen hadn't been concerned with the motivation behind Misty's murder or Riessen's and, so far as the media were concerned, it was a case of sexual jealousy, with bizarre embellishments. Much was made of the dogs' involvement and in that respect probably everyone got it right. Hubbell had set up camp in the forest as much to find his missing

184

hound as to stalk and kill his two-timing wife. Some newspapers called it 'two-timing'; no one went further in print. Editors had heard rumours that Misty was a hooker and Riessen her pimp; they had wondered about AIDS; they knew that Grady had been questioned after her murder. But the Gradys were rich and they had a son who was a lawyer; editors were not about to open a can of worms here.

Prosper had most of the truth and those who didn't know guessed, one guess confirmed by Grady's sudden elation, which he explained as Constance having at last forgiven him for getting drunk at Angel's Camp. It was Robin who spotted the connection between the blackmail that had originated at Angel's – and the timing. She remembered Grady's trip to Seattle with Paul. "The poor guy thought he could have contracted HIV," she told Owen. "He's just now had the result of his tests and he's over the moon."

They were preparing dinner at Win's place, Grady, Win and Bill outside, enjoying the afterglow from the deck. Both door and screen were wide open but the cats were all over the cooks' feet, waiting for scraps. The kitten, sitting bolt upright on the window sill, licked his lips, eyes riveted on a prawn.

"You think Grady was HIV," Owen murmured.

"No! He was afraid he was. Owen, you're not with me. What's eating you?"

There was a whisky on the counter. He drank and stared at her. "He could never have hit anyone, you know. Bill was stuck there in the mud at the top of the landslide and Hubbell couldn't even hit *him*: a stationary target! The man was at his last gasp, and I pushed his face in the water."

"Now look. Suppose you'd pulled him out, and a chopper came in, flew him to Seattle: intensive care, and they'd nursed him back to health. What for, Owen? Trial and conviction and hanging, that's what." She considered saying that on the other hand, if Hubbell had been so close to death, Owen had merely speeded the process. Instead she asked lightly, "Are all the Welsh obsessed by guilt?"

"It's the chapel upbringing: sin, retribution, hellfire. When I was growing up I thought hell was Blaenau Ffestiniog on a wet Sunday afternoon in autumn."

Her mouth twitched. "Are you aware that kitten's just stolen a prawn?"

"Nurture, not nature. I'm teaching him to live on his wits."

"You don't live on your wits." She was relieved to see him smile.

The tortoiseshell queen drifted out to the deck, seeking attention.

Grady was leaving, thanking Win for the drink, saying they must get together, have a party now that things were back to normal.

"He's happy," Bill observed, watching the heavy figure walk away down the darkening slope.

"He's right, things are back to normal – except that we have no one to clean for us." She smiled. It was a joke.

Bill didn't look at her. He said quietly, "You have Owen – who does everything." In the face of her silence he did turn. "You do have him? He's not getting itchy feet?"

"The kitten will keep him for a while. He can't travel with a cat."

"I'm next door, my dear."

She smiled wryly. "You can't – collaborate."

The colours in the west were almost gone. Something splashed offshore. A gull called. "Does it matter?" he asked. "You've written a raft of books."

"The money's useful. But I'm blackmailing him, d'you see? The man isn't going to leave, because—" She stopped deliberately.

"Because he writes the books. Well, he wrote the last one."

"He told you?"

"No, he let it slip." He had guessed before that but he would leave the initiative to her.

"He derives nothing from it," she said in wonder. "I'm going senile and he does everything for me; he even writes books under my name, and all I can do is offer him a roof."

"You're wrong there. He does it for love. And, as I see it, the fellow has a talent which you foster – and no doubt you've taught him literary English. He may have the flair but you will be the muse."

"Silly man! He's like a son, you know?" Without a change in tone she went on, "Look at that cat: free to walk through the long grass again. I don't have to call her back. We owe you everything."

"I didn't kill the hound, Win." He hesitated, about to say that the hound had been loyal too, returning to its master, fighting the Shepherd . . .

"The hound must have found Hubbell's camp while he was away strangling Misty," came her dreamy voice, her face now a pale disc in the gloom. "Poetic justice, of a sort: one hound killed a cat, its companion was killed by the Shepherd. Savage beasts."

"Who is?" Robin emerged, carrying a drink. "Who's savage?"

"Dogs and men." Bill changed the subject: "We were speculating how Hubbell managed to come past here that night without anyone seeing—" He checked, sparing their feelings.

186

"The night he killed Misty? Sumner said: he must have parked the Jeep in the willows on the river bank beyond the Manton place and he carried the body past here. It wasn't like now, Dad; it was late. Owen saw him on the point."

"Bad blood," Win said. "Stupid and very powerful: fatal combination. There was too much intermarriage among these remote communities. Hubbell was the last of a dying line and it threw up a mad bull. And he had to marry a wayward girl. Why did he make for the shore?"

Owen, standing in the doorway, accustomed to her wild mental leaps, said, "Because the shore was downhill and he'd broken his hip. He crawled back for the rifle but that was the most he could manage. The shore was nearer than the Jeep."

"He was making for Prosper," Win said. "Crawling along the shore and through the Hole, carrying two guns, although he only had the magnum at the end. But that could have caused some deaths. He was like those multiple killers who run amok, except that he couldn't run, and you stopped him in time."

Owen reached inside the door and light flooded the deck. "Lovely," he said, "to sit out here and enjoy the evening again. How's the ankle, Bill?"

"It's healing, my boy. Unfortunately I have no one to blame for *my* stupidity. I knew that slope was waterlogged; I told you, didn't I? And then I have to go and get stuck myself."

"A good thing Hubbell had only one arm when he was firing at you."

Robin said quickly, before they could start on Hubbell's injuries again, "He'd done enough harm when he had two arms. I'm sorry for Riessen; he'd done nothing really. OK, so he got Grady drunk, set him up for Misty, but the poor guy probably went down the road that night to see if he could help someone who had crashed his car – and he got shot for his trouble."

"I'm not so sure about that." Owen had given this a lot of thought. "That was the night Misty was so badly beaten, remember? The Nelsons met her the Prosper side of Angel's Camp. She'd never have passed Angel's without stopping, so Riessen would have seen what Hubbell had done to her. When he heard the crash – or the gunfire, or both – he may have started out with the intention of helping, but when he discovered the Stingray – and Hubbell inside: concussed? or just drunk? – the opportunity was staring him in the face. He could have loved Misty, you know. I think Riessen decided to do what everyone

187

thought he did – send the Stingray into the river with Hubbell inside – but Hubbell came round and shot him. Turned the tables."

"I know your trouble," Robin said. "You think too much about what goes on in people's minds."

"That's bad?" He was genuinely surprised.

"It depends."

"It's the mark of an author," Win said, and the fog horn lowed like an old sea-cow.

"Fog coming up from the south," Bill observed.

Owen walked down the steps. Pale moths rose from the grass and the kitten leapt and batted at them on the edge of the light. The fog horn boomed. Owen stood still, his back turned.

"He's feeling the night," Win said. "Times like this I wish I still had the gift but there, I handed on the torch, right?"